The Coming of Bill

P. G. WODEHOUSE

The Manor Wodehouse Collection

TARK CLASSIC FICTION

AN IMPRINT OF

MANOR

Rockville, Maryland

2008

ISBN: 978-1-60450-052-3

Published by TARK Classic Fiction
An Imprint of Arc Manor
P. O. Box 10339
Rockville, MD 20849-0339
www.ArcManor.com

Printed in the United States of America/United Kingdom

Contents

Please Visit

www.ManorWodehouse.com

for a complete list of titles available in our
Manor Wodehouse Collection

BOOK ONE

CHAPTER 1
A PAWN OF FATE

MRS. Lora Delane Porter dismissed the hireling who had brought her automobile around from the garage and seated herself at the wheel. It was her habit to refresh her mind and improve her health by a daily drive between the hours of two and four in the afternoon.

The world knows little of its greatest women, and it is possible that Mrs. Porter's name is not familiar to you. If this is the case, I am pained, but not surprised. It happens only too often that the uplifter of the public mind is baulked by a disinclination on the part of the public mind to meet him or her half-way. The uplifter does his share. He produces the uplifting book. But the public, instead of standing still to be uplifted, wanders off to browse on coloured supplements and magazine stories.

If you are ignorant of Lora Delane Porter's books that is your affair. Perhaps you are more to be pitied than censured. Nature probably gave you the wrong shape of forehead. Mrs. Porter herself would have put it down to some atavistic tendency or pre-natal influence. She put most things down to that. She blamed nearly all the defects of the modern world, from weak intellects to in-growing toe-nails, on long-dead ladies and gentlemen who, safe in the family vault, imagined that they had established their alibi. She subpoenaed grandfathers and even great-grandfathers to give evidence to show that the reason Twentieth-Century Willie squinted or had to spend his winters in Arizona was their own shocking health 'way back in the days beyond recall.

Mrs. Porter's mind worked backward and forward. She had one eye on the past, the other on the future. If she was strong on hered-

7

ity, she was stronger on the future of the race. Most of her published works dealt with this subject. A careful perusal of them would have enabled the rising generation to select its ideal wife or husband with perfect ease, and, in the event of Heaven blessing the union, her little volume, entitled "The Hygienic Care of the Baby," which was all about germs and how to avoid them, would have insured the continuance of the direct succession.

Unfortunately, the rising generation did not seem disposed to a careful perusal of anything except the baseball scores and the beauty hints in the Sunday papers, and Mrs. Porter's public was small. In fact, her only real disciple, as she sometimes told herself in her rare moods of discouragement, was her niece, Ruth Bannister, daughter of John Bannister, the millionaire. It was not so long ago, she reflected with pride, that she had induced Ruth to refuse to marry Basil Milbank – a considerable feat, he being a young man of remarkable personal attractions and a great match in every way. Mrs. Porter's objection to him was that his father had died believing to the last that he was a teapot.

There is nothing evil or degrading in believing oneself a teapot, but it argues a certain inaccuracy of the thought processes; and Mrs. Porter had used all her influence with Ruth to make her reject Basil. It was her success that first showed her how great that influence was. She had come now to look on Ruth's destiny as something for which she was personally responsible – a fact which was noted and resented by others, in particular Ruth's brother Bailey, who regarded his aunt with a dislike and suspicion akin to that which a stray dog feels towards the boy who saunters towards him with a tin can in his hand.

To Bailey, his strong-minded relative was a perpetual menace, a sort of perambulating yellow peril, and the fact that she often alluded to him as a worm consolidated his distaste for her.

Mrs. Porter released the clutch and set out on her drive. She rarely had a settled route for these outings of hers, preferring to zigzag about New York, livening up the great city at random. She always drove herself and, having, like a good suffragist, a contempt for male prohibitions, took an honest pleasure in exceeding a man-made speed limit.

One hesitates to apply the term "joy-rider" to so eminent a leader of contemporary thought as the authoress of "The Dawn of Better Things," "Principles of Selection," and "What of To-morrow?" but candour compels the admission that she was a somewhat reckless driver. Perhaps it was due to some atavistic tendency. One of her ancestors may have been a Roman charioteer or a coach-racing maniac of the Regency days. At any rate, after a hard morning's work on her new book she felt that her mind needed cooling, and found that the rush of air against her face effected this satisfactorily. The greater the rush, the quicker the cooling. However, as the alert inhabitants of Manhattan Island, a hardy race trained from infancy to dodge taxi-cabs and ambulance wagons, had always removed themselves from her path with their usual agility, she had never yet had an accident.

But then she had never yet met George Pennicut. And George, pawn of fate, was even now waiting round the corner to upset her record.

George, man of all work to Kirk Winfield, one of the youngest and least efficient of New York's artist colony, was English. He had been in America some little time, but not long enough to accustom his rather unreceptive mind to the fact that, whereas in his native land vehicles kept to the left, in the country of his adoption they kept to the right; and it was still his bone-headed practice, when stepping off the sidewalk, to keep a wary look-out in precisely the wrong direction.

The only problem with regard to such a man is who will get him first. Fate had decided that it should be Lora Delane Porter.

To-day Mrs. Porter, having circled the park in rapid time, turned her car down Central Park West. She was feeling much refreshed by the pleasant air. She was conscious of a glow of benevolence toward her species, not excluding even the young couple she had almost reduced to mincemeat in the neighbourhood of Ninety-Seventh Street. They had annoyed her extremely at the time of their meeting by occupying till the last possible moment a part of the road which she wanted herself.

On reaching Sixty-First Street she found her way blocked by a lumbering delivery wagon. She followed it slowly for a while; then, growing tired of being merely a unit in a procession, tugged at the steering-wheel, and turned to the right.

George Pennicut, his anxious eyes raking the middle distance – as usual, in the wrong direction – had just stepped off the kerb. He received the automobile in the small of the back, uttered a yell of surprise and dismay, performed a few improvised Texas Tommy steps, and fell in a heap.

In a situation which might have stimulated another to fervid speech, George Pennicut contented himself with saying "Goo!" He was a man of few words.

Mrs. Porter stopped the car. From all points of the compass citizens began to assemble, many swallowing their chewing-gum in their excitement. One, a devout believer in the inscrutable ways of Providence, told a friend as he ran that only two minutes before he had almost robbed himself of this spectacle by going into a moving-picture palace.

Mrs. Porter was annoyed. She had never run over anything before except a few chickens, and she regarded the incident as a blot on her escutcheon. She was incensed with this idiot who had flung himself before her car, not reflecting in her heat that he probably had a pre-natal tendency to this sort of thing inherited from some ancestor who had played "last across" in front of hansom cabs in the streets of London.

She bent over George and passed experienced hands over his portly form. For this remarkable woman was as competent at first aid as at anything else. The citizens gathered silently round in a circle.

"It was your fault," she said to her victim severely. "I accept no liability whatever. I did not run into you. You ran into me. I have a jolly good mind to have you arrested for attempted suicide."

This aspect of the affair had not struck Mr. Pennicut. Presented to him in these simple words, it checked the recriminatory speech which, his mind having recovered to some extent from the first shock of the meeting, he had intended to deliver. He swallowed his words, awed. He felt dazed and helpless. Mrs. Porter had that effect upon men.

Some more citizens arrived.

"No bones broken," reported Mrs. Porter, concluding her examination. "You are exceedingly fortunate. You have a few bruises, and one knee is slightly wrenched. Nothing to signify. More frightened than hurt. Where do you live?"

"There," said George meekly.

"Where?"

"Them studios."

"No. 90?"

"Yes, ma'am." George's voice was that of a crushed worm.

"Are you an artist?"

"No, ma'am. I'm Mr. Winfield's man."

"Whose?"

"Mr. Winfield's, ma'am."

"Is he in?"

"Yes, ma'am."

"I'll fetch him. And if the policeman comes along and wants to know why you're lying there, mind you tell him the truth, that you ran into me."

"Yes, ma'am."

"Very well. Don't forget."

"No, ma'am."

She crossed the street and rang the bell over which was a card bearing the name of "Kirk Winfield". Mr. Pennicut watched her in silence.

Mrs. Porter pressed the button a second time. Somebody came at a leisurely pace down the passage, whistling cheerfully. The door opened.

It did not often happen to Lora Delane Porter to feel insignificant, least of all in the presence of the opposite sex. She had well-defined views upon man. Yet, in the interval which elapsed between the opening of the door and her first words, a certain sensation of smallness overcame her.

The man who had opened the door was not, judged by any standard of regularity of features, handsome. He had a rather boyish face, pleasant eyes set wide apart, and a friendly mouth. He was rather an outsize in young men, and as he stood there he seemed to fill the doorway.

It was this sense of bigness that he conveyed, his cleanness, his magnificent fitness, that for the moment overcame Mrs. Porter. Physical fitness was her gospel. She stared at him in silent appreciation.

To the young man, however, her forceful gaze did not convey this quality. She seemed to him to be looking as if she had caught him in the act of endeavouring to snatch her purse. He had been thrown a little off his balance by the encounter.

Resource in moments of crisis is largely a matter of preparedness, and a man, who, having opened his door in the expectation of seeing a ginger-haired, bow-legged, grinning George Pennicut, is confronted by a masterful woman with eyes like gimlets, may be excused for not guessing that her piercing stare is an expression of admiration and respect.

Mrs. Porter broke the silence. It was ever her way to come swiftly to the matter in hand.

"Mr. Kirk Winfield?"

"Yes."

"Have you in your employment a red-haired, congenital idiot who ambles about New York in an absent-minded way, as if he were on a desert island? The man I refer to is a short, stout Englishman, clean-shaven, dressed in black."

"That sounds like George Pennicut."

"I have no doubt that that is his name. I did not inquire. It did not interest me. My name is Mrs. Lora Delane Porter. This man of yours has just run into my automobile."

"I beg your pardon?"

"I cannot put it more lucidly. I was driving along the street when this weak-minded person flung himself in front of my car. He is out there now. Kindly come and help him in."

"Is he hurt?"

"More frightened than hurt. I have examined him. His left knee appears to be slightly wrenched."

Kirk Winfield passed a hand over his left forehead and followed her. Like George, he found Mrs. Porter a trifle overwhelming.

Out in the street George Pennicut, now the centre of quite a substantial section of the Four Million, was causing a granite-faced policeman to think that the age of miracles had returned by informing him that the accident had been his fault and no other's. He greeted the relief-party with a wan grin.

"Just broke my leg, sir," he announced to Kirk.

"You have done nothing of the sort," said Mrs. Porter. "You have wrenched your knee very slightly. Have you explained to the policeman that it was entirely your fault?"

"Yes, ma'am."

"That's right. Always speak the truth."

"Yes, ma'am."

"Mr. Winfield will help you indoors."

"Thank you, ma'am."

She turned to Kirk.

"Now, Mr. Winfield."

Kirk bent over the victim, gripped him, and lifted him like a baby.

"He's got his," observed one interested spectator.

"I should worry!" agreed another. "All broken up."

"Nothing of the kind," said Mrs. Porter severely. "The man is hardly hurt at all. Be more accurate in your remarks."

She eyed the speaker sternly. He wilted.

"Yes, ma'am," he mumbled sheepishly.

The policeman, with that lionlike courage which makes the New York constabulary what it is, endeavoured to assert himself at this point.

"Hey!" he boomed.

Mrs. Porter turned her gaze upon him, her cold, steely gaze.

"I beg your pardon?"

"This won't do, ma'am. I've me report to make. How did this happen?"

"You have already been informed. The man ran into my automobile."

"But—"

"I shall not charge him."

She turned and followed Kirk.

"But, say—" The policeman's voice was now almost plaintive.

Mrs. Porter ignored him and disappeared into the house. The policeman, having gulped several times in a disconsolate way, relieved his feelings by dispersing the crowd with well-directed prods of his locust stick. A small boy who lingered, squeezing the automobile's hooter, in a sort of trance he kicked. The boy vanished. The crowd melted. The policeman walked slowly toward Ninth Avenue. Peace reigned in the street.

"Put him to bed," said Mrs. Porter, as Kirk laid his burden on a couch in the studio. "You seem exceedingly muscular, Mr. Winfield. I noticed that you carried him without an effort. He is a stout man, too. Grossly out of condition, like ninety-nine per cent of men to-day."

"I'm not so young as I was, ma'am," protested George. "When I was in the harmy I was a fine figure of a man."

"The more shame to you that you have allowed yourself to deteriorate," commented Mrs. Porter. "Beer?"

A grateful smile irradiated George's face.

"Thank you, ma'am. It's very kind of you, ma'am. I don't mind if I do."

"The man appears a perfect imbecile," said Mrs. Porter, turning abruptly to Kirk. "I ask him if he attributes his physical decay to beer and he babbles."

"I think he thought you were offering him a drink," suggested Kirk. "As a matter of fact, a little brandy wouldn't hurt him, after the shock he has had."

"On no account. The worst thing possible."

"This isn't your lucky day, George," said Kirk. "Well, I guess I'll phone to the doctor."

"Quite unnecessary."

"I beg your pardon?"

"Entirely unnecessary. I have made an examination. There is practically nothing the matter with the man. Put him to bed, and let him sponge his knee with warm water."

"Are you a doctor, Mrs. Porter?"

"I have studied first aid."

"Well, I think, if you don't mind, I should like to have your opinion confirmed."

This was rank mutiny. Mrs. Porter stared haughtily at Kirk. He met her gaze with determination.

"As you please," she snapped.

"Thank you," said Kirk. "I don't want to take any risks with George. I couldn't afford to lose him. There aren't any more like him: they've mislaid the pattern."

He went to the telephone.

Mrs. Porter watched him narrowly. She was more than ever impressed by the perfection of his physique. She appraised his voice as he spoke to the doctor. It gave evidence of excellent lungs. He was a wonderfully perfect physical specimen.

An idea concerning this young man came into her mind, startling as all great ideas are at birth. The older it grew, the more she approved of it. She decided to put a few questions to him. She had a habit of questioning people, and it never occurred to her that they might resent it. If it had occurred to her, she would have done it just the same. She was like that.

"Mr. Winfield?"

"Yes?"

"I should like to ask you a few questions."

This woman delighted Kirk.

"Please do," he said.

Mrs. Porter scanned him closely.

"You are an extraordinarily healthy man, to all appearances. Have you ever suffered from bad health?"

"Measles."

"Immaterial."

"Very unpleasant, though."

"Nothing else?"

"Mumps."

"Unimportant."

"Not to me. I looked like a water-melon."

"Nothing besides? No serious illnesses?"

"None."

"What is your age?"

"Twenty-five."

"Are your parents living?"

"No."

"Were they healthy?"

"Fit as fiddles."

"And your grandparents?"

"Perfect bear-cats. I remember my grandfather at the age of about a hundred or something like that spanking me for breaking his pipe. I thought it was a steam-hammer. He was a wonderfully muscular old gentleman."

"Excellent."

"By the way," said Kirk casually, "my life *is* insured."

"Very sensible. There has been no serious illness in your family at all, then, as far as you know?"

"I could hunt up the records, if you like; but I don't think so."

"Consumption? No? Cancer? No? As far as you are aware, nothing? Very satisfactory."

"I'm glad you're pleased."

"Are you married?"

"Good Lord, no!"

"At your age you should be. With your magnificent physique and remarkable record of health, it is your duty to the future of the race to marry."

"I'm not sure I've been worrying much about the future of the race."

"No man does. It is the crying evil of the day, men's selfish absorption in the present, their utter lack of a sense of duty with regard to the future. Have you read my 'Dawn of Better Things'?"

"I'm afraid I read very few novels."

"It is not a novel. It is a treatise on the need for implanting a sense of personal duty to the future of the race in the modern young man."

"It sounds a crackerjack. I must get it."

"I will send you a copy. At the same time I will send you my 'Principles of Selection' and 'What of To-morrow?' They will make you think."

"I bet they will. Thank you very much."

"And now," said Mrs. Porter, switching the conversation to the gaping George, "you had better put this man to bed."

George Pennicut's opinion of Mrs. Porter, to which he was destined to adhere on closer acquaintance, may be recorded.

"A hawful woman, sir," he whispered as Kirk bore him off.

"Nonsense, George," said Kirk. "One of the most entertaining ladies I have ever met. Already I love her like a son. But how she escaped from Bloomingdale beats me. There's been carelessness somewhere."

The bedrooms attached to the studio opened off the gallery that ran the length of the east wall. Looking over the edge of the gallery before coming downstairs Kirk perceived his visitor engaged in a tour of the studio. At that moment she was examining his masterpiece, "Ariadne in Naxos." He had called it that because that was what it had turned into.

At the beginning he had had no definite opinion as to its identity. It was rather a habit with his pictures to start out in a vague spirit of adventure and receive their label on completion. He had an airy and a dashing way in his dealings with the goddess Art.

Nevertheless, he had sufficient of the artist soul to resent the fact that Mrs. Porter was standing a great deal too close to the masterpiece to get its full value.

"You want to stand back a little," he suggested over the rail.

Mrs. Porter looked up.

"Oh, there you are!" she said.

"Yes, here I am," agreed Kirk affably.

"Is this yours?"

"It is."

"You painted it?"

"I did."

"It is poor. It shows a certain feeling for colour, but the drawing is weak," said Mrs. Porter. For this wonderful woman was as competent at art criticism as at automobile driving and first aid. "Where did you study?"

"In Paris, if you could call it studying. I'm afraid I was not the model pupil."

"Kindly come down. You are giving me a crick in the neck."

Kirk descended. He found Mrs. Porter still regarding the masterpiece with an unfavourable eye.

"Yes," she said, "the drawing is decidedly weak."

"I shouldn't wonder," assented Kirk. "The dealers to whom I've tried to sell it have not said that in so many words, but they've all begged me with tears in their eyes to take the darned thing away, so I guess you're right."

"Do you depend for a living on the sale of your pictures?"

"Thank Heaven, no. I'm the only artist in captivity with a private income."

"A large income?"

"'Tis not so deep as a well, nor so wide as a church door, but 'tis enough, 'twill serve. All told, about five thousand iron men per annum."

"Iron men?"

"Bones."

"Bones?"

"I should have said dollars."

"You should. I detest slang."

"Sorry," said Kirk.

Mrs. Porter resumed her tour of the studio. She was interrupted by the arrival of the doctor, a cheerful little old man with the bearing of one sure of his welcome. He was an old friend of Kirk's.

"Well, what's the trouble? I couldn't come sooner. I was visiting a case. *I* work."

"There is no trouble," said Mrs. Porter. The doctor spun round, startled. In the dimness of the studio he had not perceived her. "Mr. Winfield's servant has injured his knee very superficially. There is practically nothing wrong with him. I have made a thorough examination."

The doctor looked from one to the other.

"Is the case in other hands?" he asked.

"You bet it isn't," said Kirk. "Mrs. Porter just looked in for a family chat and a glimpse of my pictures. You'll find George in bed, first floor on the left upstairs, and a very remarkable sight he is. He is wearing red hair with purple pyjamas. Why go abroad when you have not yet seen the wonders of your native land?"

༈

That night Lora Delane Porter wrote in the diary which, with that magnificent freedom from human weakness that marked every aspect of her life, she kept all the year round instead of only during the first week in January.

This is what she wrote:

"Worked steadily on my book. It progresses. In the afternoon an annoying occurrence. An imbecile with red hair placed himself in front of my automobile, fortunately without serious injury to the machine – though the sudden application of the brake cannot be good for the tyres. Out of evil, however, came good, for I have made the acquaintance of his employer, a Mr. Winfield, an artist. Mr. Winfield is a man of remarkable physique. I questioned him narrowly, and he appears thoroughly sound. As to his mental attainments, I cannot speak so highly; but all men are fools, and Mr. Winfield is not more so than most. I have decided that he shall marry my dear Ruth. They will make a magnificent pair."

Chapter 2
Ruth States Her Intentions

At about the time when Lora Delane Porter was cross-examining Kirk Winfield, Bailey Bannister left his club hurriedly.

Inside the club a sad, rabbit-faced young gentleman, who had been unburdening his soul to Bailey, was seeking further consolation in an amber drink with a cherry at the bottom of it. For this young man was one of nature's cherry-chasers. It was the only thing he did really well. His name was Grayling, his height five feet three, his socks pink, and his income enormous.

So much for Grayling. He is of absolutely no importance, either to the world or to this narrative, except in so far that the painful story he has been unfolding to Bailey Bannister has so wrought upon that exquisite as to send him galloping up Fifth Avenue at five miles an hour in search of his sister Ruth.

Let us now examine Bailey. He is a faultlessly dressed young man of about twenty-seven, who takes it as a compliment when people think him older. His mouth, at present gaping with agitation and the unwonted exercise, is, as a rule, primly closed. His eyes, peering through gold-rimmed glasses, protrude slightly, giving him something of the dumb pathos of a codfish.

His hair is pale and scanty, his nose sharp and narrow. He is a junior partner in the firm of Bannister & Son, and it is his unalterable conviction that, if his father would only give him a chance, he could show Wall Street some high finance that would astonish it.

The afternoon was warm. The sun beat down on the avenue. Bailey had not gone two blocks before it occurred to him that swifter and more comfortable progress could be made in a taxicab than on his admirably trousered legs. No more significant proof of the magnitude of his agitation could be brought forward than the fact that he had so far forgotten himself as to walk at all. He hailed a cab and gave the address of a house on the upper avenue.

He leaned back against the cushions, trying to achieve a coolness of mind and body. But the heat of the day kept him unpleasantly soluble, and dismay, that perspiration of the soul, refused to be absorbed by the pocket-handkerchief of philosophy.

Bailey Bannister was a young man who considered the minding of other people's business a duty not to be shirked. Life is a rocky road for such. His motto was "Let *me* do it!" He fussed about the affairs of Bannister & Son; he fussed about the welfare of his friends at the club; especially, he fussed about his only sister Ruth.

He looked on himself as a sort of guardian to Ruth. Their mother had died when they were children, and old Mr. Bannister was indifferently equipped with the paternal instinct. He was absorbed, body and soul, in the business of the firm. He lived practically a hermit life in the great house on Fifth Avenue; and, if it had not been for Bailey, so Bailey considered, Ruth would have been allowed to do just whatever she pleased. There were those who said that this was precisely what she did, despite Brother Bailey.

It is a hard world for a conscientious young man of twenty-seven.

Bailey paid the cab and went into the house. It was deliciously cool in the hall, and for a moment peace descended on him. But the distant sound of a piano in the upper regions ejected it again by reminding him of his mission. He bounded up the stairs and knocked at the door of his sister's private den.

The piano stopped as he entered, and the girl on the music-stool glanced over her shoulder.

"Well, Bailey," she said, "you look warm."

"I *am* warm," said Bailey in an aggrieved tone. He sat down solemnly.

"I want to speak to you, Ruth."

Ruth shut the piano and caused the music-stool to revolve till she faced him.

"Well?" she said.

Ruth Bannister was an extraordinarily beautiful girl, "a daughter of the gods, divinely tall, and most divinely fair." From her mother she had inherited the dark eyes and ivory complexion which went so well with her mass of dark hair; from her father a chin of peculiar determination and perfect teeth. Her body was strong and supple. She radiated health.

To her friends Ruth was a source of perplexity. It was difficult to understand her. In the set in which she moved girls married young; yet season followed season, and Ruth remained single, and this so obviously of her own free will that the usual explanation of such a state of things broke down as soon as it was tested.

In shoals during her first two seasons, and lately with less una-
nimity, men of every condition, from a prince – somewhat battered,
but still a prince – to the Bannisters' English butler – a good man,
but at the moment under the influence of tawny port, had laid their
hearts at her feet. One and all, they had been compelled to pick
them up and take them elsewhere. She was generally kind on these
occasions, but always very firm. The determined chin gave no hope
that she might yield to importunity. The eyes that backed up the
message of the chin were pleasant, but inflexible.

Generally it was with a feeling akin to relief that the rejected,
when time had begun to heal the wound, contemplated their position. There was something about this girl, they decided, which no
fellow could understand: she frightened them; she made them feel
that their hands were large and red and their minds weak and empty.
She was waiting for something. What it was they did not know, but
it was plain that they were not it, and off they went to live happily
ever after with girls who ate candy and read best-sellers. And Ruth
went on her way, cool and watchful and mysterious, waiting.

The room which Ruth had taken for her own gave, like all rooms
when intelligently considered, a clue to the character of its owner. It
was the only room in the house furnished with any taste or simplicity. The furniture was exceedingly expensive, but did not look so.
The key-note of the colour-scheme was green and white. All round
the walls were books. Except for a few prints, there were no pictures;
and the only photograph visible stood in a silver frame on a little
table.

It was the portrait of a woman of about fifty, square-jawed,
tight-lipped, who stared almost threateningly out of the frame; exceedingly handsome, but, to the ordinary male, too formidable to
be attractive. On this was written in a bold hand, bristling with
emphatic down-strokes and wholly free from feminine flourish: "To
my dear Ruth from her Aunt Lora." And below the signature, in
what printers call "quotes," a line that was evidently an extract from
somebody's published works: "Bear the torch and do not falter."

Bailey inspected this photograph with disfavour. It always irritated him. The information, conveyed to him by amused friends,
that his Aunt Lora had once described Ruth as a jewel in a dust-bin,
seemed to him to carry an offensive innuendo directed at himself
and the rest of the dwellers in the Bannister home. Also, she had

called him a worm. Also, again, his actual encounters with the lady, though few, had been memorably unpleasant. Furthermore, he considered that she had far too great an influence on Ruth. And, lastly, that infernal sentence about the torch, which he found perfectly meaningless, had a habit of running in his head like a catch-phrase, causing him the keenest annoyance.

He pursed his lips disapprovingly and averted his eyes.

"Don't sniff at Aunt Lora, Bailey," said Ruth. "I've had to speak to you about that before. What's the matter? What has sent you flying up here?"

"I have had a shock," said Bailey. "I have been very greatly disturbed. I have just been speaking to Clarence Grayling."

He eyed her accusingly through his gold-rimmed glasses. She remained tranquil.

"And what had Clarence to say?"

"A great many things."

"I gather he told you I had refused him."

"If it were only that!"

Ruth rapped the piano sharply.

"Bailey," she said, "wake up. Either get to the point or go or read a book or do some tatting or talk about something else. You know perfectly well that I absolutely refuse to endure your impressive manner. I believe when people ask you the time you look pained and important and make a mystery of it. What's troubling you? I should have thought Clarence would have kept quiet about insulting me. But apparently he has no sense of shame."

Bailey gaped. Bailey was shocked and alarmed.

"Insulting you! What do you mean? Clarence is a gentleman. He is incapable of insulting a woman."

"Is he? He told me I was a suitable wife for a wretched dwarf with the miserably inadequate intelligence which nature gave him reduced to practically a minus quantity by alcohol! At least, he implied it. He asked me to marry him."

"I have just left him at the club. He is very upset."

"I should imagine so." A soft smile played over Ruth's face. "I spoke to Clarence. I explained things to him. I lit up Clarence's little mind like a searchlight."

Bailey rose, tremulous with just wrath.

"You spoke to him in a way that I can only call outrageous and improper, and – er – outrageous."

He paced the room with agitated strides. Ruth watched him calmly.

"If the overflowing emotion of a giant soul in torment makes you knock over a table or smash a chair," she said, "I shall send the bill for repairs to you. You had far better sit down and talk quietly. What *is* worrying you, Bailey?"

"Is it nothing," demanded her brother, "that my sister should have spoken to a man as you spoke to Clarence Grayling?"

With an impassioned gesture he sent a flower-vase crashing to the floor.

"I told you so," said Ruth. "Pick up the bits, and don't let the water spoil the carpet. Use your handkerchief. I should say that that would cost you about six dollars, dear. Why will you let yourself be so temperamental? Now let me try and think what it was I said to Clarence. As far as I can remember it was the mere A B C of eugenics."

Bailey, on his knees, picking up broken glass, raised a flushed and accusing face.

"Ah! Eugenics! You admit it!"

"I think," went on Ruth placidly, "I asked him what sort of children he thought we were likely to have if we married."

"A nice girl ought not to think about such things."

"I don't think about anything else much. A woman can't do a great deal, even nowadays, but she can have a conscience and feel that she owes something to the future of the race. She can feel that it is her duty to bring fine children into the world. As Aunt Lora says, she can carry the torch and not falter."

Bailey shied like a startled horse at the hated phrase. He pointed furiously at the photograph of the great thinker.

"You're talking like that – that damned woman!"

"Bailey *precious!* You mustn't use such wicked, wicked words."

Bailey rose, pink and wrathful.

"If you're going to break another vase," said Ruth, "you will really have to go."

"Ever since that – that—" cried Bailey. "Ever since Aunt Lora—"

Ruth smiled indulgently.

"That's more like my little man," she said. "He knows as well as I do how wrong it is to swear."

"Be quiet! Ever since Aunt Lora got hold of you, I say, you have become a sort of gramophone, spouting her opinions."

"But what sensible opinions!"

"It's got to stop. Aunt Lora! My God! Who is she? Just look at her record. She disgraces the family by marrying a grubby newspaper fellow called Porter. He has the sense to die. I will say that for him. She thrusts herself into public notice by a series of books and speeches on subjects of which a decent woman ought to know nothing. And now she gets hold of you, fills you up with her disgusting nonsense, makes a sort of disciple of you, gives you absurd ideas, poisons your mind, and – er – er—"

"Bailey! This is positive eloquence!"

"It's got to stop. It's bad enough in her; but every one knows she is crazy, and makes allowances. But in a young girl like you."

He choked.

"In a young girl like me," prompted Ruth in a low, tragic voice.

"It – it's not right. It – it's not proper." He drew a long breath. "It's all wrong. It's got to stop."

"He's perfectly wonderful!" murmured Ruth. "He just opens his mouth and the words come out. But I knew he was somebody, directly I saw him, by his forehead. Like a dome!" Bailey mopped the dome.

"Perhaps you don't know it," he said, "but you're getting yourself talked about. You go about saying perfectly impossible things to people. You won't marry. You have refused nearly every friend I have."

Ruth shuddered.

"Your friends are awful, Bailey. They are all turned out on a pattern, like a flock of sheep. They bleat. They have all got little, narrow faces without chins or big, fat faces without foreheads. Ugh!"

"None of them good enough for you, is that it?"

"Not nearly."

Emotion rendered Bailey – for him – almost vulgar.

"I guess you hate yourself!" he snapped.

"No *sir*" beamed Ruth. "I think I'm perfectly beautiful."

Bailey grunted. Ruth came to him and gave him a sisterly kiss. She was very fond of Bailey, though she declined to reverence him.

"Cheer up, Bailey boy," she said. "Don't you worry yourself. There's a method in my madness. I'll find him sooner or later, and then you'll be glad I waited."

"Him? what do you mean?"

"Why, *him*, of course. The ideal young man. That's who – or is it whom? – I'm waiting for. Bailey, shall I tell you something? You're so scarlet already – poor boy, you ought not to rush around in this hot weather – that it won't make you blush. It's this. I'm ambitious. I mean to marry the finest man in the world and have the greatest little old baby you ever dreamed of. By the way, now I remember, I told Clarence that."

Bailey uttered a strangled exclamation.

"It *has* made you blush! You turned purple. Well, now you know. I mean my baby to be the most splendid baby that was ever born. He's going to be strong and straight and clever and handsome, and – oh, everything else you can think of. That's why I'm waiting for the ideal young man. If I don't find him I shall die an old maid. But I shall find him. We may pass each other on Fifth Avenue. We may sit next each other at a theatre. Wherever it is, I shall just reach right out and grab him and whisk him away. And if he's married already, he'll have to get a divorce. And I shan't care who he is. He may be any one. I don't mind if he's a ribbon clerk or a prize-fighter or a policeman or a cab-driver, so long as he's the right man."

Bailey plied the handkerchief on his streaming forehead. The heat of the day and the horror of this conversation were reducing his weight at the rate of ounces a minute. In his most jaundiced mood he had never imagined these frightful sentiments to be lurking in Ruth's mind.

"You can't mean that!" he cried.

"I mean every word of it," said Ruth. "I hope, for your sake, he won't turn out to be a waiter or a prize-fighter, but it won't make any difference to me."

"You're crazy!"

"Well, just now you said Aunt Lora was. If she is, I am."

"I knew it! I said she had been putting these ghastly ideas into your head. I'd like to strangle that woman."

"Don't you try! Have you ever felt Aunt Lora's biceps? It's like a man's. She does dumb-bells every morning."

"I've a good mind to speak to father. Somebody's got to make you stop this insanity."

"Just as you please. But you know how father hates to be worried about things that don't concern business."

Bailey did. His father, of whom he stood in the greatest awe, was very little interested in any subject except the financial affairs of the firm of Bannister & Son. It required greater courage than Bailey possessed to place this matter before him. He had an uneasy feeling that Ruth knew it.

"I would, if it were necessary," he said. "But I don't believe you're serious."

"Stick to that idea as long as ever you can, Bailey dear," said Ruth. "It will comfort you."

CHAPTER 3
THE MATES MEET

KIRK Winfield was an amiable, if rather weak, young man with whom life, for twenty-five years, had dealt kindly. He had perfect health, an income more than sufficient for his needs, a profession which interested without monopolizing him, a thoroughly contented disposition, and the happy knack of surrounding himself with friends.

That he had to contribute to the support of the majority of these friends might have seemed a drawback to some men. Kirk did not object to it in the least. He had enough money to meet their needs, and, being a sociable person who enjoyed mixing with all sorts and conditions of men, he found the Liberty Hall regime pleasant.

He liked to be a magnet, attracting New York's Bohemian population. If he had his preferences among the impecunious crowd who used the studio as a chapel of ease, strolling in when it pleased them, drinking his whisky, smoking his cigarettes, borrowing his money, and, on occasion, his spare bedrooms and his pyjamas, he never showed it. He was fully as pleasant to Percy Shanklyn, the elegant, perpetually resting English actor, whom he disliked as far as he was capable of disliking any one, as he was to Hank Jardine, the prospector, and Hank's prize-fighter friend, Steve Dingle, both of whom he liked enormously.

It seemed to him sometimes that he had drifted into the absolutely ideal life. He lived entirely in the present. The passage of time left him untouched. Day followed day, week followed week, and nothing seemed to change. He was never unhappy, never ill, never bored.

He would get up in the morning with the comfortable knowledge that the day held no definite duties. George Pennicut would produce one of his excellent breakfasts. The next mile-stone would be the arrival of Steve Dingle. Five brisk rounds with Steve, a cold bath, and a rub-down took him pleasantly on to lunch, after which it amused him to play at painting.

There was always something to do when he wearied of that until, almost before the day had properly begun, up came George with one of his celebrated dinners. And then began the incursion of his friends. One by one they would drop in, making themselves very much at home, to help their host through till bedtime. And another day would slip into the past.

It never occurred to Kirk that he was wasting his life. He had no ambitions. Ambition is born of woman, and no woman that he had ever met had ever stirred him deeply. He had never been in love, and he had come to imagine that he was incapable of anything except a mild liking for women. He considered himself immune, and was secretly glad of it. He enjoyed his go-as-you-please existence too much to want to have it upset. He belonged, in fact, to the type which, when the moment arrives, falls in love very suddenly, very violently, and for all time.

Nothing could have convinced him of this. He was like a child lighting matches in a powder-magazine. When the idea of marriage crossed his mind he thrust it from him with a kind of shuddering horror. He could not picture to himself a woman who could compensate him for the loss of his freedom and, still less, of his friends.

His friends were men's men; he could not see them fitting into a scheme of life that involved the perpetual presence of a hostess. Hank Jardine, for instance. To Kirk, the great point about Hank was that he had been everywhere, seen everything, and was, when properly stimulated with tobacco and drink, a fountain of reminiscence. But he could not talk unless he had his coat off and his feet up on the back of a chair. No hostess could be expected to relish that.

Hank was a bachelor's friend; he did not belong in a married household. The abstract wife could not be reconciled to him, and Kirk, loving Hank like a brother, firmly dismissed the abstract wife.

He came to look upon himself as a confirmed bachelor. He had thought out the question of marriage in all its aspects, and decided against it. He was the strong man who knew his own mind and could not be shaken.

Yet, on the afternoon of the day following Mrs. Lora Delane Porter's entry into his life, Kirk sat in the studio, feeling, for the first time in recent years, a vague discontent. He was uneasy, almost afraid. The slight dislocation in the smooth-working machinery of his existence, caused by the compulsory retirement of George Pennicut, had made him thoroughly uncomfortable. With discomfort had come introspection, and with introspection this uneasiness that was almost fear.

A man, living alone, without money troubles to worry him, sinks inevitably into a routine. Fatted ease is good for no one. It sucks the soul out of a man. Kirk, as he sat smoking in the cool dusk of the studio, was wondering, almost in a panic, whether all was well with himself.

This mild domestic calamity had upset him so infernally. It could not be right that so slight a change in his habits should have such an effect upon him. George had been so little hurt – the doctor gave him a couple of days before complete recovery – that it had not seemed worth while to Kirk to engage a substitute. It was simpler to go out for his meals and make his own bed. And it was the realization that this alteration in his habits had horribly disturbed and unsettled him that was making Kirk subject himself now to an examination of quite unusual severity.

He hated softness. Physically, he kept himself always in perfect condition. Had he become spiritually flabby? Certainly this unexpected call on his energies would appear to have found him unprepared. It spoiled his whole day, knowing, when he got out of bed in the morning, that he must hunt about and find his food instead of sitting still and having it brought to him. It frightened him to think how set he had become.

Forty-eight hours ago he would have scorned the suggestion that he coddled himself. He would have produced as evidence to the contrary his cold baths, his exercises, his bouts with Steve Dingle. To-day he felt less confidence. For all his baths and boxing, the fact remained that he had become, at the age of twenty-six, such a slave to habit that a very trifling deviation from settled routine had been enough to poison life for him.

Bachelors have these black moments, and it is then that the abstract wife comes into her own. To Kirk, brooding in the dusk, the figure of the abstract wife seemed to grow less formidable, the fact that she might not get on with Hank Jardine of less importance.

The revolutionary thought that life was rather a bore, and would become more and more of a bore as the years went on, unless he had some one to share it with, crept into his mind and stayed there.

He shivered. These were unpleasant thoughts, and in his hour of clear vision he knew whence they came. They were entirely due to the knowledge that, instead of sitting comfortably at home, he would be compelled in a few short hours to go out and get dinner at some restaurant. To such a pass had he come in the twenty-sixth year of his life.

Once the gods have marked a bachelor down, they give him few chances of escape. It was when Kirk's mood was at its blackest, and the figure of the abstract wife had ceased to be a menace and become a shining angel of salvation, that Lora Delane Porter, with Ruth Bannister at her side, rang the studio bell.

Kirk went to the door. He hoped it was a tradesman; he feared it was a friend. In his present state of mind he had no use for friends. When he found himself confronting Mrs. Porter he became momentarily incapable of speech. It had not entered his mind that she would pay him a second visit. Possibly it was joy that rendered him dumb.

"Good afternoon, Mr. Winfield," said Mrs. Porter. "I have come to inquire after the man Pennicut. Ruth, this is Mr. Winfield. Mr. Winfield, my niece, Miss Bannister."

And Kirk perceived for the first time that his visitor was not alone. In the shadow behind her a girl was standing. He stood aside to let Mrs. Porter pass, and Ruth came into the light.

If there are degrees in speechlessness, Kirk's aphasia became doubled and trebled at the sight of her. It seemed to him that he went all to pieces, as if he had received a violent blow. Curious physical changes were taking place in him. His legs, which only that morning he had looked upon as eminently muscular, he now discovered to be composed of some curiously unstable jelly.

He also perceived – a fact which he had never before suspected – that he had heart-disease. His lungs, too, were in poor condition; he found it practically impossible to breathe. The violent trembling fit which assailed him he attributed to general organic weakness.

He gaped at Ruth.

Ruth, outwardly, remained unaffected by the meeting, but inwardly she was feeling precisely the same sensation of smallness which had come to Mrs. Porter on her first meeting with Kirk. If this sensation had been novel to Mrs. Porter, it was even stranger to Ruth.

To think humbly of herself was an experience that seldom happened to her. She was perfectly aware that her beauty was remarkable even in a city of beautiful women, and it was rarely that she permitted her knowledge of that fact to escape her. Her beauty, to her, was a natural phenomenon, impossible to overlook. The realization of it did not obtrude itself into her mind, it simply existed subconsciously.

Yet for an instant it ceased to exist. She was staggered by a sense of inferiority.

It lasted but a pin-point of time, this riotous upheaval of her nature. She recovered herself so swiftly that Kirk, busy with his own emotions, had no suspicion of it.

A moment later he, too, was himself again. He was conscious of feeling curiously uplifted and thrilled, as if the world had suddenly become charged with ozone and electricity, and for some reason he felt capable of great feats of muscle and energy; but the aphasia had left him, and he addressed himself with a clear brain to the task of entertaining his visitors.

"George is better to-day," he reported.

"He never was bad," said Mrs. Porter succinctly.

"He doesn't think so."

"Possibly not. He is hopelessly weak-minded."

Ruth laughed. Kirk thrilled at the sound.

"Poor George!" she observed.

"Don't waste your sympathy, my dear," said Mrs. Porter. "That he is injured at all is his own fault. For years he has allowed himself to become gross and flabby, with the result that the collision did damage which it would not have done to a man in hard condition. You, Mr. Winfield," she added, turning abruptly to Kirk, "would scarcely have felt it. But then you," went on Mrs. Porter, "are in good condition. Cold baths!"

"I beg your pardon?"

"Do you take cold baths?"

"I do."

"Do you do Swedish exercises?"

"I go through a series of evolutions every morning, with the utmost loathing. I started them as a boy, and they have become a habit like dram-drinking. I would leave them off if I could, but I can't."

"Do nothing of the kind. They are invaluable."

"But undignified."

"Let me feel your biceps, Mr. Winfield," said Mrs. Porter. She nodded approvingly. "Like iron." She poised a finger and ran a meditative glance over his form. Kirk eyed her apprehensively. The finger darted forward and struck home in the region of the third waistcoat button. "Wonderful!" she exclaimed. "Ruth!"

"Yes, aunt."

"Prod Mr. Winfield where my finger is pointing. He is extraordinarily muscular."

"I say, really!" protested Kirk. He was a modest young man, and this exploration of his more intimate anatomy by the finger-tips of the girl he loved was not to be contemplated.

"Just as you please," said Mrs. Porter. "If I were a man of your physique, I should be proud of it."

"Wouldn't you like to go up and see George?" asked Kirk. It was hard on George, but it was imperative that this woman be removed somehow.

"Very well. I have brought him a little book to read, which will do him good. It is called 'Elementary Rules for the Preservation of the Body'."

"He has learned one of them, all right, since yesterday," said Kirk. "Not to walk about in front of automobiles."

"The rules I refer to are mainly concerned with diet and wholesome exercise," explained Mrs. Porter. "Careful attention to them may yet save him. His case is not hopeless. Ruth, let Mr. Winfield show you his pictures. They are poor in many respects, but not entirely without merit."

Ruth, meanwhile, had been sitting on the couch, listening to the conversation without really hearing it. She was in a dreamy, content-ed mood. She found herself curiously soothed by the atmosphere of the studio, with its shaded lights and its atmosphere of peace. That was the keynote of the place, peace.

From outside came the rumble of an elevated train, subdued and softened, like faintly heard thunder. Somebody passed the window, whistling. A barrier seemed to separate her from these noises of the city. New York was very far away.

"I believe I could be wonderfully happy in a place like this," she thought.

She became suddenly aware, in the midst of her meditations, of eyes watching her intently. She looked up and met Kirk's.

She could read the message in them as clearly as if he had spo-ken it, and she was conscious of a little thrill of annoyance at the thought of all the tiresome formalities which must be gone through before he could speak it. They seemed absurd.

It was all so simple. He wanted her; she wanted him. She had known it from the moment of their meeting. The man had found his woman, the woman her man. Nature had settled the whole affair in an instant. And now civilization, propriety, etiquette, whatever one cared to call it, must needs step in with the rules and regulations and precedents.

The goal was there, clear in sight, but it must be reached by the winding road appointed. She, being a woman and, by virtue of her sex, primeval, scorned the road, and would have ignored it. But she knew men, and especially, at that moment as their eyes met, she knew Kirk; and she understood that to him the road was a thing that could not be ignored. The mere idea of doing so would seem grotesque and impossible, probably even shocking, to him. Men were odd, formal creatures, slaves to precedent.

He must have time, it was the prerogative of the male; time to reveal himself to her, to strut before her, to go through the solemn comedy of proving to her, by the exhibition of his virtues and the careful suppression of his defects, what had been clear to her from the first instant, that here was her mate, the man nature had set apart for her.

He would begin by putting on a new suit of clothes and having his hair cut.

She smiled. It was silly and tiresome, but it was funny.

"Will you show me your pictures, Mr. Winfield?" she asked.

"If you'd really care to see them. I'm afraid they're pretty bad."

"Exhibit A. Modesty," thought Ruth.

The journey had begun.

CHAPTER 4
TROUBLED WATERS

IT is not easy in this world to take any definite step without annoying somebody, and Kirk, in embarking on his wooing of Ruth Bannister, failed signally to do so. Lora Delane Porter beamed graciously upon him, like a pleased Providence, but the rest of his circle of acquaintances were ill at ease.

The statement does not include Hank Jardine, for Hank was out of New York; but the others – Shanklyn, the actor; Wren, the newspaper-man; Bryce, Johnson, Willis, Appleton, and the rest – sensed impending change in the air, and were uneasy, like cattle before a thunder-storm. The fact that the visits of Mrs. Porter and Ruth to inquire after George, now of daily occurrence, took place in the afternoon, while they, Kirk's dependents, seldom or never appeared in the studio till drawn there by the scent of the evening meal, it being understood that during the daytime Kirk liked to work undisturbed, kept them ignorant of the new development.

All they knew was that during the last two weeks a subtle change had taken place in Kirk. He was less genial, more prone to irritability than of old. He had developed fits of absent-mindedness, and was frequently to be found staring pensively at nothing. To slap him on the back at such moments, as Wren ventured to do on one occasion, Wren belonging to the jovial school of thought which holds that nature gave us hands in order to slap backs, was to bring forth a new and unexpected Kirk, a Kirk who scowled and snarled and was hardly to be appeased with apology. Stranger still, this new Kirk could be summoned into existence by precisely the type of story at which, but a few weeks back, he would have been the first to laugh.

Percy Shanklyn, whose conversation consisted of equal parts of autobiography and of stories of the type alluded to, was the one to discover this. His latest, which he had counted on to set the table in a roar, produced from Kirk criticism so adverse and so crisply delivered that he refrained from telling his latest but one and spent the rest of the evening wondering, like his fellow visitors, what had happened to Kirk and whether he was sickening for something.

Not one of them had the faintest suspicion that these symptoms indicated that Kirk, for the first time in his easy-going life, was in love. They had never contemplated such a prospect. It was not till his conscientious and laborious courtship had been in progress for over two weeks and was nearing the stage when he felt that the possibility of revealing his state of mind to Ruth was not so remote as it had been, that a chance visit of Percy Shanklyn to the studio during the afternoon solved the mystery.

One calls it a chance visit because Percy had not been meaning to borrow twenty dollars from Kirk that day at all. The man slated for the loan was one Burrows, a kindly member of the Lambs Club. But fate and a telegram from a manager removed Burrows to Chicago, while Percy was actually circling preparatory to the swoop, and the only other man in New York who seemed to Percy good for the necessary sum at that precise moment was Kirk.

He flew to Kirk and found him with Ruth. Kirk's utter absence of any enthusiasm at the sight of him, the reluctance with which he made the introduction, the glumness with which he bore his share of the three-cornered conversation – all these things convinced Percy that this was no ordinary visitor.

Many years of living by his wits had developed in Percy highly sensitive powers of observation. Brief as his visit was, he came away as certain that Kirk was in love with this girl, and the girl was in love with Kirk, as he had ever been of anything in his life.

As he walked slowly down-town he was thinking hard. The subject occupying his mind was the problem of how this thing was to be stopped.

Percy Shanklyn was a sleek, suave, unpleasant youth who had been imported by a theatrical manager two years before to play the part of an English dude in a new comedy. The comedy had been what its enthusiastic backer had described in the newspaper advertisements as a "rousing live-wire success." That is to say, it had staggered along for six weeks on Broadway to extremely poor houses, and after three weeks on the road, had perished for all time, leaving Percy out of work.

Since then, no other English dude part having happened along, he had rested, living in the mysterious way in which out-of-work actors do live. He had a number of acquaintances, such as the amiable Burrows, who were good for occasional loans, but Kirk Winfield was the king of them all. There was something princely about the careless open-handedness of Kirk's methods, and Percy's whole soul rose in revolt against the prospect of being deprived of this source of revenue, as something, possibly Ruth's determined chin, told him that he would be, should Kirk marry this girl.

He had placed Ruth at once, directly he had heard her name. He remembered having seen her photograph in the society section of the Sunday paper which he borrowed each week. This was the daughter of old John Bannister. There was no doubt about that. How she had found her way to Kirk's studio he could not understand; but there she certainly was, and Percy was willing to bet the twenty dollars which, despite the excitement of the moment, he had forgotten to extract from Kirk in a hurried conversation at the door, that her presence there was not known and approved by her father.

The only reasonable explanation that Kirk was painting her portrait he dismissed. There had been no signs of any portrait, and Kirk's embarrassment had been so obvious that, if there had been any such explanation, he would certainly have given it. No, Ruth had been there for other reasons than those of art.

"Unchaperoned, too, by Jove!" thought Percy virtuously, ignorant of Mrs. Lora Delane Porter, who at the time of his call, had been busily occupied in a back room instilling into George Pennicut the gospel of the fit body. For George, now restored to health, had ceased to be a mere student of "Elementary Rules for the Preservation of the Body" and had become an active, though unwilling, practiser of its precepts.

Every morning Mrs. Porter called and, having shepherded him into the back room, put him relentlessly through his exercises. George's groans, as he moved his stout limbs along the dotted lines indicated in the book's illustrated plates, might have stirred a faint heart to pity. But Lora Delane Porter was made of sterner stuff. If George so much as bent his knees while touching his toes he heard of it instantly, in no uncertain voice.

Thus, in her decisive way, did Mrs. Porter spread light and sweetness with both hands, achieving the bodily salvation of George while, at the same time, furthering the loves of Ruth and Kirk by leaving them alone together to make each other's better acquaintance in the romantic dimness of the studio.

Percy proceeded down-town, pondering. His first impulse, I regret to say, was to send Ruth's father an anonymous letter. This plan he abandoned from motives of fear rather than of self-respect. Anonymous letters are too frequently traced to their writers, and the prospect of facing Kirk in such an event did not appeal to him.

As he could think of no other way of effecting his object, he had begun to taste the bitterness of futile effort, when fortune, always his friend, put him in a position to do what he wanted in the easiest possible way with the minimum of unpleasantness.

Bailey Bannister, that strong, keen Napoleon of finance, was not above a little relaxation of an evening when his father happened to be out of town. That giant mind, weary with the strain of business, needed refreshment.

And so, at eleven thirty that night, his father being in Albany, and not expected home till next day, Bailey might have been observed, beautifully arrayed and discreetly jovial, partaking of lobster at one of those Broadway palaces where this fish is in brisk demand. He was in company with his rabbit-faced friend, Clarence Grayling, and two members of the chorus of a neighbouring musical comedy.

One of the two, with whom Clarence was conversing in a lively manner that showed his heart had not been irreparably broken as the result of his recent interview with Ruth, we may dismiss. Like Clarence, she is of no importance to the story. The other, who, not finding Bailey's measured remarks very gripping, was allowing her gaze to wander idly around the room, has this claim to a place in the scheme of things, that she had a wordless part in the comedy in which Percy Shanklyn had appeared as the English dude and was on terms of friendship with him.

Consequently, seeing him enter the room, as he did at that moment, she signalled him to approach.

"It's a little feller who was with me in 'The Man from Out West'," she explained to Bailey as Percy made his way toward them. At which Bailey's prim mouth closed with an air of disapproval.

The feminine element of the stage he found congenial to his business- harassed brain, but with the "little fellers" who helped them to keep the national drama sizzling he felt less in sympathy; and he resented extremely his companion's tactlessness in inciting this infernal mummer to intrude upon his privacy.

He prepared to be cold and distant with Percy. And when Bailey, never a ray of sunshine, deliberately tried to be chilly, those with him at the time generally had the sensation that winter was once more in their midst.

Percy, meanwhile, threaded his way among the tables, little knowing that fate had already solved the problem which had worried him the greater part of the day.

He had come to the restaurant as a relief from his thoughts. If he could find some kind friend who would invite him to supper, well and good. If not, he was feeling so tired and depressed that he was ready to take the bull by the horns and pay for his meal himself. He had obeyed Miss Freda Reece's signal because it was impossible to avoid doing so; but one glance at Bailey's face had convinced him that not there was his kind host.

"Why, Perce," said Miss Reece, "I ain't saw you in years. Where you been hiding yourself?"

Percy gave a languid gesture indicative of the man of affairs whose time is not his own.

"Percy," continued Miss Reece, "shake hands with my friend Mr. Bannister. I been telling him about how you made such a hit as the pin in 'Pinafore'!"

The name galvanized Percy like a bugle-blast.

"Mr. Bannister!" he exclaimed. "Any relation to Mr. John Bannister, the millionaire?"

Bailey favoured him with a scrutiny through the gold-rimmed glasses which would have frozen his very spine.

"My father's name is – ah – John, and he is a millionaire."

Percy met the scrutiny with a suave smile.

"By Jove!" he said. "I know your sister quite well, Mr. Bannister. I meet her frequently at the studio of my friend Kirk Winfield. Very frequently. She is there nearly every day. Well, I must be moving on. Got a date with a man. Goodbye, Freda. Glad you're going strong. Good night, Mr. Bannister. Delighted to have made your acquaintance. You must come round to the studio one of these days. Good night."

He moved softly away. Miss Reece watched him go with regret.

"He's a good little feller, Percy," she said. "And so he knows your sister. Well, ain't that nice!"

Bailey did not reply. And to the feast of reason and flow of soul that went on at the table during the rest of the meal he contributed so little that Miss Reece, in conversation that night with her friend alluded to him, not without justice, first as "that stiff," and, later, as "a dead one."

If Percy Shanklyn could have seen Bailey in the small hours of that night he would have been satisfied that his words had borne fruit. Like a modern Prometheus, Bailey writhed, sleepless, on his bed till daylight appeared. The discovery that Ruth was in the habit of paying clandestine visits to artists' studios, where she met men like the little bounder who had been thrust upon him at supper, rent his haughty soul like a bomb.

He knew no artists, but he had read novels of Bohemian life in Paris, and he had gathered a general impression that they were, as a class, shock-headed, unwashed persons of no social standing whatever, extremely short of money and much addicted to orgies. And his sister had lowered herself by association with one of these.

He rose early. His appearance in the mirror shocked him. He looked positively haggard.

Dressing with unwonted haste, he inquired for Ruth, and was told that a telephone message had come from her late the previous evening to say that she was spending the night at the apartment of Mrs. Lora Delane Porter. The hated name increased Bailey's indignation. He held Mrs. Porter responsible for the whole trouble. But for her pernicious influence, Ruth would have been an ordinary sweet American girl, running as, Bailey held, a girl should, in a decent groove.

It increased his troubles that his father was away from New York. Bailey, who enjoyed the dignity of being temporary head of the firm of Bannister & Son, had approved of his departure. But now he would have given much to have him on the spot. He did not doubt his own ability to handle this matter, but he felt that his father ought to know what was going on.

His wrath against this upstart artist who secretly entertained his sister in his studio grew with the minutes. It would be his privilege very shortly to read that scrubby dauber a lesson in deportment which he would remember.

In the interests of the family welfare he decided to stay away from the office that day. The affairs of Bannister & Son would be safe for the time being in the hands of the head clerk. Having telephoned to Wall Street to announce his decision, he made a moody breakfast and then proceeded, as was his custom of a morning, to the gymnasium for his daily exercise.

The gymnasium was a recent addition to the Bannister home. It had been established as the result of a heart-to-heart talk between old John Bannister and his doctor. The doctor spoke earnestly of nervous prostration and stated without preamble the exact number of months which would elapse before Mr. Bannister living his present life, would make first-hand acquaintance with it. He insisted on a regular routine of exercise. The gymnasium came into being, and Mr. Steve Dingle, physical instructor at the New York Athletic Club, took up a position in the Bannister household which he was wont to describe to his numerous friends as a soft snap.

Certainly his hours were not long. Thirty minutes with old Mr. Bannister and thirty minutes with Mr. Bailey between eight and nine in the morning and his duties were over for the day. But Steve was conscientious and checked any disposition on the part of his two clients to shirk work with a firmness which Lora Delane Porter might have envied.

There were moments when he positively bullied old Mr. Bannister. It would have amazed the clerks in his Wall Street office to see the meekness with which the old man obeyed orders. But John Bannister was a man who liked to get his money's worth, and he knew that Steve was giving it to the last cent.

Steve at that time was twenty-eight years old. He had abandoned an active connection with the ring, which had begun just after his seventeenth birthday, twelve months before his entry into the Bannister home, leaving behind him a record of which any boxer might have been proud. He personally was exceedingly proud of it, and made no secret of the fact.

He was a man in private life of astonishingly even temper. The only thing that appeared to have the power to ruffle him to the slightest extent was the contemplation of what he described as the bunch of cheeses who pretended to fight nowadays. He would have considered it a privilege, it seemed, to be allowed to encounter all the middle-weights in the country in one ring in a single night without training. But it appeared that he had promised his mother to quit, and he had quit.

Steve's mother was an old lady who in her day had been the best washerwoman on Cherry Hill. She was, moreover, completely lacking in all the qualities which go to make up the patroness of sport. Steve had been injudicious enough to pay her a visit the day after his celebrated unpleasantness with that rugged warrior, Pat O'Flaherty (*ne* Smith), and, though he had knocked Pat out midway through the second round, he bore away from the arena a black eye of such a startling richness that old Mrs. Dingle had refused to be comforted until he had promised never to enter the ring again. Which, as Steve said, had come pretty hard, he being a man who would rather be a water-bucket in a ring than a president outside it.

But he had given the promise, and kept it, leaving the field to the above-mentioned bunch of cheeses. There were times when the temptation to knock the head off Battling Dick this and Fighting Jack that became almost agony, but he never yielded to it. All of which suggests that Steve was a man of character, as indeed he was.

Bailey, entering the gymnasium, found Steve already there, punching the bag with a force and precision which showed that the bunch of cheeses ought to have been highly grateful to Mrs. Dingle for her anti-pugilistic prejudices.

"Good morning, Dingle," said Bailey precisely.

Steve nodded. Bailey began to don his gymnasium costume. Steve gave the ball a final punch and turned to him. He was a young man who gave the impression of being, in a literal sense, perfectly square. This was due to the breadth of his shoulders, which was quite out of proportion to his height. His chest was extraordinarily deep, and his stomach and waist small, so that to the observer seeing him for the first time in boxing trunks, he seemed to begin as a big man and, half-way down, change his mind and become a small one.

His arms, which were unusually long and thick, hung down nearly to his knees and were decorated throughout with knobs and ridges of muscle that popped up and down and in and out as he moved, in a manner both fascinating and frightening. His face increased the illusion of squareness, for he had thick, straight eyebrows, a straight mouth, and a chin of almost the minimum degree of roundness. He inspected Bailey with a pair of brilliant brown eyes which no detail of his appearance could escape. And Bailey, that morning, as has been said, was not looking his best.

"You're lookin' kind o' sick, bo," was Steve's comment. "I guess you was hittin' it up with the gang last night in one of them lobster parlours."

Bailey objected to being addressed as "bo," and he was annoyed that Steve should have guessed the truth respecting his overnight movements. Still more was he annoyed that Steve's material mind should attribute to a surfeit of lobster a pallor that was superinduced by a tortured soul.

"I did – ah – take supper last night, it is true," he said. "But if I am a little pale to-day, that is not the cause. Things have occurred to annoy me intensely."

"You should worry!" advised Steve. "Catch!"

The heavy medicine-ball struck Bailey in the chest before he could bring up his hands and sent him staggering back.

"Damn it, Dingle," he gasped. "Kindly give me warning before you do that sort of thing."

Steve was delighted. It amused his simple, honest soul to catch Bailey napping, and the incident gave him a text on which to hang a lecture. And, next to fighting, he loved best the sound of his own voice.

"Warning? Nix!" he said. "Ain't it just what I been telling you every day for weeks? You gotta be ready *always*. You seen me holding the pellet. You should oughter have been saying to yourself: 'I gotta keep an eye on that gink, so's he don't soak me one with that thing when I ain't looking.' Then you would have caught it and whizzed it back at me, and maybe, if I hadn't been ready for it, you might have knocked the breeze out of me."

"I should have derived no pleasure—"

"Why, say, suppose a plug-ugly sasshays up to you on the street to take a crack at your pearl stick-pin, do you reckon he's going to drop you a postal card first? You gotta be *ready* for him. See what I mean?"

41

"Let us spar," said Bailey austerely. He had begun to despair of ever making Steve show him that deference and respect which he considered due to the son of the house. The more frigid he was, the more genial and friendly did Steve become. The thing seemed hopeless.

It was a pleasing sight to see Bailey spar. He brought to the task the measured dignity which characterized all his actions. A left jab from him had all the majesty of a formal declaration of war. If he was a trifle slow in his movements for a pastime which demands a certain agility from its devotees he at least got plenty of exercise and did himself a great deal of good.

He was perspiring freely as he took off the gloves. A shower-bath, followed by brisk massage at the energetic hands of Steve, made him feel better than he had imagined he could feel after that night of spiritual storm and stress. He was glowing as he put on his clothes, and a certain high resolve which had come to him in the night watches now returned with doubled force.

"Dingle," he said, "how did I seem to-day?"

"Fine," answered Steve courteously. "You're gettin' to be a regular terror."

"You think I shape well?"

"Sure."

"I am glad. This morning I am going to thrash a man within an inch of his life."

"What!"

Steve spun round. Bailey's face was set and determined.

"You are?" said Steve feebly.

"I am."

"What's he been doing to you?"

"I am afraid I cannot tell you that. But he richly deserves what he will get."

Steve eyed him with affectionate interest.

"Well, ain't you the wildcat!" he said. "Who'd have thought it? I'd always had you sized up as a kind o' placid guy."

"I can be roused."

"Gee, can't I see it! But, say, what sort of a gook is this gink, anyway?"

"In what respect?"

"Well, I mean is he a heavy or a middle or a welter or what? It makes a kind o' difference, you know."

"I cannot say. I have not seen him."

"What! Not seen him? Then how's there this fuss between you?"

"That is a matter into which I cannot go."

"Well, what's his name, then? Maybe I know him. I know a few good people in this burg."

"I have no objection to telling you that. He is an artist, and his name is – his name is—"

Wrinkles appeared in Bailey's forehead. His eyes bulged anxiously behind their glasses.

"I've forgotten," he said blankly.

"For the love of Mike! Know where he lives?"

"I am afraid not."

Steve patted him kindly on the shoulder.

"Take my advice, bo," he said. "Let the poor fellow off this time."

And so it came about that Bailey, instead of falling upon Kirk Winfield, hailed a taxicab and drove to the apartment of Mrs. Lora Delane Porter.

CHAPTER 5
WHEREIN OPPOSITES AGREE

THE maid who opened the door showed a reluctance to let Bailey in. She said that Mrs. Porter was busy with her writing and had given orders that she was not to be disturbed.

Nothing could have infuriated Bailey more. He, Bailey Bannister, was to be refused admittance because this preposterous woman wished to write! It was the duty of all decent citizens to stop her writing. If it had not been for her and her absurd books Ruth would never have made it necessary for him to pay this visit at all.

"Kindly take my card to Mrs. Porter and tell her that I must see her at once on a matter of the utmost urgency," he directed.

The domestic workers of America had not been trained to stand up against Bailey's grand manner. The maid vanished meekly with the card, and presently returned and requested him to step in.

Bailey found himself in a comfortable room, more like a man's study than a woman's boudoir. Books lined the walls. The furniture was strong and plain. At the window, on a swivel-chair before a roll-top desk, Mrs. Porter sat writing, her back to the door.

"The gentleman, ma'am," announced the maid.

"Sit down," said his aunt, without looking round or ceasing to write.

The maid went out. Bailey sat down. The gentle squeak of the quill pen continued.

Bailey coughed.

"I have called this morning—"

The left hand of the writer rose and waggled itself irritably above her left shoulder.

"Aunt Lora," spoke Bailey sternly.

"Shish!" said the authoress. Only that and nothing more. Bailey, outraged, relapsed into silence. The pen squeaked on.

After what seemed to Bailey a considerable time, the writing ceased. It was succeeded by the sound of paper vigorously blotted. Then, with startling suddenness, Mrs. Porter whirled round on the swivel-chair, tilted it back, and faced him.

"Well, Bailey?" she said.

She looked at Bailey. Bailey looked at her. Her eyes had the curious effect of driving out of his head what he had intended to say.

"Well?" she said again.

He tried to remember the excellent opening speech which he had prepared in the cab.

"Good gracious, Bailey!" cried Mrs. Porter, "you have not come here and ruined my morning's work for the pleasure of looking at me surely? Say something."

Bailey found his voice.

"I have called to see Ruth, who, I am informed, is with you."

"She is in her room. I made her breakfast in bed. Is there any message I can give her?"

Bailey suddenly remembered the speech he had framed in the cab.

"Aunt Lora," he said, "I am sorry to have to intrude upon you at so early an hour, but it is imperative that I see Ruth and ask her to explain the meaning of a most disturbing piece of news that has come to my ears."

Mrs. Porter did not appear to have heard him.

"A man of your height should weigh more," she said. "What is your weight?"

"My weight; beside the point—"

"Your weight is under a hundred and forty pounds, and it ought to be over a hundred and sixty. Eat more. Avoid alcohol. Keep regular hours."

"Aunt Lora!"

"Well?"

"I wish to see my sister."

"You will have to wait. What did you wish to see her about?"

"That is a matter that concerns—No! I will tell you, for I believe you to be responsible for the whole affair."

"Well?"

"Last night, quite by chance, I found out that Ruth has for some time been paying visits to the studio of an artist."

Mrs. Porter nodded.

"Quite right. Mr. Kirk Winfield. She is going to marry him."

Bailey's hat fell to the floor. His stick followed. His mouth opened widely. His glasses shot from his nose and danced madly at the end of their string.

"What!"

"It will be a most suitable match in every way," said Mrs. Porter.

Bailey bounded to his feet.

"It's incredible!" he shouted. "It's ridiculous! It's abominable! It's – it's incredible!"

Mrs. Porter gazed upon his transports with about the same amount of interest which she would have bestowed upon a whirling dervish at Coney Island.

"You have not seen Mr. Winfield, I gather?"

"When I do, he will have reason to regret it. I—"

"Sit down."

Bailey sat down.

"Ruth and Mr. Winfield are both perfect types. Mr. Winfield is really a splendid specimen of a man. As to his intelligence, I say nothing. I have ceased to expect intelligence in man, and I am grateful for the smallest grain. But physically, he is magnificent. I could not wish dear Ruth a better husband."

Bailey had pulled himself together with a supreme effort and had achieved a frozen calm.

"Such a marriage is, of course, out of the question," he said.

"Why?"

"My sister cannot marry a – a nobody, an outsider—"

"Mr. Winfield is not a nobody. He is an extraordinarily healthy young man."

"Are you aware that Ruth, if she had wished, could have married a prince?"

"She told me. A little rat of a man, I understand. She had far too much sense to do any such thing. She has a conscience. She knows what she owes to the future of the—"

"Bah!" cried Bailey rudely.

"I suppose," said Mrs. Porter, "that, like most men, you care nothing for the future of the race? You are not interested in eugenics?"

Bailey quivered with fury at the word, but said nothing.

"If you have ever studied even so elementary a subject as the colour heredity of the Andalusian fowl—"

The colour heredity of the Andalusian fowl was too much for Bailey.

"I decline to discuss any such drivel," he said, rising. "I came here to see Ruth, and – "

"And here she is," said Mrs. Porter.

The door opened, and Ruth appeared. She looked, to Bailey, insufferably radiant and pleased with herself.

"Bailey!" she cried. "Whatever brings my little Bailey here, when he ought to be working like a good boy in Wall Street?"

"I will tell you," Bailey's demeanour was portentous.

"He's frowning," said Ruth. "You have been stirring his hidden depths, Aunt Lora!"

Bailey coughed.

"Ruth!"

"Bailey, *don't!* You don't know how terrible you look when you're roused."

"Ruth, kindly answer me one question. Aunt Lora informs me that you are going to marry this man Winfield. Is it or is it not true?"

"Of course it's true."

Bailey drew in his breath. He gazed coldly at Ruth, bowed to Mrs. Porter, and smoothed the nap of his hat.

"Very good," he said stonily. "I shall now call upon this Mr. Winfield and thrash him." With that he walked out of the room.

He directed his cab to the nearest hotel, looked up Kirk's address in the telephone-book, and ten minutes later was ringing the studio bell.

A look of relief came into George Pennicut's eyes as he opened the door. To George, nowadays, every ring at the bell meant a possible visit from Lora Delane Porter.

"Is Mr. Kirk Winfield at home?" inquired Bailey.

"Yes, sir. Who shall I say, sir?"

"Kindly tell Mr. Winfield that Mr. Bannister wishes to speak to him."

"Yes, sir. Will you step this way, sir?"

Bailey stepped that way.

While Bailey was driving to the studio in his taxicab, Kirk, in boxing trunks and a sleeveless vest, was engaged on his daily sparring exercise with Steve Dingle.

This morning Steve seemed to be amused at something. As they rested, at the conclusion of their fifth and final round, Kirk perceived that he was chuckling, and asked the reason.

"Why, say," explained Steve, "I was only thinking that it takes all kinds of ivory domes to make a nuttery. I ran across a new brand of simp this morning. Just before I came to you I'm scheduled to show up at one of these Astorbilt homes t'other side of the park. First I mix it with the old man, then son and heir blows in and I attend to him.

"Well, this morning, son acts like he's all worked up. He's one of these half-portion Willie-boys with Chippendale legs, but he throws out a line of talk that would make you wonder if it's safe to let him run around loose. Says his mind's made up; he's going to thrash a gink within an inch of his life; going to muss up his features so bad he'll have to have 'em replanted.

"'Why?' I says. 'Never you mind,' says he. 'Well, who is he?' I asks. What do you think happens then? He thinks hard for a spell, rolls his eyes, and says: 'Search me. I've forgotten.' 'Know where he lives?' I asks him. 'Nope,' he says.

"Can you beat it! Seems to me if I had a kink in my coco that big I'd phone to an alienist and have myself measured for a strait-jacket. Gee! You meet all kinds, going around the way I do."

Kirk laughed and lit a cigarette.

"If you want to use the shower, Steve," he said, "you'd better get up there now. I shan't be ready yet awhile. Then, if this is one of your energetic mornings and you would care to give me a rub-down—"

"Sure," said Steve obligingly. He picked up his clothes and went upstairs to the bathroom, which, like the bedrooms, opened on to the gallery. Kirk threw himself on the couch, fixed his eyes on the ceiling, and began to think of Ruth.

"Mr. Bannister," announced George Pennicut at the door.

Kirk was on his feet in one bound. The difference, to a man whose mind is far away, between "Mr. Bannister" and "Miss Bannister" is not great, and his first impression was that it was Ruth who had arrived.

He was acutely conscious of his costume, and was quite relieved when he saw, not Ruth, but a severe-looking young man, who advanced upon him in a tight-lipped, pop-eyed manner that suggested dislike and hostility. The visitor was a complete stranger to him, but, his wandering wits returning to their duties, he deduced that this must be one of Ruth's relatives.

It is a curious fact that the possibility of Ruth having other relatives than Mrs. Porter had not occurred to him till now. She herself filled his mind to such an extent that he had never speculated on any possible family that might be attached to her. To him Ruth was Ruth. He accepted the fact that she was Mrs. Porter's niece. That she might also be somebody's daughter or sister had not struck him. The look on Bailey's face somehow brought it home to him that the world was about to step in and complicate the idyllic simplicity of his wooing.

Bailey, meanwhile, as Kirk's hundred and eighty pounds of bone and muscle detached themselves from the couch and loomed up massively before him, was conscious of a weakening of his determination to inflict bodily chastisement. The truth of Steve's remark, that it made a difference whether one's intended victim is a heavyweight, a middle, or a welter, came upon him with some force.

Kirk, in a sleeveless vest that showed up his chest and shoulders was not an inviting spectacle for a man intending assault and battery. Bailey decided to confine himself to words. There was nothing to be gained by a vulgar brawl. A dignified man of the world avoided violence.

"Mr. Winfield?"

"Mr. Bannister?"

It was at this point that Steve, having bathed and dressed, came out on the gallery. The voices below halted him, and the sound of Bailey's decided him to remain where he was. Steve was not above human curiosity, and he was anxious to know the reason for Bailey's sudden appearance.

"That is my name. It is familiar to you. My sister," said Bailey bitterly, "has made it so."

"Won't you sit down?" said Kirk.

"No, thank you. I will not detain you long, Mr. Winfield."

"My dear fellow! There's no hurry. Will you have a cigarette?"

"No, thank you."

Kirk was puzzled by his visitor's manner. So, unseen in the shadows of the gallery, was Steve.

"I can say what I wish to say in two words, Mr. Winfield," said Bailey. "This marriage is quite out of the question."

"Eh?"

"My father would naturally never consent to it. As soon as he hears of what has happened he will forbid it absolutely. Kindly dismiss from your mind entirely the idea that my sister will ever be permitted to marry you, Mr. Winfield."

Steve, in the gallery, with difficulty suppressed a whoop of surprise. Kirk laughed ruefully.

"Aren't you a little premature, Mr. Bannister? Aren't you taking a good deal for granted?"

"In what way?"

"Well, that Miss Bannister cares the slightest bit for me, for instance; that I've one chance in a million of ever getting her to care the slightest bit for me?"

Bailey was disgusted at this futile attempt to hide the known facts of the case from him.

"You need not trouble to try and fool me, Mr. Winfield," he said tartly. "I know everything. I have just seen my sister, and she told me herself in so many words that she intended to marry you."

To his amazement he found his hand violently shaken.

"My dear old man!" Kirk was stammering in his delight. "My dear old sport, you don't know what a weight you've taken off my mind. You know how it is. A fellow falls in love and instantly starts thinking he hasn't a chance on earth. I hadn't a notion she felt that way about me. I'm not fit to shine her shoes. My dear old man, if you hadn't come and told me this I never should have had the nerve to say a word to her.

"You're a corker. You've changed everything. You'll have to excuse me. I must go to her. I can't wait a minute. I must rush and dress. Make yourself at home here. Have you breakfasted? George! George! Say, George, I've got to rush away. See that Mr. Bannister has everything he wants. Get him some breakfast. Good-bye, old man." He gripped Bailey's hand once more. "You're all right. Good-bye!"

He sprang for the staircase. George Pennicut turned to the speechless Bailey.

"How would it be if I made you a nice cup of hot tea and a rasher of 'am, sir?" he inquired with a kindly smile.

Bailey eyed him glassily, then found speech.

"Go to hell!" he shouted. He strode to the door and shot into the street, a seething volcano.

George, for his part, was startled, but polite.

"Yes, sir," he said. "Very good, sir," and withdrew.

Kirk, having reached the top of the stairs, had to check the wild rush he was making for the bathroom in order not to collide with Steve, whom he found waiting for him with outstretched hand and sympathetic excitement writ large upon his face.

"Excuse *me*, squire," said Steve, "I've been playing the part of Rubberneck Rupert in that little drama you've just been starring in. I just couldn't help listening. Say, this mitt's for you. Shake it! So you're going to marry Bailey's sister, Ruth, are you? You're the lucky guy. She's a queen!"

"Do *you* know her, Steve?"

"Do I know her! Didn't I tell you I was the tame physical instructor in that palace? I wish I had a dollar for every time I've thrown the medicine-ball at her. Why, I'm the guy that gave her that figure of hers. She don't come to me regular, like Bailey and the old man, but do I know her? I should say I did know her."

Kirk shook his hand.

"You're all right, Steve!" he said huskily, and vanished into the bathroom. A sound as of a tropical deluge came from within.

Steve hammered upon the door. The downpour ceased.

"Say!" called Steve.

"Hello?"

"I don't want to discourage you, squire, but—"

The door opened and Kirk's head appeared.

"What's the matter?"

"Well, you heard what Bailey said?"

"About his father?"

"Sure. It goes."

Kirk came out into the gallery, towelling himself vigorously.

"Who *is* her father?" he asked, seating himself on the rail.

"He's a son of a gun," said Steve with emphasis. "As rich as John D. pretty nearly and about as chummy as a rattlesnake. Were you thinking of calling and asking him for a father's blessing?"

"Something of the sort, I suppose."

"Forget it! He'd give you the hook before you'd got through asking if you might call him daddy."

"You're comforting, Steve. They call you Little Sunbeam at home, don't they?"

"Hell!" said Steve warmly, "I'm not shooting this at you just to make you feel bad. I gotta reason. I want to make you see this ain't going to be no society walk-over, with the Four Hundred looking on from the pews and poppa signing cheques in the background. Say, did I ever tell you how I beat Kid Mitchell?"

"Does it apply to the case in hand?"

"Does it what to the which?"

"Had it any bearing on my painful position? I only ask, because that's what is interesting me most just now, and, if you're going to change the subject, there's a chance that my attention may wander."

"Sure it does. It's a – what d'you call it when you pull something that's got another meaning tucked up its sleeve?"

"A parable?"

"That's right. A – what you said. Well, this Kid Mitchell was looked on as a coming champ in those days. He had cleaned up some good boys, while I had only gotten a rep about as big as a nickel with a hole in it. I guess I looked pie to him. He turkey-trotted up to me for the first round and stopped in front of me as if he was wondering what had blown in and whether the Gerry Society would stand for his hitting it. I could see him thinking 'This is too easy' as plain as if he'd said it. And then he took another peek at me, as much as to say, 'Well, let's get it over. Where shall I soak him first?' And while he's doing this I get in range and I put my left pretty smart into his lunch-wagon and I pick up my right off the carpet and hand it to him, and down he goes. And when he gets up again it's pretty nearly to-morrow morning and I've drawn the winner's end and gone home."

"And the moral?"

"Why, don't spar. Punch! Don't wait for the wallop. Give it."

"You mean?"

"Why, when old man Bannister says: 'Nix! You shall never marry my child!' come back at him by saying: 'Thanks very much, but I've just done it!'"

"Good heavens, Steve!"

"You'll never win out else. You don't know old man Bannister. I do."

"But—"

The door-bell rang.

"Who on earth's that?" said Kirk. "It can't be Bailey back again."

"Good morning, Pennicut," spoke the clear voice of Mrs. Lora Delane Porter. "I wish to see Mr. Winfield."

"Yes, ma'am. He's upstairs in 'is bath!"

"I will wait in the studio."

"Good Lord!" cried Kirk, bounding from his seat on the rail. "For Heaven's sake, Steve, go and talk to her while I dress. I'll be down in a minute."

"Sure. What's her name?"

"Mrs. Porter. You'll like her. Tell her all about yourself – where you were born, how much you are round the chest, what's your favourite breakfast food. That's what she likes to chat about. And tell her I'll be down in a second."

Steve, reaching the studio, found Mrs. Porter examining the boxing-gloves which had been thrown on a chair.

"Eight-ounce, ma'am," he said genially, by way of introduction. "Kirk'll be lining up in a moment. He's getting into his rags."

Mrs. Porter looked at him with the gimlet stare which made her so intensely disliked by practically every man she knew.

"Are you a friend of Mr. Winfield?" she said.

"Sure. We just been spieling together up above. He sent me down to tell you he won't be long."

Mrs. Porter concluded her inspection.

"What is your name?"

"Dingle, ma'am."

"You are extraordinarily well developed. You have unusually long arms for a man of your height."

"Yep. I got a pretty good reach."

"Are you an artist?"

"A which?"

"An artist. A painter."

Steve smiled broadly.

"I've been called a good many things, but no one's ever handed me that. No, ma'am, I'm a has-been."

"I beg your pardon."

"Granted."

"What did you say you were?" asked Mrs. Porter after a pause.

"A has-been. I used to be a middle, but mother kicked, and I quit. All through taking a blue eye home! Wouldn't that jar you?"

"I have no doubt you intend to be explicit—"

"Not on your life!" protested Steve. "I may be a rough-neck, but I've got me manners. I wouldn't get explicit with a lady."

Mrs. Porter sat down.

"We appear to be talking at cross-purposes," she said. "I still do not gather what your profession is or was."

"Why, ain't I telling you? I used to be a middle—"

"What is a middle?"

"Why, it's in between the light-heavies and the welters. I was a welter when I broke into the fighting game, but—"

"Now I understand. You are a pugilist?"

"Used to be. But mother kicked."

"Kicked whom?"

"You don't get me, ma'am. When I say she kicked, I mean my blue eye threw a scare into her, and she put a crimp in my career. Made me quit when I should have been champ in another couple of fights."

"I am afraid I cannot follow these domestic troubles of yours. And why do you speak of your blue eye? Your eyes are brown."

"This one wasn't. It was the fattest blue eye you ever seen. I ran up against a short right hook. I put him out next round, ma'am, mind you, but that didn't help me any with mother. Directly she seen me blue eye she said: 'That'll be all from you, Steve. You stop it this minute.' So I quit. But gee! It's tough on a fellow to have to sit out of the game and watch a bunch of cheeses like this new crop of middle-weights swelling around and calling themselves fighters when they couldn't lick a postage-stamp, not if it was properly trained. Hell! Beg pardon, ma'am."

"I find you an interesting study, Mr. Dingle," said Mrs. Porter thoughtfully. "I have never met a pugilist before. Do you box with Mr. Winfield?"

"Sure. Kirk and me go five rounds every morning."

"You have been boxing with him to-day? Then perhaps you can tell me if an absurd young man in eye-glasses has called here yet? He is wearing a grey—"

"Do you mean Bailey, ma'am. Bailey Bannister?"

"You know my nephew, Mr. Dingle?"

"Sure. I box with him every morning."

"I never expected to hear that my nephew Bailey did anything so sensible as to take regular exercise. He does not look as if he did."

"He certainly is a kind o' half-portion, ma'am. But say, if he's your nephew, Miss Ruth's your niece."

"Perfectly correct."

"Then you know all about this business?"

"Which business, Mr. Dingle?"

"Why, Kirk and Miss Ruth."

Mrs. Porter raised her eyebrows.

"Really, Mr. Dingle! Has Mr. Winfield made you his confidant?"

"How's that?"

"Has Mr. Winfield told you about my niece and himself?"

"Hell, no! You don't find a real person like Kirk shooting his head about that kind of thing. I had it from Bailey."

"From Bailey?"

"Surest thing you know. He blew in here and shouted it all out at the top of his voice."

"Indeed! I was wondering if he had arrived yet. He left my apartment saying he was going to thrash Mr. Winfield. I came here to save him from getting hurt. Was there any trouble?"

"Not so's you could notice it. I guess when he'd taken a slant at Kirk he thought he wouldn't bother to swat him. Say, ma'am – "

"Well?"

"Whose corner are you in for this scrap?"

"I don't understand you."

"Well, are you rooting for Kirk, or are you holding the towel for old man Bannister?"

"You mean, do I wish Mr. Winfield to marry my niece?"

"You're hep."

"Most certainly I do. It was I who brought them together."

"Bully for you! Well, say, I just been shooting the dope into Kirk upstairs. I been – you didn't happen to read the report of a scrap I once had with a gazook called Kid Mitchell, did you, ma'am?"

"I seldom, I may say never, read the sporting section of the daily papers."

Steve looked at her in honest wonder.

"For the love of Pete! What else do you find to read in 'em?" he said. "Well, I was telling Kirk about it. The Kid came at me to soak me, but I soaked him first and put him out. It's the only thing to do, ma'am, when you're up against it. Get in the first wallop before the other guy can get himself set for his punch. 'Kirk,' I says, 'don't you wait for old man Bannister to tell you you can't marry Miss Ruth. Marry her before he can say it.' I wish you'd tell him the same thing, ma'am. You know the old man as well as I do – better, I guess – and you know that Kirk ain't got a chance in a million with him if he don't rush him. Ain't that right?"

"Mr. Dingle," said Mrs. Porter, "I should like to shake you by the hand. It is amazing to me to find such sound sense in a man. You have expressed my view exactly. If I have any influence with Mr. Winfield, he shall marry my niece to-day. You are a man of really exceptional intelligence, Mr. Dingle."

"Aw, check it with your hat, ma'am!" murmured Steve modestly. "Nix on the bouquets! I'm only a roughneck. But I fall for Miss Ruth, and there ain't many like Kirk, so I'd like to see them happy. It would sure get my goat the worst way to have the old man gum the game for them."

"I cannot understand a word you say," said Mrs. Porter, "but I fancy we mean the same thing. Here comes Mr. Winfield at last. I will speak to him at once."

"Spiel away, ma'am," said Steve. "The floor's yours."

Kirk entered the studio.

CHAPTER 6
BREAKING THE NEWS

OLD John Bannister returned that night. Learning from Bailey's trembling lips the tremendous events that had been taking place in his absence, he was first irritated, then coldly amused. His coolness dampened, while it comforted, Bailey.

A bearer of sensational tidings likes to spread a certain amount of dismay and terror; but, on the other hand, it was a relief to him to find that his father appeared to consider trivial a crisis which, to Bailey, had seemed a disaster without parallel in the annals of American social life.

"She said she was going to *marry* him!"

Old Bannister opened the nut-cracker mouth that always had the appearance of crushing something. His pale eyes glowed for an instant.

"Did she?" he said.

"She seemed very – ah – determined."

"*Did* she!"

Silence falling like a cloud at this point, Bailey rightly conjectured that the audience was at an end and left the room. His father bit the end off a cigar and began to smoke.

Smoking, he reviewed the situation, and his fighting spirit rose to grapple with it. He was not sorry that this had happened. His was a patriarchal mind, and he welcomed opportunities of exercising his authority over his children. It had always been his policy to rule them masterfully, and he had often resented the fact that his daughter, by the nature of things, was to a great extent outside his immediate rule.

During office hours business took him away from her. The sun never set on his empire over Bailey, but it needed a definite crisis like the present one to enable him to jerk at the reins which guided Ruth, and he was glad of the chance to make his power felt.

The fact that this affair brought him into immediate contact with Mrs. Porter added to his enjoyment. Of all the people, men or women, with whom his business or social life had brought him into conflict, she alone had fought him squarely and retired with the honours of war. When his patriarchal mind had led him to bully his late wife, it was Mrs. Porter who had fought her cause. It was Mrs. Porter who openly expressed her contempt for his money and certain methods of making it. She was the only person in his immediate sphere over whom he had no financial hold.

He was a man who liked to be surrounded by dependents, and Mrs. Porter stoutly declined to be a dependent. She moved about the world, blunt and self-sufficing, and he hated her as he hated no one else. The thought that she had now come to grips with him and that he could best her in open fight was pleasant to him. All his life, except in his conflicts with her, he had won. He meant to win now.

Bailey's apprehensions amused him. He had a thorough contempt for all actors, authors, musicians, and artists, whom he classed together in one group as men who did not count, save in so far as they gave mild entertainment to the men who, like himself, did count. The idea of anybody taking them seriously seemed too fantastic to be considered.

Of affection for his children he had little. Bailey was useful in the office, and Ruth ornamental at home. They satisfied him. He had never troubled to study their characters. It had never occurred to him to wonder if they were fond of him. They formed a necessary part of his household, and beyond that he was not interested in them. If he had ever thought about Ruth's nature, he had dismissed her as a feminine counterpart of Bailey, than whom no other son and heir in New York behaved so exactly as a son and heir should.

That Ruth, even under the influence of Lora Delane Porter, should have been capable of her present insubordination, was surprising, but the thing was too trivial to be a source of anxiety. The mischief could be checked at once before it amounted to anything.

Bailey had not been gone too long before Ruth appeared. She stood in the doorway looking at him for a moment. Her face was pale and her eyes bright. She was breathing quickly.

"Are you busy, father? I – I want to tell you something."

John Bannister smiled. He had a wintry smile, a sort of muscular affection of the mouth, to which his eyes contributed nothing. He had made up his mind to be perfectly calm and pleasant with Ruth. He had read in novels and seen on the stage situations of this kind, where the father had stormed and blustered. The foolishness of such a policy amused him. A strong man had no need to behave like that.

"I think I have heard it already," he said. "I have just been seeing Bailey."

"What did Bailey tell you, father?"

"That you fancied yourself in love with some actor or artist or other whose name I have forgotten."

"It is not fancy. I do love him."

"Yes?"

There was a pause.

"Are you very angry, father?"

"Why should I be? Let's talk it over quietly. There's no need to make a tragedy of it."

"I'm glad you feel like that, father."

John Bannister lit another cigar.

"Tell me all about it," he said.

Ruth found herself surprisingly near tears. She had come into the room with every nerve in her body braced for a supreme struggle. Her father's unexpected gentleness weakened her, exactly as he had foreseen. The plan of action which he had determined upon was that of the wrestler who yields instead of resisting, in order to throw an antagonist off his balance.

"How did it begin?" he asked.

"Well," said Ruth, "it began when Aunt Lora took me to his studio."

"Yes, I heard that it was she who set the whole thing going. She is a friend of this fellow-what is his name?"

"Kirk Winfield. Yes, she seemed to know him quite well."

"And then?"

In spite of her anxiety, Ruth smiled.

"Well, that's all," she said. "I just fell in love with him."

Mr. Bannister nodded.

"You just fell in love with him," he repeated. "Pretty quick work, wasn't it?"

"I suppose it was."

"You just took one look at him and saw he was the affinity, eh?"

"I suppose so."

"And what did he do? Was he equally sudden?"

Ruth laughed. She was feeling quite happy now.

"He would have liked to be, poor dear, but he felt he had to be cautious and prepare the way before telling me. If it hadn't been for Bailey, he might be doing it still. Apparently, Bailey went to him and said I had said I was going to marry him, and Kirk came flying round, and – well, then it was all right."

Mr. Bannister drew thoughtfully at his cigar. He was silent for a few moments.

"Well, my dear," he said at last. "I think you had better consider the engagement broken off."

Ruth looked at him quickly. He still smiled, but his eyes were cold and hard. She realized suddenly that she had been played with, that all his kindliness and amiability had been merely a substitute for the storm which she had expected. After all, it was to be war between them, and she braced herself for it!

"Father!" she cried.

Mr. Bannister continued to puff serenely at his cigar.

"We needn't get worked up about it," he said. "Let's keep right on talking it over quietly."

"Very well," said Ruth. "But, after what you have just said, what is there to talk over?"

"You might be interested to hear my reasons for saying it."

"And I will argue my side."

Mr. Bannister waved his hand gently.

"You don't have to argue. You just listen."

Ruth bit her lip.

"Well?"

"In the first place," said her father, "about this young man. What is he? Bailey says he is an artist. Well, what has he ever done? Why don't I know his name? I buy a good many pictures, but I don't remember ever signing a cheque for one of his. I read the magazines

now and then, but I can't recall seeing his signature to any of the illustrations. How does he live, anyway, without going into the question of how he intends to support a wife?"

"Aunt Lora told me he had private means."

"How much?"

"Five thousand dollars a year."

"Exactly the amount necessary to let him live without working. I
have him placed now. I know his type. I could show you a thousand
men in this city in exactly the same position. They don't starve and
they don't work. This young man of yours is a loafer."

"Well?"

Ruth's voice was quiet, but a faint colour had crept into her face
and her eyes were blazing.

"Now perhaps you would care to hear what I think of his principles. How do you feel that he comes out of this business? Does he
show to advantage? Isn't there just a suspicion of underhandedness
about his behaviour?"

"No."

"No? He lets you pay these secret visits—"

Ruth interrupted.

"There was nothing secret about them – to him. Aunt Lora
brought me to the studio in the first place, and she kept on bringing
me. I don't suppose it ever occurred to Kirk to wonder who I was
and who my father might be. He has been perfectly straight. If you
like to say I have been underhanded, I admit it. I have. More so
than you imagine. I just wanted him, and I didn't care for anything
except that."

"It did not strike you that you owed anything to me, for
instance?"

"No."

"I should have thought that, as your father, I had certain
claims."

Ruth was silent.

Mr. Bannister sighed.

"I thought you were fond of me, Ruth," he said wistfully. It was
the wrestler yielding instead of resisting. Ruth's hard composure
melted instantly. She flung her arms round his neck in a burst of
remorseful affection.

"Of course I am, father dear. You're making this awfully hard for me."

Mr. Bannister chuckled inwardly. It seemed to him that victory was in sight. He always won, he told himself, always.

"I only want you to be sensible."

Ruth stiffened at the word. It jarred upon her. She felt that they were leagues apart, that they could never be in sympathy with each other.

"Father," she said.

"Yes?"

"Would you like to see Kirk?"

"I have been wondering when he was going to appear on the scene. I always thought it was customary on these occasions for the young man to present himself in person, and not let the lady fight his battles for him. Is this Mr. Winfield a little deficient in nerve?"

Ruth flushed angrily.

"I particularly asked Kirk not to come here before I had seen you. I insisted on it. Naturally, he wanted to."

"Of course!"

There was a sneer in his voice which he did not try to hide. It flicked Ruth like a whip. Her painfully preserved restraint broke up under it.

"Do you think Kirk is afraid of you, father?"

"It crossed my mind."

"He is not."

"I have only your word for it."

"You can have his if you want it. There is the telephone. You can have him here in ten minutes if you want to see him."

"A very good idea. But, as it happens, I do not want to see him. There is no necessity. His views on this matter do not interest me. I—"

There was a hurried knock at the door. Bailey burst in, ruffled and wild as to the eyes.

"Father," he cried, "I don't want to interrupt you, but that infernal woman, Aunt Lora, has arrived, and says she won't go till she has seen you. She's downstairs now."

"Not now," said Lora Delane Porter, moving him to one side and entering the room. "I thought it would be a comfort to you, Ruth, to have me with you to help explain exactly how matters stand. Good evening, John. Go away, Bailey. Now let us discuss things quietly."

"She is responsible for the whole thing, father," cried Bailey.

Mr. Bannister rose.

"There is nothing to discuss," he said shortly. "I have no wish to speak to you at all. As you appear to have played a large part in this affair, I may as well tell you that it is settled. Ruth will not marry Mr. Winfield."

Lora Delane Porter settled herself comfortably in a chair. She drew off her gloves and placed them on the table.

"Please ask that boy Bailey to go," she said. "He annoys me. I cannot marshal my thoughts in his presence."

Quelled by her eye, Bailey removed himself. His father remained standing. Ruth, who had risen at her aunt's entry, sat down again. Mrs. Porter looked round the room with some approval.

"You have a nice taste in pictures, John," she said. "That is a Corot, surely, above the mantelpiece?"

"Will you—"

"But about this little matter. You dislike the idea of Ruth marrying Mr. Winfield? Have you seen Mr. Winfield?"

"I have not."

"Then how can you possibly decide whether he is a fit husband for Ruth?"

"I know all about him."

"What do you know?"

"What Ruth has told me. That he is a loafer who pretends to be an artist."

"He is a poor artist. I grant you that. His drawing is weak. But are you aware that he is forty-three inches round the chest, six feet tall, and in perfect physical condition?"

"What has that got to do with it?"

"Everything. You have not read my 'Principles of Selection'?"

"I have not."

"I will send you a copy to-morrow."

"I will burn it directly it arrives."

"Then you will miss a great deal of valuable information," said Mrs. Porter tranquilly.

There was a pause. John Bannister glared furiously at Mrs. Porter, but her gaze was moving easily about the room, taking in each picture in turn in a leisurely inspection.

An exclamation from Ruth broke the silence, a sharp cry like that of an animal in pain. She sprang up, her face working, her eyes filled with tears.

"I can't stand it!" she cried. "I can't stand it any longer! Father, Kirk and I were married this afternoon."

Mrs. Porter went quickly to her and put her arm round her. Ruth was sobbing helplessly. The strain had broken her. John Bannister's face was leaden. The veins stood out on his forehead. His mouth twisted dumbly.

Mrs. Porter led Ruth gently to the door and pushed her out. Then she closed it and turned to him.

"So now you know, John," she said. "Well, what are you going to do about it?"

Self-control was second nature with John Bannister. For years he had cultivated it as a commercial asset. Often a fortune had depended on his mastery of his emotions. Now, in an instant, he had himself under control once more. His face resumed its normal expression of cold impassiveness. Only his mouth twitched a little.

"Well?" asked Mrs. Porter.

"Take her away," he said quietly. "Take her out of here. Let her go to him. I have done with her."

"I suppose so," said Mrs. Porter, and left the room.

CHAPTER 7
SUFFICIENT UNTO THEMSELVES

SOME months after John Bannister had spoken his ultimatum in the library two drought-stricken men met on the Rialto. It was a close June evening, full of thirst.

"I could do with a drink," said the first man. "Several."

"My tongue is black clear down to the roots," said the second.

"Let's go up to Kirk Winfield's," proposed the first man, inspired.

"Not for me," said the other briefly. "Haven't you heard about Kirk? He's married!"

"I know – but—"

"And when I say married, I mean *married*. She's old John Bannister's daughter, you know, and I guess she inherits her father's character. She's what I call a determined girl. She seems to have made up her mind that the old crowd that used to trail around the studio aren't needed any longer, and they've been hitting the sidewalk on one ear ever since the honeymoon.

"If you want to see her in action, go up there now. She'll be perfectly sweet and friendly, but somehow you'll get the notion that you don't want to go there again, and that she can bear up if you don't. It's something in her manner. I guess it's a trick these society girls learn. You've seen a bouncer handling a souse. He doesn't rough-house him. He just puts his arm round his waist and kind of suggests he should leave the place. Well, it's like that."

"But doesn't Kirk kick? He used to like having us around."

His friend laughed.

"Kick? Kirk? You should see him! He just sits there waiting for you to go, and, when you do go, shuts the door on you so quick you have to jump to keep from getting your coat caught in it. I tell you, those two are about all the company either of them needs. They've got the Newly-weds licked to a whisper."

"It's always the best fellows that get it the worse," said the other philosophically, "and it's always the fellows you think are safe too. I could have bet on Kirk. Six months ago I'd have given you any odds you wanted that he would never marry."

"And I wouldn't have taken you. It's always the way."

The criticisms of the two thirsty men, though prejudiced, were accurate. Marriage had undeniably wrought changes in Kirk Winfield. It had blown up, decentralized, and re-arranged his entire scheme of life. Kirk's was one of those natures that run to extremes. He had been a whole-hearted bachelor, and he was assuredly a much-married man. For the first six months Ruth was almost literally his whole world. His friends, the old brigade of the studio, had dropped away from him in a body. They had visited the studio once or twice at first, but after that had mysteriously disappeared. He was too engrossed in his happiness to speculate on the reasons for this defection: he only knew that he was glad of it.

Their visits had not been a success. Conversation had flowed fitfully. Some sixth sense told him that Ruth, though charming to them all, had not liked them; and he himself was astonished to find what bull dogs they really were. It was odd how out of sympathy he felt with them. They seemed so unnecessary: yet what a large part of his life they had once made up!

Something had come between him and them. What it was he did not know.

Ruth could have told him. She was the angel with the flaming sword who guarded their paradise. Marriage was causing her to make unexpected discoveries with regard to herself. Before she had always looked on herself as a rather unusually reasonable, and certainly not a jealous, woman. But now she was filled with an active dislike for these quite harmless young men who came to try and share Kirk with her.

She knew it was utterly illogical. A man must have friends. Life could not be forever a hermitage of two. She tried to analyse her objection to these men, and came to the conclusion that it was the fact that they had known Kirk before she did that caused it.

She made a compromise with herself. Kirk should have friends, but they must be new ones. In a little while, when this crazy desire to keep herself and him alone together in a world of their own should have left her, they would begin to build up a circle. But these men whose vocabulary included the words "Do you remember?" must be eliminated one and all.

Kirk, blissfully unconscious that his future was being arranged for him and the steering-wheel of his life quietly taken out of his hands, passed his days in a state of almost painful happiness. It never crossed his mind that he had ceased to be master of his fate and captain of his soul. The reins were handled so gently that he did not feel them. It seemed to him that he was travelling of his own free will along a pleasant path selected by himself.

He saw his friends go from him without a regret. Perhaps at the bottom of his heart he had always had a suspicion of contempt for them. He had taken them on their surface value, as amusing fellows who were good company of an evening. There was not one of them whom he had ever known as real friends know each other – not one, except Hank Jardine; and Hank had yet to be subjected to the acid test of the new conditions.

There were moments when the thought of Hank threw a shadow across his happiness. He could let these others go, but Hank was different. And something told him that Ruth would not like Hank.

But these shadows were not frequent. Ruth filled his life too completely to allow him leisure to brood on possibilities of future trouble.

Looking back, it struck him that on their wedding-day they had been almost strangers. They had taken each other blindly, trusting to instinct. Since then he had been getting to know her. It was astonishing how much there was to know. There was a fresh discovery to be made about her every day. She was a perpetually recurring miracle.

The futility of his old life made him wince whenever he dared think of it. How he had drifted, a useless log on a sluggish current!

He was certainly a whole-hearted convert. As to Saul of Tarsus, so to him there had come a sudden blinding light. He could hardly believe that he was the same person who had scoffed at the idea of a man giving up his life to one woman and being happy. But then the abstract wife had been a pale, bloodless phantom, and Ruth was real.

It was the realness of her that kept him in a state of perpetual amazement. To see her moving about the studio, to touch her, to look at her across the dinner-table, to wake in the night and hear her breathing at his side.... It seemed to him that centuries might pass, yet these things would still be wonderful.

And always in his heart there was the gratitude for what she had done for him. She had given up everything to share his life. She had weighed him in the balance against wealth and comfort and her place among the great ones of the world, and had chosen him. There were times when the thought filled him with a kind of delirious pride: times, again, when he felt a grateful humility that made him long to fall down and worship this goddess who had stooped to him.

In a word, he was very young, very much in love, and for the first time in his life was living with every drop of blood in his veins.

❦

Hank returned to New York in due course. He came to the studio the same night, and he had not been there five minutes before a leaden weight descended on Kirk's soul. It was as he had feared. Ruth did not like him.

Hank was not the sort of man who makes universal appeal. Also, he was no ladies' man. He was long and lean and hard-bitten, and his supply of conventional small talk was practically non-existent. To get the best out of Hank, as has been said, you had to let him take his coat off and put his feet up on the back of a second chair and reconcile yourself to the pestiferous brand of tobacco which he affected.

Ruth conceded none of these things. Throughout the interview Hank sat bolt upright, tucking a pair of shoes of the dreadnought class coyly underneath his chair, and drew suspiciously at Turkish cigarettes from Kirk's case. An air of constraint hung over the party. Again and again Kirk hoped that Hank would embark on the epic of his life, but shyness kept Hank dumb.

He had heard, on reaching New York, that Kirk was married, but he had learned no details, and had conjured up in his mind the vision of a jolly little girl of the Bohemian type, who would make a fuss over him as Kirk's oldest friend. Confronted with Ruth, he lost a nerve which had never before failed him. This gorgeous creature, he felt, would never put up with those racy descriptions of wild adventures which had endeared him to Kirk. As soon as he could decently do so, he left, and Kirk, returning to the studio after seeing him out, sat down moodily, trying to convince himself against his judgment that the visit had not been such a failure after all.

Ruth was playing the piano softly. She had turned out all the lights except one, which hung above her head, shining on her white arms as they moved. From where he sat Kirk could see her profile. Her eyes were half closed.

The sight of her, as it always did, sent a thrill through him, but he was conscious of an ache behind it. He had hoped so much that Hank would pass, and he knew that he had not. Why was it that two people so completely one as Ruth and himself could not see Hank with the same eyes?

He knew that she had thought him uncouth and impossible. Why could not Hank have exerted himself more, instead of sitting there in that stuffed way? Why could not Ruth have unbent? Why had not he himself done something to save the situation? Of the three, he blamed himself most. He was the one who should have taken the lead and made things pleasant for everybody instead of forcing out conversational platitudes.

Once or twice he had caught Hank's eye, and had hated himself for understanding what it said and not being able to deny it. He had marked the end of their old relationship, the parting of the ways, and that a tragedy had been played out that night.

He found himself thinking of Hank as of a friend who had died. What times they had had! How smoothly they had got on together! He could not recall a single occasion on which they had fallen out, from the time when they had fought as boys at the prep. school and cemented their friendship the next day. After that there had been periods when they had parted, sometimes for more than a year, but they had always come together again and picked up the threads as neatly as if there had been no gap in their intimacy.

He had gone to college: Hank had started on the roving life which suited his temperament. But they had never lost touch with each other. And now it was all over. They would meet again, but it would not be the same. The angel with the flaming sword stood between them.

For the first time since the delirium of marriage had seized upon him, Kirk was conscious of a feeling that all was not for the best in a best of all possible worlds, a feeling of regret, not that he had married – the mere thought would have been a blasphemy – but that marriage was such a complicated affair. He liked a calm life, free from complications, and now they were springing up on every side.

There was the matter of the models. Kirk had supposed that it was only in the comic papers that the artist's wife objected to his employing models. He had classed it with the mother-in-law joke, respecting it for its antiquity, but not imagining that it ever really happened. And Ruth had brought this absurd situation into the sphere of practical politics only a few days ago.

Since his marriage Kirk had dropped his work almost entirely. There had seemed to be no time for it. He liked to spend his days going round the stores with Ruth, buying her things, or looking in at the windows of Fifth Avenue shops and choosing what he would buy her when he had made his fortune. It was agreed upon between them that he was to make his fortune some day.

Kirk's painting had always been more of a hobby with him than a profession. He knew that he had talent, but talent without hard work is a poor weapon, and he had always shirked hard work. He had an instinct for colour, but his drawing was uncertain. He hated linework, while knowing that only through steady practice at linework could he achieve his artistic salvation. He was an amateur, and a lazy amateur.

But once in a while the work fever would grip him. It had gripped him a few days before Hank's visit. An idea for a picture had come to him, and he had set to work upon it with his usual impulsiveness.

This had involved the arrival of Miss Hilda Vince at the studio. There was no harm in Miss Vince. Her morals were irreproachable. She supported a work-shy father, and was engaged to be married to a young gentleman who travelled for a hat firm. But she was of a chatty disposition and no respecter of persons. She had posed frequently for Kirk in his bachelor days, and was accustomed to call him by his first name – a fact which Kirk had forgotten until Ruth, who had been out in the park, came in.

Miss Vince was saying at the moment: "So I says to her, 'Kirk's just phoned to me to sit.' 'What! Kirk!' she says. 'Is *he* doin' a bit of work for a change? Well, it's about time.' 'Aw, Kirk don't need to work,' I says. 'He's a plute. He's got it in gobs.' So—"

"I didn't know you were busy, dear," said Ruth. "I won't interrupt you."

She went out.

"Was that your wife?" inquired Miss Vince. "She's got a sweet face. Say, I read the piece about you and her in the paper. You certainly got a nerve, Kirk, breaking in on the millionaires that way."

That night Ruth spoke her mind about Miss Vince. It was in vain that Kirk touched on the work-shy father, dwelt feelingly on the young gentleman who travelled in hats. Ruth had made up her mind. It was thumbs down for Miss Vince.

"But if I'm to paint," said Kirk, "I must have models."

"There must be hundreds who don't call you by your Christian name."

"After about five minutes they all do," said Kirk. "It's a way they've got. They mean no harm."

Ruth then made this brilliant suggestion: "Kirk, dear, why don't you paint landscapes?"

In spite of his annoyance, he laughed.

"Why don't I paint landscapes, Ruth? Because I'm not a land-scape painter, that's why."

"You could learn."

"It's a different branch of the trade altogether. You might just as well tell a catcher to pitch."

"Well, anyhow," reported Ruth with spirit, "I won't have that Vince creature in the place again."

It was the first time she had jerked at the reins or given any sign that she was holding them, and undoubtedly this was the moment at which Kirk should have said: "My dearest, the time has come for me to state plainly that my soul is my own. I decline to give in to this absurd suggestion. Marriage is an affair of give and take, not a circus where one party holds the hoop while the other jumps through and shams dead. We shall be happier later on if we get this clearly into our heads now."

What he did say was: "Very well, dear. I'll write and tell her not to come."

He knew he was being abominably weak, but he did not care. He even felt a certain pleasure in his surrender. Big, muscular men are given to this feebleness with women. Hercules probably wore an idiotic grin of happiness when he spun wool for Omphale.

Since then the picture had been laid aside, but Kirk's desire to be up and at it had grown with inaction. When a lazy man does make up his mind to assail a piece of work, he is like a dog with a bone.

The music had stopped. Ruth swung round.

"What are you dreaming about Kirk?"

Kirk came to himself with a start.

"I was thinking of a lot of things. For one, about that picture of mine."

"What about it?"

"Well, when I was going to finish it."

"Why don't you?"

Kirk laughed.

"Where's my model? You've scared her up a tree, and I can't coax her down."

Ruth came over to him and sat down on a low chair at his side. She put her arm round his waist and rested her head in the hollow of his shoulder.

"Is he pining for his horrid Vince girl, the poor boy?"

"He certainly is," said Kirk. "Or at any rate, for some understudy to her."

"We must think. Do they *all* call you Kirk?"

"I've never met one who didn't."

"What horrible creatures you artists are!"

"My dear kid, you don't understand the thing at all. When you're painting a model she ceases to be a girl at all. You don't think of her as anything except a sort of lay-figure."

"Good gracious! Does your lay-figure call you Kirk too?"

"It always looks as if it were going to."

Ruth shuddered.

"It's a repulsive thing. I hate it. It gives me the creeps. I came in here last night and switched on the light, and there it was, goggling at me."

"Are you getting nervous?"

Ruth's face grew grave.

"Do you know, Kirk, I really believe I am. This morning as I was dressing, I suddenly got the most awful feeling that something terrible was going to happen. I don't know what. It was perfectly vague. I just felt a kind of horror. It passed off in a moment or two; but, while it lasted – ugh!"

"How ghastly! Why didn't you tell me before? You must be run down. Look here, let's shut up this place and get out to Florida or somewhere for the winter!"

"Let's don't do anything of the kind. Florida indeed! For the love of Mike, as Steve would say, it's much too expensive. You know, Kirk, we are both frightfully extravagant. I'm sure we are spending too much money as it is. You know you sold out some of your capital only the other day."

"It was only that once. And you had set your heart on that pendant. Surely to goodness, if I drag you away from a comfortable home to live in a hovel, the least I can do is to—"

"You didn't drag me. I just walked in and sat down, and you couldn't think how to get rid of me, so in despair you married me."

"That was it. And now I've got to set to work and make a fortune and – what do you call it? – support you in the style to which you have been accustomed. Which brings us back to the picture. I don't suppose I shall get ten dollars for it, but I feel I shall curl up and die if I don't get it finished. Are you *absolutely* determined about the Vince girl?"

"I'm adamant. I'm granite. I'm chilled steel. Oh! Kirk, can't you find a nice, motherly old model, with white hair and spectacles? I shouldn't mind *her* calling you by your first name."

"But it's absurd. I told you just now that an artist doesn't look on his models as human beings while—"

"I know. I've read all about that in books, and I believed it then. Why, when I married you, I said to myself: 'I mustn't be foolish. Kirk's an artist, I mustn't be a comic-supplement wife and object to his using models!' Oh, I was going to be so good and reasonable. You would have loved me! And then, when it came to the real thing, I found I just could not stand it. I know it's silly of me. I know just as well as you do that Miss Vince is quite a nice girl really, and is going to make a splendid Mrs. Travelling Salesman, but that doesn't help me. It's my wicked nature, I suppose. I'm just a plain cat, and that's all there is to it. Look at the way I treat your friends!"

Kirk started.

"You jumped!" said Ruth. "You jerked my head. Do you think I didn't know you had noticed it? I knew how unhappy you were when Mr. Jardine was here, and I just hated myself."

"Didn't you like Hank?" asked Kirk.

Ruth was silent for a moment.

"I wish you would," Kirk went on. "You don't know what a real white man old Hank is. You didn't see him properly that night. He was nervous. But he's one of the very best God ever made. We've known each other all our lives. He and I—"

"Don't tell me!" cried Ruth. "Don't you see that that's just the reason why I can't like him? Don't tell me about the things you and he did together, unless you want me to hate him. Don't you understand, dear? It's the same with all your friends. I'm jealous of them for having known you before I did. And I hate these models because they come into a part of your life into which I can't. I want you all to myself. I want to be your whole life. I know it's idiotic and impossible, but I do."

"You are my whole life," said Kirk seriously. "I wasn't born till I met you. There isn't a single moment when you are not my whole life."

She pressed her head contentedly against his arm.

"Kirk."

"Yes?"

"Let *me* pose for your picture."

"What! You couldn't!"

"Why not?"

"It's terribly hard work. It's an awful strain."

"I'm sure I'm as strong as that Vince girl. You ask Steve; he's seen me throw the medicine-ball."

"But posing is different. Hilda Vince has been trained for it."

"Well let me try, at any rate."

"But—"

"Do! And I'll promise to like your Hank and not put on my grand manner when he begins telling me what fun you and he used to have in the good old days before I was born or thought of. May I?"

"But—"

"Quick! Promise!"

"Very well."

"You dear! I'll be the best model you ever had. I won't move a muscle, and I'll stand there till I drop."

"You'll do nothing of the kind. You'll come right down off that model-throne the instant you feel the least bit tired."

The picture which Kirk was painting was one of those pictures which thousands of young artists are working on unceasingly every day. Kirk's ideas about it were in a delightfully vague state. He had a notion that it might turn out in the end as "Carmen." On the other hand, if anything went wrong and he failed to insert a sufficient amount of wild devilry into it, he could always hedge by calling it "A Reverie" or "The Spanish Maiden."

Possibly, if the thing became too pensive and soulful altogether, he might give it some title suggestive of the absent lover at the bull-fight – "The Toreador's Bride" – or something of that sort. The only point on which he was solid was that it was to strike the Spanish note; and to this end he gave Ruth a costume of black and orange and posed her on the model-throne with a rose in her hair.

Privately he had decided that ten minutes would be Ruth's limit. He knew something of the strain of sitting to an artist.

"Tired?" he asked at the end of this period.

Ruth shook her head and smiled.

"You must be. Come and sit down and take a rest."

"I'm quite all right, dear. Go on with your work."

"Well, shout out the moment you feel you've had enough."

He began to paint again. The minutes went by and Ruth made no movement. He began to grow absorbed in his work. He lost count of time. Ruth ceased to be Ruth, ceased even to be flesh and blood. She was just something he was painting.

"Kirk!"

The sharp suddenness of the cry brought him to his feet, quivering. Ruth was swaying on the model-throne. Her eyes were staring straight before her and her face was twisted with fear.

As he sprang forward she fell, pitching stiffly head foremost, as he had seen men fall in the ring, her arms hanging at her sides; and he caught her.

He carried her to the couch and laid her down. He hung for an instant in doubt whether to go for water or telephone for the doctor. He decided on the telephone.

He hung up the receiver and went back to Ruth. She stirred and gave a little moan. He flew upstairs and returned with a pitcher of water. When he got back Ruth was sitting up. The look of terror was gone from her face. She smiled at him, a faint, curiously happy smile. He flung himself on his knees beside her, his arm round her waist, and burst into a babble of self-reproach.

He cursed himself for being such a brute, such a beast as to let her stand there, tiring herself to death. She must never do it again. He was a devil. He ought to have known she could not stand it. He was not fit to be married. He was not fit to live.

Ruth ruffled his hair.

"Stop abusing my husband," she said. "I'm fond of him. Did you catch me, Kirk?"

"Yes, thank God. I got to you just in time."

"That's the last thing I remember, wondering if you would. You seemed such miles and miles away. It was like looking at something in a mist through the wrong end of a telescope. Oh, Kirk!"

"Yes, honey?"

"It came again, that awful feeling as if something dreadful was going to happen. And then I felt myself going." She paused. "Kirk, I think I know now. I understand; and oh, I'm so happy!"

She buried her face on his shoulder, and they stayed there silent, till there came a ring at the bell. Kirk got up. George Pennicut ushered in the doctor. It was the same little old doctor who had ministered to George in his hour of need.

"Feeling better, Mrs. Winfield?" he said, as he caught sight of Ruth. "Your husband told me over the 'phone that you were unconscious."

"She fainted," cried Kirk. "It was all through me. I—"

The doctor took him by the shoulders. He had to stretch to do it.

"You go away, young man," he said. "Take a walk round the block. You aren't on in this scene."

Kirk was waiting in the hall when he left a few minutes later.

"Well?" he said anxiously.

"Well?" said the little doctor.

"Is she all right? There's nothing wrong, is there?"

The doctor grinned a friendly grin.

"On the contrary," he said. "You ought to be very pleased."

"What do you mean?"

"It's quite a commonplace occurrence, though I suppose it will seem like a miracle to you. But, believe me, it has happened before. If it hadn't, you and I wouldn't be here now."

Kirk looked at him in utter astonishment. His words seemed meaningless. And then, suddenly, he understood, and his heart seemed to stand still.

"You don't mean—" he said huskily.

"Yes, I do," said the doctor. "Good-bye, my boy. I've got to hurry off. You caught me just as I was starting for the hospital."

Kirk went back to the studio, his mind in a whirl. Ruth was lying on the couch. She looked up as the door opened. He came quickly to her side.

"Ruth!" he muttered.

Her eyes were shining with a wonderful light of joy. She drew his head down and kissed him.

"Oh, Kirk," she whispered. "I'm happy. I'm happy. I've wanted this so."

He could not speak. He sat on the edge of the couch and looked at her. She had been wonderful to him before. She was a thousand times more wonderful now.

CHAPTER 8

SUSPENSE

IT seemed to Kirk, as the days went by, that a mist of unreality fell like a curtain between him and the things of this world. Commonplace objects lost their character and became things to marvel at. There was a new bond of sympathy between the world and himself.

A citizen walking in the park with his children became a kind of miracle. Here was a man who had travelled the road which he was travelling now, who had had the same hopes and fear and wonder. Once he encountered a prosperous looking individual moving, like a liner among tugs, in the midst of no fewer than six offspring. Kirk fixed him with such a concentrated stare of emotion and excitement that the other was alarmed and went on his way alertly, as one in the presence of danger. It is probable that, if Kirk had happened to ask him the time at that moment, or indeed addressed him at all, he would have screamed for the police.

The mystery of childbirth and the wonder of it obsessed Kirk as time crept on. And still more was he conscious of the horrible dread that was gathering within him. Ruth's unvarying cheerfulness was to him almost uncanny. None of the doubts and fears which blackened his life appeared to touch her. Once he confided these to his friend, the little doctor, and was thoroughly bullied by him for his foolishness. But in spite of ridicule the fear crept back, cringingly, like a whipped dog.

And then, time moving on its leisurely but businesslike fashion, the day arrived, and for the first time in his life Kirk knew what fear really meant. All that he had experienced till now had, he saw, been a mild apprehension, not worthy of a stronger name. His flesh crawled with the thoughts which rose in his mind like black bubbles in a pond. There were moments when the temptation to stupefy himself with drink was almost irresistible.

It was his utter uselessness that paralysed him. He seemed destined to be of no help to Ruth at just those crises when she needed him most. When she was facing her father with the news of the marriage he had not been at her side. And now, when she was fighting for her life, he could do nothing but pace the empty, quiet studio and think.

The doctor had arrived at eight o'clock, cheery as ever, and had come downstairs after seeing Ruth to ask him to telephone to Mrs. Porter. In his overwrought state, this had jarred upon Kirk. Here, he felt, was somebody who could help where he was useless.

Mrs. Porter had appeared in a cab and had had the cold brutality to ask for a glass of sherry and a sandwich before going upstairs. She put forward the lame excuse that she had not dined. Kirk gave her the sherry and sandwich and resumed his patrol in a glow of indignation. The idea of any one requiring food at this moment struck him as gross and revolting.

His wrath did not last. In a short while fear came back into its own.

The hands of the clock pointed to ten before he stooped to following Mrs. Porter's example. George Pennicut had been sent out, so he went into the little kitchen, where he found eggs, which he mixed with milk and swallowed. After this he was aware of a momentary excess of optimism. The future looked a little brighter. But not for long. Presently he was prowling the studio as restlessly as ever.

Men of Kirk's type are not given to deep thought. Until now he had probably never spent more than a couple of minutes consecutively in self-examination. This vigil forced him upon himself and caused him to pass his character under review, with strange and unsatisfactory results. He had never realised before what a curiously contemptible and useless person he was. It seemed to him that this was all he was fit for – to hang about doing nothing while everybody else was busy and proving his or her own worth.

A door opened and the little doctor came quietly down the stairs. Kirk sprang at him.

"Well?"

"My dear man, everything's going splendidly. Couldn't be better." The doctor's eyes searched his face. "When did you have anything to eat last?"

"I don't know. I had some eggs and milk. I don't know when."

The doctor took him by the shoulders and hustled him into the kitchen, where he searched and found meat and bread.

"Eat that," he said. "I'll have some, too."

"I couldn't."

"And some whisky. Where do you keep it?"

After the first few mouthfuls Kirk ate wolfishly. The doctor munched a sandwich with the placidity of a summer boarder at a picnic. His calmness amazed and almost shocked Kirk.

"You can't help her by killing yourself," said the doctor philosophically. "I like that woman with the gimlet eyes. At least I don't, but she's got sense. Go on. You haven't done yet. Another highball won't hurt you." He eyed Kirk with some sympathy. "It's a bad time for you, of course."

"For *me?* Good God!"

"You want to keep your nerve. Nothing awful is going to happen."

"If only there was something I could do."

"'They also serve who only stand and wait,'" quoted the doctor sententiously. "There is something you can do."

"What?"

"Light your pipe and take it easy."

Kirk snorted.

"I mean it. In a very short while now you will be required to take the stage and embrace your son or daughter, as the case may be. You don't want to appear looking as if you had been run over by an automobile after a night out. You want your appearance to give Mrs. Winfield as little of a shock as possible. Bear that in mind. Well, I must be going."

And Kirk was alone again.

The food and the drink and the doctor's words had a good effect. His mind became quieter. He sat down and filled his pipe. After a few puffs he replaced it in his pocket. It seemed too callous to think of smoking now. The doctor was a good fellow, but he did not understand. All the same, he was glad that he had had that whisky. It had certainly put heart into him for the moment.

What was happening upstairs? He strained his ears, but could hear nothing.

Gradually, as he waited, his mood of morbid self-criticism returned. He had sunk once more into the depths when he was aware of a soft tapping. The door bell rang very gently. He went to the door and opened it.

"I kinder thought I'd look in and see how things were getting along," said a voice.

It was Steve. A subdued and furtive Steve. Kirk's heart leaped at the sight of him. It was as if he had found something solid to cling to in a shifting world.

"Come in, Steve."

He spoke huskily. Steve sidled into the studio, embarrassment written on every line of him.

"Don't mind my butting in, do you? I've been walking up and down and round the block till every cop on the island's standing by waiting for me to pull something. Another minute and they'd have pinched me on suspicion. I just felt I had to come and see how Miss Ruth was making out."

"The doctor was down here just now. He said everything was going well."

"I guess he knows his business."

There was a silence. Kirk's ears were straining for sounds from above.

"It's hell," said Steve.

Kirk nodded. This kind of talk was more what he wanted. The doctor meant well, but he was too professional. Steve was human.

"Go and get yourself a drink, Steve. I expect you need one."

Steve shook his head.

"Waggon," he said briefly. And there was silence again.

"Say, Kirk."

"Yes?"

"What a wonder she is. Miss Ruth, I mean. I've helped her throw that medicine-ball – often – you wouldn't believe. She's a wonder." He paused. "Say, this is hell, ain't it?"

Kirk did not answer. It was very quiet in the studio now. In the street outside a heavy waggon rumbled part. Somebody shouted a few words of a popular song. Steve sprang to his feet.

"I'll fix that guy," he said. But the singing ceased, and he sat down again.

Kirk got up and began to walk quickly up and down. Steve watched him furtively.

"You want to take your mind off it," he said. "You'll be all in if you keep on worrying about it in that way."

Kirk stopped in his stride.

"That's what the doctor said," he snapped savagely. "What do you two fools think I'm made of?" He recovered himself quickly, ashamed of the outburst. "I'm sorry, Steve. Don't mind anything I say. It's awfully good of you to have come here, and I'm not going to forget it."

Steve scratched his chin reflectively.

"Say, I'll tell you something," he said. "My mother told me once that when I was born my old dad took it just like you. Found he was getting all worked up by having to hang around and do nothing, so he says to himself: 'I've got to take my mind off this business, or it's me for the foolish-house.'

"Well, sir, there was a big guy down on that street who'd been picking on dad good and hard for a mighty long while. And this guy suddenly comes into dad's mind. He felt of his muscle, dad did. 'Gee!' he says to himself, 'I believe the way I'm feeling, I could just go and eat up that gink right away.' And the more he thought of it, the better it looked to him, so all of a sudden he grabs his hat and beats it like a streak down to the saloon on the corner, where he knew the feller would be at that time, and he goes straight up to him and hands him one.

"Back comes the guy at him – he was a great big son of a gun, weighing thirty pounds more than dad – and him and dad mixes it right there in the saloon till the barkeep and about fifty other fellers throws them out, and they goes off to a vacant lot to finish the thing. And dad's so worked up that he gives the other guy his till he hollers that that's all he'll want. And then dad goes home and waits quite quiet and happy and peaceful till they tell him I'm there."

Steve paused.

"Kirk," he said then, "how would you like a round or two with the small gloves, just to get things off your mind for a spell and pass the time? My dad said he found it eased him mighty good."

Kirk stared at him.

"Just a couple of rounds," urged Steve. "And you can go all out at that. I shan't mind. Just try to think I'm some guy that's been picking on you and let me have it. See what I mean?"

For the first time that day the faint ghost of a grin appeared on Kirk's face.

"I wonder if you're right, Steve?"

"I know I'm right. And, say, don't think I don't need it, too. I ain't known Miss Ruth all this time for nothing. You'll be doing me a kindness if you knock my face in."

The small gloves occupied a place of honour to themselves in a lower drawer. It was not often that Kirk used them in his friendly bouts with Steve. For ordinary occasions the larger and more padded species met with his approval. Steve, during these daily sparring encounters, was amiability itself; but he could not be counted upon not to forget himself for an occasional moment in the heat of the fray; and though Kirk was courageous enough, he preferred to preserve the regularity of his features at the expense of a little extra excitement.

Once, after a brisk rally, he had gone about the world looking as if he was suffering from mumps, owing to a right hook which no one regretted more than Steve himself.

But to-day was different; and Kirk felt that even a repetition of that lethal punch would be welcome.

Steve, when the contest opened, was disposed to be consolatory in word as well as deed. He kept up a desultory conversation as he circled and feinted.

"You gotta look at it this way," he began, side-stepping a left, "it ain't often you hear of anything going wrong at times like this. You gotta remember" – he hooked Kirk neatly on the jaw – "that" he concluded.

Kirk came back with a swing at the body which made his adversary grunt.

"That's true," he said.

"Sure," rejoined Steve a little breathlessly, falling into a clinch.

They moved warily round each other.

"So," said Steve, blocking a left, "that ought to comfort you some."

Kirk nodded. He guessed correctly that the other was alluding to his last speech, not to the counter which had just made the sight of his left eye a little uncertain.

Gradually, as the bout progressed, Kirk began to lose the slight diffidence which had hampered him at the start. He had been feeling so wonderfully friendly toward Steve, so grateful for his presence, and his sympathy, that it had been hard, in spite of the other's admonitions, to enter into the fray with any real conviction. Moreover, subconsciously, he was listening all the time for sounds from above which never came.

These things gave a certain lameness to his operations. It was immediately after this blow in the eye, mentioned above, that he ceased to be an individual with private troubles and a wandering mind, and became a boxer pure and simple, his whole brain concentrated on the problem of how to get past his opponent's guard.

Steve, recognizing the change in an instant, congratulated himself on the success of his treatment. It had worked even more quickly than he had hoped. He helped the cure with another swift jab which shot over Kirk's guard.

Kirk came in with a rush. Steve slipped him. Kirk rushed again. Steve, receiving a hard punch on a nose which, though accustomed to such assaults, had never grown really to enjoy them, began to feel a slight diminution of his detached attitude toward this encounter. Till now his position had been purely that of the kindly physician soothing a patient. The rapidity with which the patient was permitting himself to be soothed rendered the post of physician something of a sinecure; and Steve, as Kirk had done, began to slip back into the boxer.

It was while he was in what might be called a transition stage that an unexpected swing sent him with some violence against the wall; and from that moment nature asserted itself. A curious, set look appeared on his face; wrinkles creased his forehead; his jaw protruded slightly.

Kirk made another rush. This time Steve did not slip; he went to meet it, head down and hands busy.

Mrs. Lora Delane Porter came downstairs with the measured impressiveness of one who bears weighty news. Her determined face was pale and tired, as it had every right to be; but she bore herself proudly, as one who has fought and not been defeated.

"Mr. Winfield," she said.

There was no answer. Looking about her, she found the studio empty.

Then, from behind the closed door of the inner room, she was aware of a strange, shuffling sound. She listened, astonished. She heard a gasp, then curious thuds, finally a bump louder than the thuds. And then there was silence.

These things surprised Mrs. Porter. She opened the door and looked in.

It says much for her iron self-control that she remained quiet at this point. A lesser person, after a far less tiring ordeal than she had passed through, would have found relief in some cry or exclamation – possibly even in a scream.

Against the far wall, breathing hard and fondling his left eye with a four-ounce glove, leaned Steve Dingle. His nose was bleeding somewhat freely, but this he appeared to consider a trifle unworthy of serious attention. On the floor, an even more disturbing spectacle, Kirk lay at full length. To Mrs. Porter's startled gaze he appeared to be dead. He too, was bleeding, but he was not in a position to notice it.

"It's all right, ma'am," said Steve, removing the hand from his face and revealing an eye which for spectacular dilapidation must have rivalled the epoch-making one which had so excited his mother on a famous occasion. "It's nothing serious."

"Has Mr. Winfield fainted?"

"Not exactly fainted, ma'am. It's like this. He'd got me clear up in a corner, and I seen it's up to me if I don't want to be knocked through the wall, so I has to cross him. Maybe I'd gotten a little worked up myself by then. But it was my fault. I told him to go all out, and he sure did. This eye's going to be a pippin to-morrow."

Mrs. Porter examined the wounded organ with interest.

"That, I suppose Mr. Dingle, is what you call a blue eye?"

"It sure is, ma'am."

"What has been happening?"

"Well, it's this way. I see he's all worked up, sitting around doing nothing except wait, so I makes him come and spar a round to take his mind off it. My old dad, ma'am, when I was coming along, found that dope fixed him all right, so I reckoned it would do as much good here. My old dad went and beat the block off a fellow down our street, and it done him a lot of good."

Mrs. Porter shook his gloved hand.

"Mr. Dingle," she said with enthusiasm, "I really believe that you are the only sensible man I have ever met. Your common sense is astonishing. I have no doubt you saved Mr. Winfield from a nervous break-down. Would you be kind enough, when you are rested, to fetch some water and bring him to and inform him that he is the father of a son?"

CHAPTER 9
THE WHITE HOPE IS TURNED DOWN

WILLIAM Bannister Winfield was the most wonderful child. Of course, you had to have a certain amount of intelligence to see this. To the vapid and irreflective observer he was not much to look at in the early stages of his career, having a dough-like face almost entirely devoid of nose, a lack-lustre eye, and the general appearance of a poached egg. His immediate circle of intimates, however, thought him a model of manly beauty; and there was the undeniable fact that he had come into the world weighing nine pounds. Take him for all in all, a lad of promise.

Kirk's sense of being in a dream continued. His identity seemed to have undergone a change. The person he had known as Kirk Winfield had disappeared, to be succeeded by a curious individual bubbling over with an absurd pride for which it was not easy to find an outlet. Hitherto a rather reserved man, he was conscious now of a desire to accost perfect strangers in the street and inform them that he was not the ordinary person they probably imagined, but a father with an intensely unusual son at home, and if they did not believe him they could come right along and see for themselves.

The only flaw in his happiness at the moment was the fact that his circle of friends was so small. He had not missed the old brigade of the studio before, but now the humblest of them would have been welcome, provided he would have sat still and listened. Even Percy Shanklyn would have been acceptable as an audience.

Steve, excellent fellow, was always glad to listen to him on his favourite subject. He had many long talks with Steve on the question of William's future. Steve, as the infant's godfather, which post he had claimed and secured at an early date, had definite views on the matter.

Here, held Steve, was the chance of a lifetime. With proper training, a baby of such obvious muscular promise might be made the greatest fighter that ever stepped into the ring. He was the real White Hope. He advised Kirk to direct William's education on the lines which would insure his being, when the time was ripe, undisputed heavy-weight champion of the world. To Steve life outside the ring was a poor affair, practically barren of prizes for the ambitious.

Mrs. Lora Delane Porter, eyeing William's brow, of which there was plenty, he being at this time extremely short of hair, predicted a less robust and more intellectual future for him. Something more on the lines of president of some great university or ambassador at some important court struck her as his logical sphere.

Kirk's view was that he should combine both careers and be an ambassador who took a few weeks off every now and then in order to defend his champion's belt. In his spare time he might paint a picture or two.

Ruth hesitated between the army, the navy, the bar, and business. But every one was agreed that William was to be something special.

This remarkable child had a keen sense of humour. Thus he seldom began to cry in his best vein till the small hours of the morning; and on these occasions he would almost invariably begin again after he had been officially pronounced to be asleep. His sudden grab at the hair of any adult who happened to come within reach was very droll, too.

As to his other characteristics, he was of rather an imperious nature. He liked to be waited on. He wanted what he wanted when he wanted it. The greater part of his attention being occupied at this period with the important duty of chewing his thumb, he assigned the drudgery of life to his dependants. Their duties were to see that he got up in the morning, dressed, and took his tub; and after that to hang around on the chance of general orders.

Any idea Kirk may have had of resuming his work was abandoned during these months. No model, young and breezy or white-haired and motherly, passed the studio doors. Life was far too interesting for work. The canvas which might have become "Carmen" or "A Reverie" or even "The Toreador's Bride" lay unfinished and neglected in a corner.

It astonished Kirk to find how strong the paternal instinct was in him. In the days when he had allowed his mind to dwell upon the abstract wife he had sometimes gone a step further and conjured up the abstract baby. The result had always been to fill him with a firm conviction that the most persuasive of wild horses should not drag him from his bachelor seclusion. He had had definite ideas on babies as a class. And here he was with his world pivoting on one of them. It was curious.

The White Hope, as Steve called his godson – possibly with the idea of influencing him by suggestion – grew. The ailments which attacked lesser babies passed him by. He avoided croup, and even whooping-cough paid him but a flying visit hardly worth mentioning. His first tooth gave him a little trouble, but that is the sort of thing which may happen to anyone; and the spirited way in which he protested against the indignity of cutting it was proof of a high soul.

Such was the remarkableness of this child that it annoyed Kirk more and more that he should be obliged to give the exhibition of his extraordinary qualities to so small an audience. Ruth felt the same; and it was for this reason that the first overtures were made to the silent camp which contained her father and her brother Bailey.

Since that evening in the library there had come no sign from the house on Fifth Avenue that its inmates were aware of her existence. Life had been too full till now to make this a cause of trouble to her; but with William Bannister becoming every day more amazing the desire came to her to try and heal the breach. Her father had so ordered his life in his relation to his children that Ruth's affection was not so deep as it might have been; but, after all, he was William Bannister's grandfather, and, as such, entitled to consideration.

It was these reflections that led to Steve's state visit to John Bannister – probably the greatest fiasco on record.

Steve had been selected for the feat on the strength of his having the right of entry to the Fifth Avenue house, for John Bannister was still obeying his doctor's orders and taking his daily spell of exercise with the pugilist – and Steve bungled it hopelessly.

His task was not a simple one. He was instructed to employ tact, to hint rather than to speak, to say nothing to convey the impression that Ruth in any way regretted the step she had taken, to give the idea that it was a matter of complete indifference to her whether she ever saw her father again or not, yet at the same time to make it quite clear that she was very anxious to see him as soon as possible.

William Bannister, grown to maturity and upholding the interests of his country as ambassador at some important court, might have jibbed at the mission.

William Bannister was to accompany Steve and be produced dramatically to support verbal arguments. It seemed to Ruth that for her father to resist William when he saw him was an impossibility. William's position was that of the ace of trumps in the cards which Steve was to play.

Steve made a few objections. His chief argument against taking up the post assigned to him was that he was a roughneck, and that the job in question was one which no roughneck, however gifted in the matter of left hooks, could hope to carry through with real success. But he yielded to pressure, and the expedition set out.

William Bannister at this time was at an age when he was beginning to talk a little and walk a little and take a great interest in things. His walking was a bit amateurish, and his speech rather hard to follow unless you had the key to it. But nobody could have denied that his walk, though staggery, was a genuine walk, and his speech, though limited, genuine speech, within the meaning of the act.

He made no objections to the expedition. On being told that he was going to see his grandpa he nodded curtly and said: "Gwa-wah," after his custom. For, as a conversationalist, perhaps the best description of him is to say that he tried hard. He rarely paused for a word. When in difficulties he said something; he did not seek refuge in silence. That the something was not always immediately intelligible was the fault of his audience for not listening more carefully.

Perhaps the real mistake of the expedition was the nature of its baggage. William Bannister had stood out for being allowed to take with him his wheelbarrow, his box of bricks, and his particular favourite, the dying pig, which you blew out and then allowed to collapse with a pleasing noise. These properties had struck his parents as excessive, but he was firm; and when he gave signs of being determined to fight it out on these lines if it took all the summer, they gave in.

Steve had no difficulty in smuggling William into his grandfather's house. He was a great favourite below stairs there. His great ally was the English butler, Keggs.

Keggs was a stout, dignified, pigeon-toed old sinner, who cast off the butler when not on duty and displayed himself as something of a rounder. He was a man of many parts. It was his chief relaxation to look in at Broadway hotels while some big fight was in progress out West to watch the ticker and assure himself that the man he had backed with a portion of the loot which he had accumulated in the form of tips was doing justice to his judgment, for in private Keggs was essentially the sport.

It was this that so endeared Steve to him. A few years ago Keggs had won considerable sums by backing Steve, and the latter was always given to understand that, as far as the lower regions of it were concerned, the house on Fifth Avenue was open to him at all hours.

To-day he greeted Steve with enthusiasm and suggested a cigar in the pantry before the latter should proceed to his work.

"He ain't ready for you yet, Mr. Dingle. He's lookin' over some papers in – for goodness' sake, who's this?"

He had caught sight of William Bannister, who having wriggled free of Steve, was being made much of by the maids.

"The kid," said Steve briefly.

"Not—"

Steve nodded.

"Sure. His grandson."

Keggs' solemnity increased.

"You aren't going to take him upstairs with you?"

"Surest thing you know. That's why I brought him."

"Don't you do it, Mr. Dingle. 'E's in an awful temper this morning – he gets worse and worse – he'll fire you as soon as look at you."

"Can't be helped. I've got me instructions."

"You always were game," said Keggs admiringly. "I used to see that quick enough before you retired from active work. Well, good luck to you, Mr. Dingle."

Steve gathered up William Bannister, the wheelbarrow, the box of bricks, and the dying pig and made his way to the gymnasium.

The worst of these pre-arranged scenes is that they never happen just as one figured them in one's mind. Steve had expected to have to wait a few minutes in the gymnasium, then there would be a step outside and the old man would enter. The beauty of this, to Steve's mind, was that he himself would be "discovered," as the stage term is; the onus of entering and opening the conversation would be on Mr. Bannister. And, as everybody who has ever had an awkward interview knows, this makes all the difference.

But the minutes passed, and still no grandfather. The nervousness which he had with difficulty expelled began to return to Steve. This was exactly like having to wait in the ring while one's opponent tried to get one's goat by dawdling in the dressing room.

An attempt to relieve himself by punching the ball was a dismal failure. At the first bang of the leather against the wood William Bannister, who had been working in a pre-occupied way at the dying pig, threw his head back and howled, and would not be comforted till Steve took out the rope and skipped before him, much as dancers used to dance before oriental monarchs in the old days.

Steve was just saying to himself for the fiftieth time that he was a fool to have come, when Keggs arrived with the news that Mr. Bannister was too busy to take his usual exercise this morning and that Steve was at liberty to go.

It speaks well for Steve's character that he did not go. He would have given much to retire, for the old man was one of the few people who inspired in him anything resembling fear. But he could not return tamely to the studio with his mission unaccomplished.

"Say, ask him if he can see me for a minute. Say it is important."

Keggs' eye rested on William Bannister, and he shook his head.

"I shouldn't, Mr. Dingle. Really I shouldn't. You don't know what an ugly mood he's in. Something's been worrying him. It's what you might call courting disaster."

"Gee! Do you think I *want* to do it? I've just got to. That's all there is to it."

A few moments later Keggs returned with the news that Mr. Bannister would see Dingle in the library.

"Come along, kid," said Steve. "Gimme hold of the excess baggage, and let's get a move on."

So in the end it was Mr. Bannister who was discovered and Steve who made the entrance. And, as Steve pointed out to Kirk later, it just made all the difference.

The effect of the change on Steve was to make him almost rollicking in his manner, as if he and Mr. Bannister were the nucleus of an Old Home Week celebration or two old college chums meeting after long absence. Nervousness, on the rare occasions when he suffered from it, generally had that effect on him.

He breezed into the library, carrying the wheelbarrow, the box of bricks, and the dying pig, and trailing William in his wake. William's grandfather was seated with his back to the door, dictating a letter to one of his secretaries.

He looked up as Steve entered. He took in Steve and William in a rapid glance and guessed the latter's identity in an instant. He had expected something of this sort ever since he had heard of his grandson's birth. Indeed, he had been somewhat surprised that the visit had not occurred before.

He betrayed no surprise.

"One moment, Dingle," he said, and turned to the secretary again. A faint sneer came and went on his face.

The delay completed Steve's discomfiture. He placed the wheel harrow on the floor, the box of bricks on the wheelbarrow, and the dying pig on the box of bricks, whence it was instantly removed and inflated by William.

"'Referring to your letter of the eighth – '" said Mr. Bannister in his cold, level voice.

He was interrupted by the incisive cry of the dying pig.

"Ask your son to be quiet, Dingle," he said impassively.

Steve was staggered.

"Say, this ain't my son, squire," he began breezily.

"Your nephew, then, or whatever relation he happens to be to you."

He resumed his dictation. Steve wiped his forehead and looked helplessly at the White Hope, who, having discarded the dying pig, was now busy with the box of bricks.

Steve wished he had not come. He was accustomed to the primitive exhibition of emotions, having moved in circles where the wrathful expressed their wrath in a normal manner.

Anger which found its expression in an exaggerated politeness was out of his line and made him uncomfortable.

After what seemed to him a century, John Bannister dismissed the secretary. Even then, however, he did not come immediately to Steve. He remained for a few moments writing, with his back turned. Then, just when Steve had given up hope of ever securing his attention, he turned suddenly.

"Well?"

"Say, it's this way, colonel," Steve had begun, when a triumphant cry from the direction of the open window stopped him. The White Hope was kneeling on a chair, looking down into the street.

"Bix," he explained over his shoulder.

"Kindly ring the bell, Dingle," said Mr. Bannister, unmoved. "Your little nephew appears to have dropped his bricks into Fifth Avenue."

In answer to the summons Keggs appeared. He looked anxious.

"Keggs," said Mr. Bannister, "tell one of the footmen to go out into the avenue and pick up some wooden bricks which he will find there. Dingle's little brother has let some fall."

As Keggs left the room Steve's pent-up nervousness exploded in a whirl of words.

"Aw say, boss, quit yer kiddin'. You know this kid ain't anything to do with me. Why, say, how would he be any relation of a rough-neck like me? Come off the roof, bo. You know well enough who he is. He's your grandson. On the level."

Mr. Bannister looked at William, now engaged in running the wheelbarrow up and down the room, emitting the while a curious sound, possibly to encourage an imaginary horse. The inspection did not seem to excite him or afford him any pleasure.

"Oh!" he said.

Steve was damped, but resumed gamely:

"Say, boss, this is the greatest kid on earth. I'm not stringing you, honest. He's a wonder. On the level, did you ever see a kid that age with a pair of shoulders on him like what this kid's got? Say, squire, what's the matter with calling the fight off and starting fair? Miss Ruth would be tickled to death if you would. Can the rough stuff, colonel. I know you think you've been given a raw deal, Kirk chipping in like that and copping off Miss Ruth, but for the love of Mike, what does it matter? You seen for yourself what a dandy kid this is. Well, then, check your grouch with your hat. Do the square thing. Have out the auto and come right round to the studio and make it up. What's wrong with that, colonel? Honest, they'd be tickled clean through."

At this point Keggs entered, followed by a footman carrying wooden bricks.

"Keggs," said Mr. Bannister, "telephone for the automobile at once – "

"That's the talk, colonel," cried Steve joyfully. "I know you were a sport."

"—to take me down to Wall Street."

Keggs bowed.

"Oh Keggs," said Mr. Bannister, as he turned to leave.

"Sir?"

"Another thing. See that Dingle does not enter the house again."

And Mr. Bannister resumed his writing, while Steve, gathering up the wheelbarrow, the box of bricks, and the dying pig, took William by the hand and retreated.

That terminated Ruth's attempts to conciliate her father.

There remained Bailey. From Bailey she was prepared to stand no nonsense. Meeting him on the street, she fairly kidnapped him, driving him into a taxicab and pushing him into the studio, where he was confronted by his nephew.

Bailey came poorly through the ordeal. William Bannister, a stern critic, weighed him up in one long stare, found him wanting, and announced his decision with all the strength of powerful lungs. In the end he had to be removed, hiccupping, and Bailey, after lingering a few uneasy moments making conversation to Kirk, departed, with such a look about the back of him as he sprang into his cab that Ruth felt that the visit was one which would not be repeated.

She went back into the studio with a rather heavy heart. She was fond of Bailey.

The sight of Kirk restored her. After all, what had happened was only what she had expected. She had chosen her path, and she did not regret it.

CHAPTER 10
AN INTERLUDE OF PEACE

TWO events of importance in the small world which centred round William B. Winfield occurred at about this time. The first was the entrance of Mamie, the second the exit of Mrs. Porter.

Mamie was the last of a series of nurses who came and went in somewhat rapid succession during the early years of the White Hope's life. She was introduced by Steve, who, it seemed, had known her since she was a child. She was the nineteen-year-old daughter of a compositor on one of the morning papers, a little, mouselike thing, with tiny hands and feet, a soft voice, and eyes that took up far more than their fair share of her face.

She had had no professional experience as a nursery-maid; but, as Steve pointed out, the fact that, in the absence of her mother, who had died some years previously, she had had sole charge of three small brothers at the age when small brothers are least easily handled, and had steered them through to the office-boy age without mishap, put her extremely high in the class of gifted amateurs. Mamie was accordingly given a trial, and survived it triumphantly. William Bannister, that discerning youth, took to her at once. Kirk liked the neat way she moved about the studio, his heart being still sore at the performance of one of her predecessors, who had upset and put a substantial foot through his masterpiece, that same "Ariadne in Naxos" which Lora Delane Porter had criticised on the occasion of her first visit to the studio. Ruth, for her part, was delighted with Mamie.

As for Steve, though as an outside member of the firm he cannot be considered to count, he had long ago made up his mind about her. Some time before, when he had found it impossible for him to be in her presence, still less to converse with her, without experiencing a warm, clammy, shooting sensation and a feeling of general weakness similar to that which follows a well-directed blow at the solar plexus, he had come to the conclusion that he must be in love. The furious jealousy which assailed him on seeing her embraced by and embracing a stout person old enough to be her father convinced him of this.

The discovery that the stout man actually was her father's brother relieved his mind to a certain extent, but the episode left him shaken. He made up his mind to propose at once and get it over. When Mamie joined the garrison of No. 90 a year later the dashing feat was still unperformed. There was that about Mamie which unmanned Steve. She was so small and dainty that the ruggedness which had once been his pride seemed to him, when he thought of her, an insuperable defect. The conviction that he was a roughneck deepened in him and tied his tongue.

The defection of Mrs. Porter was a gradual affair. From a very early period in the new regime she had been dissatisfied. Accustomed to rule, she found herself in an unexpectedly minor position. She had definite views on the hygienic upbringing of children, and these she imparted to Ruth, who listened pleasantly, smiled, and ignored them.

Mrs. Porter was not used to such treatment. She found Ruth considerably less malleable than she had been before marriage, and she resented the change.

Kirk, coming in one afternoon, found Ruth laughing.

"It's only Aunt Lora," she said. "She will come in and lecture me on how to raise babies. She's crazy about microbes. It's the new idea. Sterilization, and all that. She thinks that everything a child touches ought to be sterilized first to kill the germs. Bill's running awful risks being allowed to play about the studio like this."

Kirk looked at his son and heir, who was submitting at that moment to be bathed. He was standing up. It was a peculiarity of his that he refused to sit down in a bath, being apparently under the impression, when asked to do so, that there was a conspiracy afoot to drown him.

"I don't see how the kid could be much fitter."

"It's not so much what he is now. She is worrying about what might happen to him. She can talk about bacilli till your flesh creeps. Honestly, if Bill ever did get really ill, I believe Aunt Lora could talk me round to her views about them in a minute. It's only the fact that he is so splendidly well that makes it seem so absurd."

Kirk laughed.

"It's all very well to laugh. You haven't heard her. I've caught myself wavering a dozen times. Do you know, she says a child ought not to be kissed?"

"It has struck me," said Kirk meditatively, "that your Aunt Lora, if I may make the suggestion, is the least bit of what Steve would call a shy-dome. Is there anything else she had mentioned?'

"Hundreds of things. Bill ought to be kept in a properly sterilized nursery, with sterilized toys and sterilized everything, and the temperature ought to be just so high and no higher, and just so low and no lower. Get her to talk about it to you. She makes you wonder why everybody is not dead."

"This is a new development, surely? Has she ever broken out in this place before?"

"Oh, yes. In the old days she often used to talk about it. She has written books about it."

"I thought her books were all about the selfishness of the modern young man in not marrying."

"Not at all. Some of them are about how to look after the baby. It's no good the modern young man marrying if he's going to murder his baby directly afterward, is it?"

"Something in that. There's just one objection to this sterilized nursery business, though, which she doesn't seem to have detected. How am I going to provide these things on an income of five thousand and at the same time live in that luxury which the artist soul demands? Bill, my lad, you'll have to sacrifice yourself for your father's good. When I'm a millionaire we'll see about it. Meanwhile —"

"Meanwhile," said Ruth, "come and be dried before you catch your death of cold." She gathered William Bannister into her lap.

"I pity any germ that tries to play catch-as-catch-can with that infant," remarked Kirk. "He'd simply flatten it out in a round. Did you ever see such a chest on a kid of that age?"

It was after the installation of Whiskers at the studio that the diminution of Mrs. Porter's visits became really marked. There was something almost approaching a battle over Whiskers, who was an Irish terrier puppy which Hank Jardine had presented to William Bannister as a belated birthday present.

Mrs. Porter utterly excommunicated Whiskers. Nothing, she maintained, was so notoriously supercharged with bacilli as a long-haired dog. If this was true, William Bannister certainly gave them every chance to get to work upon himself. It was his constant pleasure to clutch Whiskers to him in a vice-like clinch, to bury his face in his shaggy back, and generally to court destruction. Yet the more he clutched, the healthier did he appear to grow, and Mrs. Porter's demand for the dog's banishment was overruled.

Mrs. Porter retired in dudgeon. She liked to rule, and at No. 90 she felt that she had become merely among those present. She was in the position of a mother country whose colony has revolted. For years she had been accustomed to look on Ruth as a disciple, a weaker spirit whom she could mould to her will, and now Ruth was refusing to be moulded.

So Mrs. Porter's visits ceased. Ruth still saw her at the apartment when she cared to go there, but she kept away from the studio. She considered that in the matter of William Bannister her claim had been jumped, that she had been deposed; and she withdrew.

"I shall bear up," said Kirk, when this fact was brought home to him. "I mistrust your Aunt Lora as I should mistrust some great natural force which may become active at any moment and give you yours. An earthquake, for instance. I have no quarrel with your Aunt Lora in her quiescent state, but I fear the developments of that giant mind. We are better off without her."

"All the same," said Ruth loyally, "she's rather a dear. And we ought to remember that, if it hadn't been for her, you and I would never have met."

"I do remember it. And I'm grateful. But I can't help feeling that a woman capable of taking other people's lives and juggling with them as if they were india-rubber balls as she did with ours, is likely at any moment to break out in a new place. My gratitude to her is the sort of gratitude you would feel toward a cyclone if you were walking home late for dinner and it caught you up and deposited you on your doorstep. Your Aunt Lora is a human cyclone. No, on the whole, she's more like an earthquake. She has a habit of splitting up and altering the face of the world whenever she feels like it, and I'm too well satisfied with my world at present to relish the idea of having it changed."

Little by little the garrison of the studio had been whittled down. Except for Steve, the community had no regular members outside the family itself. Hank was generally out of town. Bailey paid one more visit, then seemed to consider that he could now absent himself altogether. And the members of Kirk's bachelor circle stayed away to a man.

Their isolation was rendered more complete by the fact that Ruth, when she had ornamented New York society, had made few real friends. Most of the girls she had known bored her. They were gushing creatures with a passion for sharing and imparting secrets, and Ruth's cool reserve had alienated her from them.

When she married she dropped out. The romance of her wedding gave people something to talk about for a few days, and then she was forgotten.

And so it came about that she had her desire and was able practically to monopolize Kirk. He and she and William Bannister lived in a kind of hermit's cell for three and enjoyed this highly unnatural state of things enormously. Life had never seemed so full either to Kirk or herself. There was always something to do, something to think about, something to look forward to, if it was only a visit to a theatre or the inspection of William Bannister's bath.

CHAPTER 11
STUNG TO ACTION

It was in the third year of the White Hope's life that the placid evenness of Kirk's existence began to be troubled. The orderly procession of the days was broken by happenings of unusual importance, one at least of them extraordinarily unpleasant. This was the failure of a certain stock in which nearly half of Kirk's patrimony was invested, that capital which had always seemed to him as solid a part of life as the asphalt on which he walked, as unchangeable a part of nature as the air he breathed. He had always had it, and he could hardly bring himself to realize that he was not always to have it.

It gave him an extraordinary feeling of panic and discomfort when at length he faced the fact squarely that his private means, on the possession of which he had based the whole lazy scheme of his life, were as much at the mercy of fate as the stake which a gambler flings on the green cloth. He did not know enough of business to understand the complicated processes by which a stock hitherto supposed to be as impregnable as municipal bonds had been hammered into a ragged remnant in the course of a single day; but the result of them was unpleasantly clear and easily grasped.

His income was cut in half, and instead of being a comfortably off young man, idly watching the pageant of life from a seat in the grand stand, he must now plunge into the crowd and endeavour to earn a living as others did.

For his losses did not begin and end with the ruin of this particular stock. At intervals during the past two years he had been nibbling at his capital, and now, forced to examine his affairs frankly and minutely, he was astonished at the inroads he had made upon it.

There had been the upkeep of the summer shack he had bought in Connecticut. There had been expenses in connection with William Bannister. There had been little treats for Ruth. There had been cigars and clothes and dinners and taxi-cabs and all the other trifles which cost nothing but mount up and make a man wander beyond the bounds of his legitimate income.

It was borne in upon Kirk, as he reflected upon these things, that the only evidence he had shown of the possession of the artistic temperament had been the joyous carelessness of his extravagance. In that only had he been the artist. It shocked him to think how little honest work he had done during the past two years. He had lived in a golden haze into which work had not entered.

He was to be shocked still more very soon.

Stung to action by his thoughts, he embarked upon a sweeping attack on the stronghold of those who exchange cash for artists' dreams. He ransacked the studio and set out on his mission in a cab bulging with large, small, and medium-sized canvases. Like a wave receding from a breakwater he returned late in the day, a branded failure.

The dealers had eyed his canvases, large, small, and medium-sized, and, in direct contravention of their professed object in life, had refused to deal. Only one of them, a man with grimy hands but a moderately golden heart, after passing a sepia thumb over some of the more ambitious works, had offered him fifteen dollars for a little sketch which he had made in an energetic moment of William Bannister crawling on the floor. This, the dealer asserted, was the sort of "darned mushy stuff" the public fell for, and he held it to be worth the fifteen, but not a cent more. Kirk, humble by now, accepted three battered-looking bills and departed.

He had a long talk with Ruth that night, and rose from it in the frame of mind which in some men is induced by prayer. Ruth was quite marvellously sensible and sympathetic.

"I wanted you," she said in answer to his self-reproaches, "and here we are, together. It's simply nonsense to talk about ruining my life and dragging me down. What *does* it matter about this money? We have got plenty left."

"We've got about as much left as you used to spend on hats in the old days."

"Well, we can easily make it do. I've thought for some time that we were growing too extravagant. And talking of hats, I had no right to have that last one you bought me. It was wickedly expensive. We can economize there, at any rate. We can get along splendidly on what you have now. Besides, directly you settle down and start to paint, we shall be quite rich again."

Kirk laughed grimly.

"I wish you were a dealer," he said. "Fifteen dollars is what I have managed to extract from them so far. One of the Great Unwashed on Sixth Avenue gave me that for that sketch I did of Bill on the floor."

"Which took you about three minutes to do," Ruth pointed out triumphantly. "You see! You're bound to make a fortune if you stick to it."

Kirk put his arm round her and gave her a silent hug of gratitude. He had dreaded this talk, and lo! it was putting new life into him.

They sat for a few moments in silence.

"I don't deserve it," said Kirk at last. "Instead of comforting me like this, and making me think I'm rather a fine sort of a fellow, you ought to be lashing me with scorpions. I don't suppose any man has ever made such a criminal idiot of himself in this city before."

"You couldn't tell that this stock was going to fail."

"No; but I could have done some work these last three years and made it not matter whether it failed or not. You can't comfort me out of that knowledge. I knew all along that I was being a waster and a loafer, but I was so happy that I didn't mind. I was so interested in seeing what you and the kid would do next that I didn't seem to have time to work. And the result is that I've gone right back.

"There was a time when I really could paint a bit. Not much, it's true, but enough to get along with. Well, I'm going to start it again in earnest now, and if I don't make good, well, there's always Hank's offer."

Ruth turned a little pale. They had discussed Hank's offer before, but then life had been bright and cloudless and Hank's offer a thing to smile at. Now it had assumed an uncomfortably practical aspect.

"You will make good," said Ruth.

"I'll do my best," said Kirk. But even as he spoke his mind was pondering on the proposition which Hank had made.

Hank, always flitting from New York into the unknown and back again, had called at the studio one evening, after a long absence, looking sick and tired. He was one of those lean, wiry men whom it is unusual to see in this condition, and Kirk was sympathetic and inquisitive.

Hank needed no pressing. He was full of his story.

"I've been in Colombia," he said. "I got back on a fruit-steamer this morning. Do you know anything of Colombia?"

Kirk reflected.

"Only that there's generally a revolution there," he said.

"There wasn't anything of that kind this trip, except in my interior." Hank pulled thoughtfully at his pipe. The odour of his remarkable brand of tobacco filled the studio. "I've had a Hades of a time," he said simply.

Kirk looked at him curiously. Hank was in a singularly chastened mood to-night.

"What took you there?"

"Gold."

"Gold? Mining?"

Hank nodded.

"I didn't know there were gold-mines in that part of the world," said Kirk.

"There are. The gold that filled the holds of Spanish galleons in the sixteenth century came from Colombia. The place is simply stiff with old Spanish relics."

"But surely the mines must have been worked out ages ago."

"Only on the surface."

Kirk laughed.

"How do you mean, only on the surface? Explain. I don't know a thing about gold, except that getting it out of picture-dealers is like getting blood out of a turnip."

"It's simple enough. The earth hoards its gold in two ways. There's auriferous rock and auriferous dirt. If the stuff is in the rock, you crush it. If it's in the dirt, you wash it."

"It sounds simple."

"It is. The difficult part is finding it."

"And you have done that?"

"I have. Or I'm practically certain I have. At any rate, I know that I have discovered the ditches made by the Spaniards three hundred years ago. If there was gold there in those days there is apt to be gold there now. Only it isn't on the surface any longer. They cleaned up as far as the surface is concerned, so I have to sink shafts and dig tunnels."

"I see. It isn't so simple as it used to be."

"It is, practically, if you have any knowledge of mining."

"Well, what's your trouble?" asked Kirk. "Why did you come back? Why aren't you out there grabbing it with both hands and getting yourself into shape to be a walking gold-mine to your friends? I don't like to see this idle spirit in you, Hank."

Hank smoked long and thoughtfully.

"Kirk," he said suddenly.

"Well?"

Hank shook his head.

"No, it's no good."

"What is no good? What do you mean?"

"I came back," said Hank, suddenly lucid, "with a wild notion of getting you to come in with me on this thing."

"What! Go to Colombia with you?"

Hank nodded.

"But, of course, it's not possible. It's no job for a married man."

"Why not? If this gold of yours is just lying about in heaps it seems to me that a married man is exactly the man who ought to be around grabbing it. Or do you believe that old yarn about two being able to live as cheaply as one? Take it from me, it's not so. If there is gold waiting to be gathered up in handfuls, me for it. When do we start? Can I bring Ruth and the kid?"

"I wish we could start. If I could have had you with me these last few months I'd never have quit. But I guess it's out of the question.

You've no idea what sort of an inferno it is, and I won't let you come into it with your eyes shut. But if ever you are in a real tight corner let me know. It might be worth your while then to take a few risks."

"Oh! there are risks?"

"Risks! My claims are located along the Atrato River in the Choco district. Does that convey anything to you?"

"Not a thing."

"The workings are three hundred miles inland. Just three hundred miles of pure Hades. You can get all the fevers you ever heard of, and a few more, I got most of them last trip."

"I thought you were looking pretty bad."

"I ought to be. I've swallowed so much quinine since I saw you last that my ears are buzzing still. And then there are the insects. They all bite. Some bite worse than others, but not much. Darn it! even the butterflies bite out there. Every animal in the country has some other animal constantly chasing it until a white man comes along, when they call a truce and both chase him. And the vegetation is so thick and grows so quickly that you have to cut down the jungle about the workings every few days or so to avoid being swamped by it. Otherwise," finished Hank, refilling his pipe and lighting it, "the place is a pretty good kind of summer resort."

"And you're going back to it? Back to the quinine and the beasts and the butterflies?"

"Sure. The gold runs up to twenty dollars the cubic yard and is worth eighteen dollars an ounce."

"When are you going?"

"I'm in no hurry. This year, next year, some time, never. No, not never. Call it some time."

"And you want me to come, too?"

"I would give half of whatever there is in the mine to have you come. But things being as they are, well, I guess we can call it off. Is there any chance in the world, Kirk, of your ever ceasing to be a bloated capitalist? Could any of your stocks go back on you?"

"I doubt it. They're pretty gilt-edged, I fancy, though I've never studied the question of stocks. My little gold-mine isn't in the same class with yours, but it's as solid as a rock, and no fevers and insects attached to it, either."

And now the gold-mine had proved of less than rock-like solidity. The most gilt-edged of all the stocks had failed. The capitalist had become in one brief day the struggling artist.

Hank's proposal seemed a good deal less fantastic now to Kirk as he prepared for his second onslaught, the grand attack, on the stronghold of those who bought art with gold.

CHAPTER 12
A CLIMAX

ONE afternoon, about two weeks later, Kirk, returning to the studio from an unprofitable raid into the region of the dealers, found on the table a card bearing the name of Mrs. Robert Wilbur. This had been crossed out, and beneath it, in a straggly hand, the name Miss Wilbur had been written.

The phenomenon of a caller at the cell of the two hermits was so strange that he awaited Ruth's arrival with more than his customary impatience. She would be able to identify the visitor. George Pennicut, questioned on the point, had no information of any value to impart. A very pretty young lady she was, said George, with what you might call a lively manner. She had seemed disappointed at finding nobody at home. No, she had left no message.

Ruth, arriving a few moments later, was met by Kirk with the card in his hand.

"Can you throw any light on this?" he said. "Who is Miss Wilbur, who has what you might call a lively manner and appears disappointed when she does not find us at home?"

Ruth looked at the card.

"Sybil Wilbur? I wonder what she wants."

"Who is she? Let's get that settled first."

"Oh, she's a girl I used to know. I haven't seen her for two years. I thought she had forgotten my existence."

"Call her up on the phone. If we don't solve this mystery we shan't sleep to-night. It's like *Robinson Crusoe* and the footprint."

Ruth went to the telephone. After a short conversation she turned to Kirk with sparkling eyes and the air of one with news to impart.

"Kirk! She wants you to paint her portrait!"

"What!"

"She's engaged to Bailey! Just got engaged! And the first thing she does is to insist on his letting her come to you for her portrait," Ruth bubbled with laughter. "It's to be a birthday present for Bailey, and Bailey has got to pay for it. That's so exactly like Sybil."

"I hope the portrait will be. She's taking chances."

"I think it's simply sweet of her. She's a real friend."

"At fairly long intervals, apparently. Did you say you had not seen her for two years?"

"She is an erratic little thing with an awfully good heart. I feel touched at her remembering us. Oh, Kirk, you must do a simply wonderful portrait, something that everybody will talk about, and then our fortune will be made! You will become the only painter that people will go to for their portraits."

Kirk did not answer. His experiences of late had developed in him an unwonted mistrust of his powers. To this was added the knowledge that, except for an impressionist study of Ruth for private exhibition only, he had never attempted a portrait. To be called upon suddenly like this to show his powers gave him much the same feeling which he had experienced when called upon as a child to recite poetry before an audience. It was a species of stage fright.

But it was certainly a chance. Portrait-painting was an uncommonly lucrative line of business. His imagination, stirred by Ruth's, saw visions of wealthy applicants turned away from the studio door owing to pressure of work on the part of the famous man for whose services they were bidding vast sums.

"By Jove!" he said thoughtfully.

Another aspect of the matter occurred to him.

"I wonder what Bailey thinks about it!"

"Oh, he's probably so much in love with her that he doesn't mind what she does. Besides, Bailey likes you."

"Does he?"

"Oh, well, if he doesn't, he will. This will bring you together."

"I suppose he knows about it?"

"Oh, yes. Sybil said he did. It's all settled. She will be here tomorrow for the first sitting."

Kirk spoke the fear that was in his mind.

"Ruth, old girl, I'm horribly nervous about this. I am taken with a sort of second sight. I see myself making a ghastly failure of this job and Bailey knocking me down and refusing to come across with the cheque."

"Sybil is bringing the cheque with her to-morrow," said Ruth simply.

"Is she?" said Kirk. "Now I wonder if that makes it worse or better. I'm trying to think!"

Sybil Wilbur fluttered in next day at noon, a tiny, restless creature who darted about the studio like a humming-bird. She effervesced with the joy of life. She uttered little squeaks of delight at everything she saw. She hugged Ruth, beamed at Kirk, went wild over William Bannister, thought the studio too cute for words, insisted on being shown all over it, and talked incessantly.

It was about two o'clock before she actually began to sit, and even then she was no statue. A thought would come into her small head and she would whirl round to impart it to Ruth, destroying in a second the pose which it had taken Kirk ten painful minutes to fix.

Kirk was too amused to be irritated. She was such a friendly little soul and so obviously devoted to Ruth that he felt she was entitled to be a nuisance as a sitter. He wondered more and more what weird principle of selection had been at work to bring Bailey and this butterfly together. He had never given any deep thought to the study of his brother-in-law's character; but, from his small knowledge of him, he would have imagined some one a trifle more substantial and serious as the ideal wife for him. Life, he conceived, was to Bailey a stately march. Sybil Wilbur evidently looked on it as a mad gallop.

Ruth felt the same. She was fond of Sybil, but she could not see her as the fore-ordained Mrs. Bailey.

"I suppose she swept him off his feet," she said. "It just shows that you never really get to know a person even if you're their sister. Bailey must have all sorts of hidden sides to his character which I never noticed – unless *she* has. But I don't think there is much of that about Sybil. She's just a child. But she's very amusing, isn't she? She enjoys life so furiously."

"I think Bailey will find her rather a handful. Does she ever sit still, by the way? If she is going to act right along as she did to-day this portrait will look like that cubist picture of the 'Dance at the Spring'."

As the sittings went on Miss Wilbur consented gradually to simmer down and the portrait progressed with a fair amount of speed. But Kirk was conscious every day of a growing sensation of panic. He was trying his very hardest, but it was bad work, and he knew it.

His hand had never had very much cunning, but what it had had it had lost in the years of his idleness. Every day showed him more clearly that the portrait of Miss Wilbur, on which so much depended, was an amateurish daub. He worked doggedly on, but his heart was cold with that chill that grips the artist when he looks on his work and sees it to be bad.

At last it was finished. Ruth thought it splendid. Sybil Wilbur pronounced it cute, as she did most things. Kirk could hardly bear to look at it. In its finished state it was worse than he could have believed possible.

In the old days he had been a fair painter with one or two bad faults. Now the faults seemed to have grown like weeds, choking whatever of merit he might once have possessed. This was a horrible production, and he was profoundly thankful when it was packed up and removed from the studio. But behind his thankfulness lurked the feeling that all was not yet over, that there was worse to come.

It came.

It was heralded by a tearful telephone call from Miss Wilbur, who rang up Ruth with the agitated information that "Bailey didn't seem to like it." And on the heels of the message came Bailey in person, pink from forehead to collar, and almost as wrathful as he had been on the great occasion of his first visit to the studio. His annoyance robbed his speech of its normal stateliness. He struck a colloquial note unusual with him.

"I guess you know what I've come about," he said.

He had found Kirk alone in the studio, as ill luck would have it. In the absence of Ruth he ventured to speak more freely than he would have done in her presence.

"It's an infernal outrage," he went on. "I've been stung, and you know it."

Kirk said nothing. His silence infuriated Bailey.

"It's the portrait I'm speaking about – the portrait, if you have the nerve to call it that, of Miss Wilbur. I was against her sitting to you from the first, but she insisted. Now she's sorry."

"It's as bad as all that, is it?" said Kirk dully. He felt curiously indisposed to fight. A listlessness had gripped him. He was even a little sorry for Bailey. He saw his point of view and sympathized with it.

"Yes," said Bailey fiercely. "It is, and you know it."

Kirk nodded. Bailey was quite right. He did know it.

"It's a joke," went on Bailey shrilly. "I can't hang it up. People would laugh at it. And to think that I paid you all that money for it. I could have got a real artist for half the price."

"That is easily remedied," said Kirk. "I will send you a cheque to-morrow."

Bailey was not to be appeased. The venom of more than three years cried out for utterance. He had always held definite views upon Kirk, and Heaven had sent him the opportunity of expressing them.

"Yes, I dare say," he said contemptuously. "That would settle the whole thing, wouldn't it? What do you think you are – a millionaire? Talking as if that amount of money made no difference to you? Where does my sister come in? How about Ruth? You sneak her away from her home and then—"

Kirk's lethargy left him. He flushed.

"I think that will be about all, Bannister?" he said. He spoke quietly, but his voice trembled.

But Bailey's long-dammed hatred, having at last found an outlet, was not to be checked in a moment.

"Will it? Will it? The hell it will. Let me tell you that I came here to talk straight to you, and I'm going to do it. It's about time you had your darned dime-novel romance shown up to you the way it strikes somebody else. You think you're a tremendous dashing twentieth-century *Young Lochinvar*, don't you? You thought you had done a pretty smooth bit of work when you sneaked Ruth away! You! You haven't enough backbone in you even to make a bluff at working to support her. You're just what my father said you were – a loafer who pretends to be an artist. You've got away with it up to now, but you've shown yourself up at last. You damned waster!"

Kirk walked to the door and flung it open.

"You're perfectly right, Bannister," he said quietly. "Everything you have said is quite true. And now would you mind going?"

"I've not finished yet."

"Yes, you have."

Bailey hesitated. The first time frenzy had left him, and he was beginning to be a little ashamed of himself for having expressed his views in a manner which, though satisfying, was, he felt, less dignified than he could have wished.

He looked at Kirk, who was standing stiffly by the door. Something in his attitude decided Bailey to leave well alone. Such had been his indignation that it was only now that for the first time it struck him that his statement of opinion had not been made without considerable bodily danger to himself. Jarred nerves had stood him in the stead of courage; but now his nerves were soothed and he saw things clearly.

He choked down what he had intended to say and walked out. Kirk closed the door softly behind him and began to pace the studio floor as he had done on that night when Ruth had fought for her life in the room upstairs.

His mind worked slowly at first. Then, as it cleared, he began to think more and more rapidly, till the thoughts leaped and ran like tongues of fire scorching him.

It was all true. That was what hurt. Every word that Bailey had flung at him had been strictly just.

He had thought himself a fine, romantic fellow. He was a waster and a loafer who pretended to be an artist. He had thrown away the little talent he had once possessed. He had behaved shamefully to Ruth, shirking his responsibilities and idling through life. He realized it now, when it was too late.

Suddenly through the chaos of his reflections there shone out clearly one coherent thought, the recollection of what Hank Jardine had offered to him. "If ever you are in a real tight corner—"

꙳

His brain cleared. He sat down calmly to wait for Ruth. His mind was made up. Hank's offer was the way out, the only way out, and he must take it.

BOOK TWO

Chapter 1
Empty-handed

THE steamship *Santa Barbara*, of the United Fruit Line, moved slowly through the glittering water of the bay on her way to dock. Out at quarantine earlier in the morning there had been a mist, through which passing ships loomed up vague and shapeless; but now the sun had dispersed it and a perfect May morning welcomed the *Santa Barbara* home.

Kirk leaned on the rail, looking with dull eyes on the city he had left a year before. Only a year! It seemed ten. As he stood there he felt an old man.

A drummer, a cheery soul who had come aboard at Porto Rico, sauntered up, beaming with well-being and good-fellowship.

"Looks pretty good, sir," said he.

Kirk did not answer. He had not heard.

"Some burg," ventured the drummer.

Again encountering silence, he turned away, hurt. This churlish attitude on the part of one returning to God's country on one of God's own mornings surprised and wounded him.

To him all was right with the world. He had breakfasted well; he was smoking a good cigar; and he was strong in the knowledge that he had done well by the firm this trip and that bouquets were due to be handed to him in the office on lower Broadway. He was annoyed with Kirk for having cast even a tiny cloud upon his contentment.

He communicated his feelings to the third officer, who happened to come on deck at that moment.

"Say, who *is* that guy?" he asked complainingly. "The big son of a gun leaning on the rail. Seems like he'd got a hangover this morning. Is he deaf and dumb or just plain grouchy?"

The third officer eyed Kirk's back with sympathy.

"I shouldn't worry him, Freddie," he said. "I guess if you had been up against it like him you'd be shy on the small talk. That's a fellow called Winfield. They carried him on board at Colon. He was about all in. Got fever in Colombia, inland at the mines, and nearly died. His pal did die. Ever met Hank Jardine?"

"Long, thin man?"

The other nodded.

"One of the best. He made two trips with us."

"And he's dead?"

"Died of fever away back in the interior, where there's nothing much else except mosquitoes. He and Winfield went in there after gold."

"Did they get any?" asked the drummer, interested.

The third officer spat disgustedly over the rail.

"You ask Winfield. Or, rather, don't, because I guess it's not his pet subject. He told me all about it when he was getting better. There was gold there, all right, in chunks. It only needed to be dug for. And somebody else did the digging. Of all the skin games! It made me pretty hot under the collar, and it wasn't *me* that was stung.

"Out there you can't buy land if you're a foreigner; you have to lease it from the natives. Poor old Hank leased his bit, all right, and when he'd got to his claim he found somebody else working on it. It seemed there had been a flaw in his agreement and the owners had let it over his head to these other guys, who had slipped them more than what Hank had done."

"What did he do?"

"He couldn't do anything. They were the right side of the law, or what they call law out there. There was nothing to do except beat it back again three hundred miles to the coast. That's where they got the fever which finished Hank. So you can understand," concluded the third officer, "that Mr. Winfield isn't in what you can call a sunny mood. If I were you, I'd go and talk to someone else, if conversation's what you need."

Kirk stood motionless at the rail, thinking. It was not what was past that occupied his thoughts, as the third officer had supposed; it was the future.

The forlorn hope had failed; he was limping back to Ruth wounded and broken. He had sent her a wireless message. She would be at the dock to meet him. How could he face her? Fate had been against him, it was true, but he was in no mood to make excuses for himself. He had failed. That was the beginning and the end of it. He had set out to bring back wealth and comfort to her, and he was returning empty-handed.

That was what the immediate future held, the meeting with Ruth. And after? His imagination was not equal to the task of considering that. He had failed as an artist. There was no future for him there. He must find some other work. But he was fit for no other work. He had no training. What could he do in a city where keenness of competition is a tradition? It would be as if an unarmed man should attack a fortress.

The thought of the years he had wasted was very bitter. Looking back, he could see how fate had tricked him into throwing away his one talent. He had had promise. With hard work he could have become an artist, a professional – a man whose work was worth money in the open market. He had never had it in him to be a great artist, but he had had the facility which goes to make a good worker of the second class. He had it still. Given the time for hard study, it was still in him to take his proper place among painters.

But time for study was out of his reach now. He must set to work at once, without a day's delay, on something which would bring him immediate money. The reflection brought his mind back abruptly to the practical consideration of the future.

Before him, as he stood there, the ragged battlements of New York seemed to frown down on him with a cold cruelty that paralysed his mind. He had seen them a hundred times before. They should have been familiar and friendly. But this morning they were strange and sinister. The skyline which daunts the emigrant as he comes up the bay to his new home struck fear into Kirk's heart.

He turned away and began to walk up and down the deck.

He felt tired and lonely. For the first time he realized just what it meant to him that he should never see Hank again. It had been hard, almost impossible, till now to force his mind to face that fact. He had winced away from it. But now it would not be avoided. It fell upon him like a shadow.

Hank had filled a place of his own in Kirk's life. Theirs had been one of those smooth friendships which absence cannot harm. Often they had not seen each other for months at a time. Indeed, now that he thought of it, Hank was generally away; and he could not remember that they had ever exchanged letters. Yet even so there had been a bond between them which had never broken. And now Hank had dropped out.

Kirk began to think about death. As with most men of his temperament, it was a subject on which his mind had seldom dwelt, never for any length of time. His parents had died when he was too young to understand; and circumstances had shielded him from the shadow of the great mystery. Birth he understood; it had forced itself into the scheme of his life; but death till now had been a stranger to him.

The realization of it affected him oddly. In a sense, he found it stimulating; not stimulating as birth had been, but more subtly. He could recall vividly the thrill that had come to him with the birth of his son. For days he had walked as one in a trance. The world had seemed unreal, like an opium-smoker's dream. There had been magic everywhere.

But death had exactly the opposite effect. It made everything curiously real – himself most of all. He had the sensation, as he thought of Hank, of knowing himself for the first time. Somehow he felt strengthened, braced for the fight, as a soldier might who sees his comrade fall at his side.

There was something almost vindictive in the feeling that came to him. It was too vague to be analysed, but it filled him with a desire to fight, gave him a sense of determination of which he had never before been conscious. It toughened him, and made the old, easy-going Kirk Winfield seem a stranger at whom he could look with detachment and a certain contempt.

As he walked back along the deck the battlements of the city met his gaze once more. But now they seemed less formidable.

In the leisurely fashion of the home-coming ship the *Santa Barbara* slid into her dock. The gangplank was thrust out. Kirk walked ashore.

For a moment he thought that Ruth had not come to meet him. Then his heart leaped madly. He had seen her.

❦

There are worse spots in the world than the sheds of the New York customs, but few more desolate; yet to Kirk just then the shadowy vastness seemed a sunlit garden. A flame of happiness blazed up in his mind, blotting out in an instant the forebodings which had lurked there like evil creatures in a dark vault. The future, with its explanations and plans, could take care of itself. Ruth was a thing of the present.

He put his arms round her and held her. The friendly drummer, who chanced to be near, observed them with interest and a good deal of pleasure. The third officer's story had temporarily destroyed his feeling that all was right with the world, and his sympathetic heart welcomed this evidence that life held compensations even for men who had been swindled out of valuable gold-mines.

"I guess he's not feeling so worse, after all," he mused, and went on his way with an easy mind to be fawned upon by his grateful firm.

Ruth was holding Kirk at arm's length, her eyes full of tears at the sight.

"You poor boy, how thin you are!"

"I had fever. It's an awful place for fever out there."

"Kirk!"

"Oh, I'm all right now. The voyage set me up. They made a great fuss over me on board."

Ruth's hand was clinging to his arm. He squeezed it against his side. It was wonderful to him, this sense of being together again after these centuries of absence. It drove from his mind the thought of all the explanations which sooner or later he had got to make. Whatever might come after, he would keep this moment in his memory golden and untarnished.

"Don't you worry about me," he said. "Now that I've found you again I'm feeling better than I ever did in my life. You wait till you see me sparring with Steve to-morrow. By the way, how is Steve?"

"Splendid."

"And Bill?"

Ruth drew herself up haughtily.

"You dare to ask about your son after Steve? How clumsy that sounds! I mean you dare to put Steve before your son. I believe you've only just realized that you have a son."

"I've only just realized there's anybody or anything in the world except my wife."

"Well, after that I suppose I've got to forgive you. Since you have asked after Bill at last, I may tell you that he's very well indeed."

Kirk's eyes glowed.

"He ought to be a great kid by now."

"He is."

"And Mamie? Have you still got her?"

"I wouldn't lose her for a million."

"And Whiskers?"

"I'm afraid Whiskers is gone."

"Not dead?"

"No. I gave him away."

"For Heaven's sake! Why?"

"Well, dear, the fact is, I've come around to Aunt Lora's way of thinking."

"Eh?"

"About germs."

Kirk laughed, the first real laugh he had had for a year.

"That insane fad of hers!"

Ruth was serious.

"I have," she said. "We're taking a great deal more care of Bill than in the old days. I hate to think of the way I used to let him run around wild then. He might have died."

"What nonsense! He was simply bursting with health all the time."

"I had a horrible shock after you left," Ruth went on. "The poor little fellow was awfully ill with some kind of a fever. The doctor almost gave him up."

"Good heavens!"

"Aunt Lora helped me to nurse him, and she made me see how I had been exposing him to all sorts of risks, and – well, now we guard against them."

There was a silence.

"I grew to rely on her a great deal, Kirk, when you were away. You know I always used to before we were married. She's so wonderfully strong. And then when your letters stopped coming—"

"There aren't any postal arrangements out there in the interior. It was the worst part of it – not being able to write to you or hear from you. Heavens, what an exile I've been this last year! Anything may have happened!"

"Perhaps something has," said Ruth mysteriously.

"What do you mean?"

"Wait and see. Oh, I know one thing that has happened. I've been looking at you all this while trying to think what it was. You've grown a beard, and it looks perfectly horrid."

"Sheer laziness. It shall come off this very day. I knew you would hate it."

"I certainly do. It makes you look so old."

Kirk's face clouded.

"I feel old."

For the first time since he had left the ship the memory of Hank had come back to him. The sight of Ruth had driven it away, but now it swept back on him. The golden moment was over. Life with all its troubles and its explanations and its burdening sense of failure must be faced.

"What's the matter?" asked Ruth, startled by the sudden change.

"I was thinking of poor old Hank."

"Where is Mr. Jardine? Didn't he come back with you?"

"He's dead, dear," said Kirk gently. "He died of fever while we were working our way back to the coast."

"Oh!"

It was the idea of death that shocked Ruth, not the particular manifestation of it. Hank had not touched her life. She had begun by disliking him and ended by feeling for him the tolerant sort of affection which she might have bestowed upon a dog or a cat. Hank as a man was nothing to her, and she could not quite keep her indifference out of her voice.

It was only later, when he looked back on this conversation, that Kirk realized this. At the moment he was unconscious of it, significant as it was of the fact that there were points at which his mind and Ruth's did not touch.

When Ruth spoke again it was to change the subject.

"Well, Kirk," she said, "have you come back with your trunk crammed with nuggets? You haven't said a word about the mine yet, and I'm dying to know."

He groaned inwardly. The moment he had been dreading had arrived more swiftly than he had expected. It was time for him to face facts.

"No," he said shortly.

Ruth looked at him curiously. She met his eyes and saw the pain in them, and intuition told her in an instant what Kirk, stumbling through his story, could not have told her in an hour. She squeezed his arm affectionately.

"Don't tell me," she said. "I understand. And it doesn't matter. It doesn't matter a bit."

"Doesn't matter? But—"

Ruth's eyes were dancing.

"Kirk, dear, I've something to tell you. Wait till we get outside."

"What do you mean?"

"You'll soon see?"

They went out into the street. Against the kerb a large red automobile was standing. The chauffeur touched his cap as he saw them. Kirk stared at him dumbly.

"In you get, dear," said Ruth.

She met his astonished gaze with a smile of triumph. This was her moment, the moment for which she had been waiting. The chauffeur started the machine.

"I don't understand. Whose car is this?"

"Mine. Yours. Ours. Oh, Kirk, darling, I was so afraid that you would come back bulging with a fortune that would make my little one look like nothing. But you haven't, you haven't, and it's just splendid." She caught his hand and pressed it. "It's simply sweet of you to look so astonished. I was hoping you would. This car belongs to us, and there's another just as big besides, and a house, and – oh – everything you can think of. Kirk, dear, we've nothing to worry us any longer. We're rich!"

Chapter 2
An Unknown Path

Kirk blinked. He closed his eyes and opened them again. The automobile was still there, and he was still in it. Ruth was still gazing at him with the triumphant look in her eyes. The chauffeur, silent emblem of a substantial bank-balance, still sat stiffly at the steering-wheel.

"Rich?" Kirk repeated.

"Rich," Ruth assured him.

"I don't understand."

Ruth's smile faded.

"Poor father—"

"Your father?"

"He died just after you sailed. Just before Bill got ill." She gave a little sigh. "Kirk, how odd life is!"

"But—"

"It was terrible. It was some kind of a stroke. He had been working too hard and taking no exercise. You know when he sent Steve away that time he didn't engage anybody else in his place. He went back to his old way of living, which the doctor had warned him against. He worked and worked, until one day, Bailey says, he fainted at the office. They brought him home, and he just went out like a burned-out candle. I – I went to him, but for a long time he wouldn't see me.

"Oh, Kirk, the hours I spent in the library hoping that he would let me come to him! But he never did till right at the end. Then I went up, and he was dying. He couldn't speak. I don't know now how he felt toward me at the last. I kissed him. He was all shrunk to nothing. I had a horrible feeling that I had never been a real daughter to him. But – but – you know, he made it difficult, awfully difficult. And then he died; Bailey was on one side of the bed and I was on the other, and the nurse and the doctor were whispering outside the door. I could hear them through the transom."

She slipped her hand into Kirk's and sat silent while the car slid into the traffic of Fifth Avenue. For the second time the shadow of the Great Mystery had fallen on the brightness of the perfect morning.

The car had stopped at Thirty-Fourth Street to allow the hurrying crowds to cross the avenue. Kirk looked at them with a feeling of sadness. It was not caused by John Bannister's death. He was too honest to be able to plunge himself into false emotion at will. His feeling was more a vague uneasiness, almost a presentiment. Things changed so quickly in this world. Old landmarks shifted as the crowd of strangers was shifting before him now, hurrying into his life and hurrying out of it.

He, too, had changed. Ruth, though he had detected no signs of it, must be different from the Ruth he had left a year ago. The old life was dead. What had the new life in store for him? Wealth for one thing – other standards of living – new experiences.

An odd sensation of regret that this stream of gold had descended upon him deepened his momentary depression. They had been so happy, he and Ruth and the kid, in the old days of the hermit's cell. Something that was almost a superstitious fear of this unexpected legacy came upon him.

It was unlucky money, grudgingly given at the eleventh hour. He seemed to feel John Bannister watching him with a sneer, and he was afraid of him. His nerves were still a little unstrung from the horror of his wanderings, and the fever had left him weak. It seemed to him that there was a curse on the old man's wealth, that somehow it was destined to bring him unhappiness.

The policeman waved his hand. The car jerked forward. The sudden movement brought him to himself. He smiled, a little ashamed of having been so fanciful; the sky was blue; the sun shone; a cool breeze put the joy of life into him; and at his side Ruth sat, smiling now. From her, too, the cloud had been lifted.

"It seems like a fairy-story," said Kirk, breaking the silence that had fallen between them.

"I think it must have been the thought of Bill that made him do it," said Ruth. "He left half his money to Bailey and half to me during my lifetime. Bailey's married now, by the way." She paused. "I'm afraid father never forgave you, dear," she added. "He made Bailey the trustee for the money, and it goes to Bill in trust after my death."

She looked at him rather nervously it seemed to Kirk. The terms of the will had been the cause of some trouble to her. Especially had she speculated on his reception of the news that Bailey was to play so important a part in the administration of the money. Kirk had never told her what had passed between him and Bailey that afternoon in the studio, but her quick intelligence had enabled her to guess at the truth; and she was aware that the minds of the two men, their temperaments, were naturally antagonistic.

Kirk's reception of the news relieved her.

"Of course," he said. "He couldn't do anything else. He knew nothing of me except that I was a kind of man with whom he was quite out of sympathy. He mistrusted all artists, I expect, in a bunch. And, anyway, an artist is pretty sure to be a bad man of business. He would know that. And – and, well, what I mean is, it strikes me as a very sensible arrangement. Why are we stopping here?"

The car had drawn up before a large house on the upper avenue, one of those houses which advertise affluence with as little reticence as a fat diamond solitaire.

"We live here," said Ruth, laughing.

Kirk drew a long breath.

"Do we? By George!" he exclaimed. "I see it's going to take me quite a while to get used to this state of things."

A thought struck him.

"How about the studio? Have you got rid of it?"

"Of course not. The idea! After the perfect times we had there! We're going to keep it on as an annex. Every now and then, when we are tired of being rich, we'll creep off there and boil eggs over the gas-stove and pretend we are just ordinary persons again."

"And oftener than every now and then this particular plutocrat is going to creep off there and try to teach himself to paint pictures."

Ruth nodded.

"Yes, I think you ought to have a hobby. It's good for you."

Kirk said nothing. But it was not as a hobby that he was regarding his painting. He had come to a knowledge of realities in the wilderness and to an appreciation of the fact that he had a soul which could not be kept alive except by honest work.

He had the decent man's distaste for living on his wife's money. He supposed it was inevitable that a certain portion of it must go to his support, but he was resolved that there should be in the sight of the gods who look down on human affairs at least a reasonable excuse for his existence. If work could make him anything approaching a real artist, he would become one.

Meanwhile he was quite willing that Ruth should look upon his life-work as a pleasant pastime to save him from ennui. Even to his wife a man is not always eager to exhibit his soul in its nakedness.

"By the way," said Ruth, "you won't find George Pennicut at the studio. He has gone back to England."

"I'm sorry. I liked George."

"He liked you. He left all sorts of messages. He nearly wept when he said good-bye. But he wouldn't stop. In a burst of confidence he told me what the trouble was. Our blue sky had got on his nerves.

He wanted a London drizzle again. He said the thought of it made him homesick."

Kirk entered the house thoughtfully. Somehow this last piece of news had put the coping-stone on the edifice of his – his what? Depression? It was hardly that. No, it was rather a kind of vague regret for the life which had so definitely ended, the feeling which the Romans called *desiderium* and the Greeks *pathos*. The defection of George Pennicut was a small thing in itself, but it meant the removal of another landmark.

"We had some bully good times in that studio," he said.

The words were a requiem.

The first person whom he met in this great house, in the kingdom of which he was to be king-consort, was a butler of incredible stateliness. This was none other than Steve's friend Keggs. But round the outlying portions of this official he had perceived, as the door opened, a section of a woman in a brown dress.

The butler moving to one side, he found himself confronting Mrs. Lora Delane Porter.

If other things in Kirk's world had changed, time had wrought in vain upon the great authoress. She looked as masterful, as unyielding, and as efficient as she had looked at the time of his departure. She took his hand without emotion and inspected him keenly.

"You are thinner," she remarked.

"I said that, Aunt Lora," said Ruth. "Poor boy, he's a skeleton."

"You are not so robust."

"I have been ill."

Ruth interposed.

"He's had fever, Aunt Lora, and you are not to tease him."

"I should be the last person to tease any man. What sort of fever?"

"I think it was a blend of all sorts," replied Kirk. "A kind of Irish stew of a fever."

"You are not infectious?"

"Certainly not."

Mrs. Porter checked Ruth as she was about to speak.

"We owe it to William to be careful," she explained. "After all the trouble we have taken to exclude him from germs it is only reasonable to make these inquiries."

"Come along, dear," said Ruth, "and I'll show you the house. Don't mind Aunt Lora," she whispered; "she means well, and she really is splendid with Bill."

Kirk followed her. He was feeling chilled again. His old mistrust of Mrs. Porter revived. If their brief interview was to be taken as evidence, she seemed to have regained entirely her old ascendancy over Ruth. He felt vaguely uneasy, as a man might who walks in a powder magazine.

"Aunt Lora lives here now," observed Ruth casually, as they went upstairs.

Kirk started.

"Literally, do you mean? Is this her home?"

Ruth smiled at him over her shoulder.

"She won't interfere with you," she said. "Surely this great house is large enough for the three of us. Besides, she's so devoted to Bill. She looks after him all the time; of course, nowadays I don't get quite so much time to be with him myself. One has an awful lot of calls on one. I feel Bill is so safe with Aunt Lora on the premises."

She stopped at a door on the first floor.

"This is Bill's nursery. He's out just now. Mamie takes him for a drive every morning when it's fine."

Something impelled Kirk to speak.

"Don't you ever take him for walks in the morning now?" he asked. "He used to love it."

"Silly! Of course I do, when I can manage it. For drives, rather. Aunt Lora is rather against his walking much in the city. He might so easily catch something, you know."

She opened the door.

"There!" she said. "What do you think of that for a nursery?"

If Kirk had spoken his mind he would have said that of all the ghastly nurseries the human brain could have conceived this was the ghastliest. It was a large, square room, and to Kirk's startled eyes had much the appearance of an operating theatre at a hospital.

There was no carpet on the tiled floor. The walls, likewise tiled, were so bare that the eye ached contemplating them. In the corner by the window stood the little white cot. Beside it on the wall hung a large thermometer. Various knobs of brass decorated the opposite wall. At the farther end of the room was a bath, complete with shower and all the other apparatus of a modern tub.

It was probably the most horrible room in all New York.

"Well, what do you think of it?" demanded Ruth proudly.

Kirk gazed at her, speechless. This, he said to himself, was Ruth, his wife, who had housed his son in the spare bedroom of the studio and allowed a shaggy Irish terrier to sleep on his bed; who had permitted him to play by the hour in the dust of the studio floor, who had even assisted him to do so by descending into the dust herself in the role of a bear or a snake.

What had happened to this world from which he had been absent but one short year? Was everybody mad, or was he hopelessly behind the times?

"Well?" Ruth reminded him.

Kirk eyed the dreadful room.

"It looks clean," he said at last.

"It is clean," said the voice of Lora Delane Porter proudly behind him. She had followed them up the stairs to do the honours of the nursery, the centre of her world. "It is essentially clean. There is not an object in that room which is not carefully sterilized night and morning with a weak solution of boric acid!"

"Even Mamie?" inquired Kirk.

It had been his intention to be mildly jocular, but Mrs. Porter's reply showed him that in jest he had spoken the truth.

"Certainly. Have you any idea, Kirk, of the number of germs there are on the surface of the human body? It runs into billions. You" – she fixed him with her steely eye – "you are at the present moment one mass of microbes."

"I sneaked through quarantine all right."

"To the adult there is not so much danger in these microbes, provided he or she maintains a reasonable degree of personal cleanliness. That is why adults may be permitted to mix with other adults without preliminary sterilization. But in the case of a growing child it is entirely different. No precaution is excessive. So—"

From below at this point there came the sound of the front-door bell. Ruth went to the landing and looked over the banisters.

"That ought to be Bill and Mamie back from their drive," she said.

The sound of a child's voice came to Kirk as he stood listening; and as he heard it all the old feeling of paternal pride and excitement, which had left him during his wanderings, swept over him like a wave. He reproached himself that, while the memory of Ruth had been with him during every waking moment of the past year, there had been occasions when that of William Bannister had become a little faded.

He ran down the stairs.

"Hello, Mamie!" he said. "How are you? You're looking well."

Mamie greeted him with the shy smile which was wont to cause such havoc in Steve's heart.

"And who's this you've got with you? Mamie, you know you've no business going about with young men like this. Who is he?"

He stood looking at William Bannister, and William Bannister stood looking at him, Kirk smiling, William staring with the intense gravity of childhood and trying to place this bearded stranger among his circle of friends. He seemed to be thinking that the familiarity of the other's manner indicated a certain amount of previous acquaintanceship.

"Watch that busy brain working," said Kirk. "He's trying to place me. It's all right, Bill, old man; it's my fault. I had no right to spring myself on you with eight feet of beard. It isn't giving you a square deal. Never mind, it's coming off in a few minutes, never to return, and then, perhaps, you'll remember that you've a father."

"Fa-a-a-ar!" shrieked William Bannister triumphantly, taking the cue with admirable swiftness.

He leaped at Kirk, and Kirk swung him up in the air. It was quite an effort, for William Bannister had grown astonishingly in the past year.

"Pop," said he firmly, as if resolved to prevent any possibility of mistake. "Daddy," he added, continuing to play upon the theme. He summed up. "You're my pop."

Then, satisfied that this was final and that there could now be no chance for Kirk to back out of the contract, he reached out a hand and gave a tug at the beard which had led to all the confusion.

"What's this?"

"You may well ask," said Kirk. "I got struck that way because I left you and mummy for a whole year. But now I'm back I'm going to be allowed to take it off and give it away. Whom shall I give it to? Steve? Do you think Steve would like it? Yes, you can go on pulling it; it won't break. On the other hand, I should just like to mention that it's hurting something fierce, my son. It's fastened on at the other end, you know."

"Why?"

"Don't ask me. That's the way it's built."

William Bannister obligingly disentangled himself from the beard.

"Where you been?" he inquired.

"Miles and miles away. You know the Battery?"

William Bannister nodded.

"Well, a long way past that. First I took a ship and went ever so many miles. Then I landed and went ever so many more miles, with all sorts of beasts trying to bite pieces out of me."

This interested William Bannister.

"Tigers?" he inquired.

"I didn't actually see any tigers, but I expect they were sneaking round. There were mosquitoes, though. You know what a mosquito is?"

William nodded.

"Bumps," he observed crisply.

"That's right. You see this lump here, just above my mouth? Well, that's not a mosquito-bite; that's my nose; but think of something about that size and you'll have some idea of what a mosquito-bite is like out there. But why am I boring you with my troubles? Tell me all about yourself. You've certainly been growing, whatever else you may have been doing while I've been away; I can hardly lift you. Has Steve taught you to box yet?"

At this moment he was aware that he had become the centre of a small group. Looking round he found himself gazing into a face so stiff with horror and disapproval that he was startled almost into dropping William. What could have happened to induce Mrs. Porter to look like that he could not imagine; but her expression checked his flow of light conversation as if it had been turned off with a switch. He lowered Bill to the ground.

"What on earth's the matter?" he asked. "What has happened?"

Without replying, Mrs. Porter made a gesture in the direction of the nursery, which had the effect of sending Mamie and her charge off again on the journey upstairs which Kirk's advent had interrupted. Bill seemed sorry to go, but he trudged sturdily on without remark. Kirk followed him with his eyes till he disappeared at the bend of the stairway.

"What's the matter?" he repeated.

"Are you mad, Kirk?" demanded Mrs. Porter in a tense voice.

Kirk turned helplessly to Ruth.

"You had better let me explain, Aunt Lora," she said. "Of course Kirk couldn't be expected to know, poor boy. You seem to forget that he has only this minute come into the house."

Aunt Lora was not to be appeased.

"That is absolutely no excuse. He has just left a ship where he cannot have failed to pick up bacilli of every description. He has himself only recently recovered from a probably infectious fever. He is wearing a beard, notoriously the most germ-ridden abomination in existence."

Kirk started. He was not proud of his beard, but he had not regarded it as quite the pestilential thing which it seemed to be in the eyes of Mrs. Porter.

"And he picks up the child!" she went on. "Hugs him! Kisses him! And you say he could not have known better! Surely the most elementary common sense – "

"Aunt Lora!" said Ruth.

She spoke quietly, but there was a note in her voice which acted on Mrs. Porter like magic. Her flow of words ceased abruptly. It was a small incident, but it had the effect of making Kirk, grateful as he was for the interruption, somehow vaguely uneasy for a moment.

It seemed to indicate some subtle change in Ruth's character, some new quality of hardness added to it. The Ruth he had left when he sailed for Colombia would, he felt, have been incapable of quelling her masterful aunt so very decisively and with such an economy of words. It suggested previous warfare, in which the elder women had been subdued to a point where a mere exclamation could pull her up when she forgot herself.

Kirk felt uncomfortable. He did not like these sudden discoveries about Ruth.

"I will explain to Kirk," she said. "You go up and see that everything is right in the nursery."

And – amazing spectacle! – off went Mrs. Porter without another word.

Ruth put her arm in Kirk's and led him off to the smoking-room.

"You may smoke a cigar while I tell you all about Bill," she said.

Kirk lit a cigar, bewildered. It is always unpleasant to be the person to whom things have to be explained.

"Poor old boy," Ruth went on, "you certainly are thin. But about Bill. I am afraid you are going to be a little upset about Bill, Kirk. Aunt Lora has no tact, and she will make a speech on every possible occasion; but she was right just now. It really was rather dangerous, picking Bill up like that and kissing him."

Kirk stared.

"I don't understand. Did you expect me to wave my hand to him? Or would it have been more correct to bow?"

"Don't be so satirical, Kirk; you wither me. No, seriously, you really mustn't kiss Bill. I never do. Nobody does."

"What!"

"I dare say it sounds ridiculous to you, but you were not here when he was so ill and nearly died. You remember what I was telling you at the dock? About giving Whiskers away? Well, this is all part of it. After what happened I feel, like Aunt Lora, that we simply can't take too many precautions. You saw his nursery. Well, it would be simply a waste of money giving him a nursery like that if he was allowed to be exposed to infection when he was out of it."

"And I am supposed to be infectious?"

"Not more than anybody else. There's no need to be hurt about it. It's just as much a sacrifice for me."

"So nobody makes a fuss over Bill now – is that it?"

"Well, no. Not in the way you mean."

"Pretty dreary outlook for the kid, isn't it?"

"It's all for his good."

"What a ghastly expression!"

Ruth left her chair and came and sat on the arm of Kirk's. She ruffled his hair lightly with the tips of her fingers. Kirk, who had been disposed to be militant, softened instantly. The action brought back a flood of memories. It conjured up recollections of peaceful evenings in the old studio, for this had been a favourite habit of Ruth's. It made him feel that he loved her more than he had ever done in his life; and – incidentally – that he was a brute to try and thwart her in anything whatsoever.

"I know it's horrid for you, dear old boy," said Ruth coaxingly; "but do be good and not make a fuss about it. Not kissing Bill doesn't mean that you need be any the less fond of him. I know it will be strange at first – I didn't get used to it for ever so long – but, honestly, it is for his good, however ghastly the expression of the thing may sound."

"It's treating the kid like a wretched invalid," grumbled Kirk.

"You wait till you see him playing, and then you'll know if he's a wretched invalid or not!"

"May I see him playing?"

"Don't be silly. Of course."

"I thought I had better ask. Being the perambulating plague-spot I am, I was not taking any risks."

"How horribly self-centred you are! You will talk as if you were in some special sort of quarantine. I keep on telling you it's the same for all of us."

"I suppose when I'm with him I shall have to be sterilized?"

"I don't think it necessary myself, but Aunt Lora does, so it's always done. It humours her, and it really isn't any trouble. Besides, it may be necessary after all. One never knows, and it's best to be on the safe side."

Kirk laid down his cigar firmly, the cold cigar which stress of emotion had made him forget to keep alight.

"Ruth, old girl," he said earnestly, "this is pure lunacy."

Ruth's fingers wandered idly through his hair. She did not speak for some moments.

"You will be good about it, won't you, Kirk dear?" she said at last.

It is curious what a large part hair and its treatment may play in the undoing of strong men. The case of Samson may be recalled in this connection. Kirk, with Ruth ruffling the wiry growth that hid his scalp, was incapable of serious opposition. He tried to be morose and resolute, but failed miserably.

"Oh, very well," he grunted.

"That's a good boy. And you promise you won't go hugging Bill again?"

"Very well."

"There's an angel for you. Now I'll fix you a cocktail as a reward."

"Well, mind you sterilize it carefully."

Ruth laughed. Having gained her point she could afford to. She made the cocktail and brought it to him.

"And now I'll be off and dress, and then you can take me out to lunch somewhere."

"Aren't you dressed?"

"My goodness, no. Not for going to restaurants. You forget that I'm one of the idle rich now. I spend my whole day putting on different kinds of clothes. I've a position to keep up now, Mr. Winfield."

Kirk lit a fresh cigar and sat thinking. The old feeling of desolation which had attacked him as he came up the bay had returned. He felt like a stranger in a strange world. Life was not the same. Ruth was not the same. Nothing was the same.

The more he contemplated the new regulations affecting Bill the chillier and more unfriendly did they seem to him. He could not bring himself to realize Ruth as one of the great army of cranks preaching and carrying out the gospel of Lora Delane Porter. It seemed so at variance with her character as he had known it. He could not seriously bring himself to believe that she genuinely approved of these absurd restrictions. Yet, apparently she did.

He looked into the future. It had a grey and bleak aspect. He seemed to himself like a man gazing down an unknown path full of unknown perils.

CHAPTER 3
THE MISADVENTURE OF STEVE

KIRK was not the only person whom the sudden change in the financial position of the Winfield family had hit hard. The blighting effects of sudden wealth had touched Steve while Kirk was still in Colombia.

In a sense, it had wrecked Steve's world. Nobody had told him to stop or even diminish the number of his visits, but the fact remained that, by the time Kirk returned to New York, he had practically ceased to go to the house on Fifth Avenue.

For all his roughness, Steve possessed a delicacy which sometimes almost amounted to diffidence; and he did not need to be told that there was a substantial difference, as far as he was concerned, between the new headquarters of the family and the old. At the studio he had been accustomed to walk in when it pleased him, sure of a welcome; but he had an idea that he did not fit as neatly into the atmosphere of Fifth Avenue as he had done into that of Sixty-First Street; and nobody disabused him of it.

It was perhaps the presence of Mrs. Porter that really made the difference. In spite of the compliments she had sometimes paid to his common sense, Mrs. Porter did not put Steve at his ease. He was almost afraid of her. Consequently, when he came to Fifth Avenue, he remained below stairs, talking pugilism with Keggs.

It was from Keggs that he first learned of the changes that had taken place in the surroundings of William Bannister.

"I've 'ad the privilege of serving in some of the best houses in England," said the butler one evening, as they sat smoking in the pantry, "and I've never seen such goings on. I don't hold with the pampering of children."

"What do you mean, pampering?" asked Steve.

"Well, Lord love a duck!" replied the butler, who in his moments of relaxation was addicted to homely expletives of the lower London type. "If you don't call it pampering, what do you call pampering? He ain't allowed to touch nothing that ain't been – it's slipped my memory what they call it, but it's got something to do with microbes. They sprinkle stuff on his toys and on his clothes and on his nurse; what's more, and on any one who comes to see him. And his nursery ain't what *I* call a nursery at all. It's nothing more or less than a private 'ospital, with its white tiles and its antiseptics and what not, and the temperature just so and no lower nor higher. I don't call it 'aving a proper faith in Providence, pampering and fussing over a child to that extent."

"You're stringing me!"

"Not a bit of it, Mr. Dingle. I've seen the nursery with my own eyes, and I 'ave my information direct from the young person who looks after the child."

"But, say, in the old days that kid was about the dandiest little sport that ever came down the pike. You seen him that day I brought him round to say hello to the old man. He didn't have no nursery at all then, let alone one with white tiles. I've seen him come up off the studio floor looking like a coon with the dust. And Miss Ruth tickled to see him like that, too. For the love of Mike, what's come to her?"

"It's all along of this Porter," said Keggs morosely. "She's done it all. And if," he went on with sudden heat, "she don't break her 'abit of addressing me in a tone what the 'umblest dorg would resent, I'm liable to forget my place and give her a piece of my mind. Coming round and interfering!"

"Got *your* goat, has she?" commented Steve, interested. "She's what you'd call a tough proposition, that dame. I used to have my eye on her all the time in the old days, waiting for her to start something. But say, I'd like to see this nursery you've been talking about. Take me up and let me lamp it."

Keggs shook his head.

"I daren't, Mr. Dingle. It 'ud be as much as my place is worth."

"But, darn it! I'm the kid's godfather."

"That wouldn't make no difference to that Porter. She'd pick on me just the same. But, if you care to risk it, Mr. Dingle, I'll show you where it is. You'll find the young person up there. She'll tell you more about the child's 'abits and daily life than I can."

"Good enough," said Steve.

He had not seen Mamie for some time, and absence had made the heart grow fonder. It embittered him that his meetings with her were all too rare nowadays. She seemed to have abandoned the practice of walking altogether, for, whenever he saw her now she was driving in the automobile with Bill. Keggs' information about the new system threw some light upon this and made him all the more anxious to meet her now.

It was a curious delusion of Steve's that he was always going to pluck up courage and propose to Mamie the very next time he saw her. This had gone on now for over two years, but he still clung to it. Repeated failures to reveal his burning emotions never caused him to lose the conviction that he would do it for certain next time.

It was in his customary braced-up, do-or-die frame of mind that he entered the nursery now.

His visit to Keggs had been rather a late one and had lasted some time before the subject of the White Hope had been broached, with the result that, when Steve arrived among the white tiles and antiseptics, he found his godson in bed and asleep. In a chair by the cot Mamie sat sewing.

Her eyes widened with surprise when she saw who the visitor was, and she put a finger to her lip and pointed to the sleeper. And, as we have to record another of the long list of Steve's failures to propose we may say here, in excuse, that this reception took a great deal of the edge off the dashing resolution which had been his up to that moment. It made him feel self-conscious from the start.

"Whatever brings you up here, Steve?" whispered Mamie.

It was not a very tactful remark, perhaps, considering that Steve was the child's godfather, and, as such, might reasonably expect to be allowed a free pass to his nursery; but Mamie, like Keggs, had fallen so under the domination of Lora Delane Porter that she had grown to consider it almost a natural law that no one came to see Bill unless approved of and personally conducted by her.

Steve did not answer. He was gaping at the fittings of the place in which he found himself. It was precisely as Keggs had described it, white tiles and all.

He was roused from his reflections by the approach of Mamie, or, rather, not so much by her approach as by the fact that at this moment she suddenly squirted something at him. It was cold and wet and hit him in the face before, as he put it to Keggs later, he could get his guard up.

"For the love of—"

"Sh!" said Mamie warningly.

"What's the idea? What are you handing me?"

"I've got to. It's to sterilize you. I do it to every one."

"Gee! You've got a swell job! Well, go to it, then. Shoot! I'm ready."

"It's boric acid," explained Mamie.

"I shouldn't wonder. Is this all part of the Porter circus?"

"Yes."

"Where is she?" inquired Steve in sudden alarm. "Is she likely to butt in?"

"No. She's out."

"Good," said Steve, and sat down, relieved, to resume his inspection of the room.

When he had finished he drew a deep breath.

"Well!" he said softly. "Say, Mamie, what do you think about it?"

"I'm not paid to think about it, Steve."

"That means you agree with me that it's the punkest state of things you ever struck. Well, you're quite right. It is. It's a shame to think of that innocent kid having this sort of deal handed to him. Why, just think of him at the studio!"

But Mamie, whatever her private views, was loyal to her employers. She refused to be drawn into a discussion on the subject.

"Have you been downstairs with Mr. Keggs, Steve?"

"Yes. It was him that told me about all this. Say, Mame, we ain't seen much of each other lately."

"No."

"Mighty little."

"Yes."

Having got as far as this, Steve should, of course, have gone resolutely ahead. After all, it is not a very long step from telling a girl in a hushed whisper with a shake in it that you have not seen much of her lately to hinting that you would like to see a great deal more of her in the future.

Steve was on the right lines, and he knew it; but that fatal lack of nerve which had wrecked him on all the other occasions when he had got as far as this undid him now. He relapsed into silence, and Mamie went on sewing.

In a way, if you shut your eyes to the white tiles and the thermometer and the brass knobs and the shower-bath, it was a peaceful scene; and Steve, as he sat there and watched Mamie sew, was stirred by it. Remove the white tiles, the thermometer the brass knobs, and the shower-bath, and this was precisely the sort of scene his imagination conjured up when the business of life slackened sufficiently to allow him to dream dreams.

There he was, sitting in one chair; there was Mamie, sitting in another; and there in the corner was the little white cot – well, perhaps that was being a shade too prophetic; on the other hand, it always came into these dreams of his. There, in short, was everything arranged just as he pictured it; and all that was needed to make the picture real was for him to propose and Mamie to accept him.

It was the disturbing thought that the second condition did not necessarily follow on to the first that had kept Steve from taking the plunge for the last two years. Unlike the hero of the poem, he feared his fate too much to put it to the touch, to win or lose it all.

Presently the silence began to oppress Steve. Mamie had her needlework, and that apparently served her in lieu of conversation; but Steve had nothing to occupy him, and he began to grow restless. He always despised himself thoroughly for his feebleness on these occasions; and he despised himself now. He determined to make a big effort.

"Mamie!" he said.

As he was nervous and had been silent so long that his vocal cords had gone off duty under the impression that their day's work was over, the word came out of him like a husky gunshot. Mamie started, and the White Hope, who had been sleeping peacefully, stirred and muttered.

"S-sh!" hissed Mamie.

Steve collapsed with the feeling that it was not his lucky night, while Mamie bent anxiously over the cot. The sleeper, however, did not wake. He gurgled, gave a sigh, then resumed his interrupted repose. Mamie returned to her seat.

"Yes?" she said, as if nothing had occurred, and as if there had been no interval between Steve's remark and her reply.

Steve could not equal her calmness. He had been strung up when he spoke, and the interruption had undone him. He reflected ruefully that he might have said something to the point if he had been allowed to go straight on; now he had forgotten what he had meant to say.

"Oh, nothing," he replied.

Silence fell once more on the nursery.

Steve was bracing himself up for another attack when suddenly there came a sound of voices from the stairs. One voice was a mere murmur, but the other was sharp and unmistakable, the incisive note of Lora Delane Porter. It brought Steve and Mamie to their feet simultaneously.

"What's it matter?" said Steve stoutly, answering the panic in Mamie's eyes. "It's not her house, and I got a perfect right to be here."

"You don't know her. I shall get into trouble."

Mamie was pale with apprehension. She knew her Lora Delane Porter, and she knew what would happen if Steve were to be discovered there. It was, as Keggs put it, as much as her place was worth.

For a brief instant Mamie faced a future in which she was driven from Bill's presence into outer darkness, dismissed, and told never to return. That was what would happen. Sitting and talking with Steve in the sacred nursery at this time of night was a crime, and she had known it all the time. But she had been glad to see Steve again after all this while – if Steve had known how glad, he would certainly have found courage and said what he had so often failed to say – and, knowing that Mrs. Porter was out, she had thought the risk of his presence worth taking. Now, with discovery imminent, panic came upon her.

The voices were quite close now. There was no doubt of the destination of the speakers. They were heading slowly but directly for the nursery.

Steve, not being fully abreast of the new rules and regulations of the sacred apartment, could not read Mamie's mind completely. He did not know that, under Mrs. Porter's code, the admission of a visitor during the hours of sleep was a felony in the first degree, punishable by instant dismissal. But Mamie's face and her brief reference to trouble were enough to tell him that the position was critical, and with the instinct of the trapped he looked round him for cover.

But the White Hope's nursery was not constructed with a view to providing cover for bulky gentlemen who should not have been there. It was as bare as a billiard-table as far as practicable hiding-places were concerned.

And then his eye caught the water-proof sheet of the shower-bath. Behind that there was just room for concealment.

With a brief nod of encouragement to Mamie, he leaped at it. The door opened as he disappeared.

Mrs. Porter's rules concerning visitors, though stringent as regarded Mamie, were capable of being relaxed when she herself was the person to relax them. She had a visitor with her now – a long, severe-looking lady with a sharp nose surmounted by spectacles, who, taking in the white tiles, the thermometer, the cot, and the brass knobs in a single comprehensive glance, observed: "Admirable!"

Mrs, Porter was obviously pleased with this approval. Her companion was a woman doctor of great repute among the advanced apostles of hygiene; and praise from her was praise indeed. She advanced into the room with an air of suppressed pride.

"These tiles are thoroughly cleaned twice each day with an antiseptic solution."

"Just so," said the spectacled lady.

"You notice the thermometer."

"Exactly."

"Those knobs you see on the wall have various uses."

"Quite."

They examined the knobs with an air of profound seriousness, Mrs. Porter erect and complacent, the other leaning forward and peering through her spectacles. Mamie took advantage of their backs and turned to cast a hurried glance at the water-proof curtain. It was certainly an admirable screen; no sign of Steve was visible; but nevertheless she did not cease to quake.

"This," said Mrs. Porter, "controls the heat. This, this, and this are for the ventilation."

"Just so, just so, just so," said the doctor. "And this, of course, is for the shower-bath? I understand!"

And, extending a firm finger, she gave the knob a forceful push. Mrs. Porter nodded.

"That is the cold shower," she said. "This is the hot. It is a very ingenious arrangement, one of Malcolmson's patents. There is a regulator at the side of the bath which enables the nurse to get just the correct temperature. I will turn on both, and then—"

It was as Mrs. Porter's hand was extended toward the knob that the paralysis which terror had put upon Mamie relaxed its grip. She had stood by without a movement while the cold water splashed down upon the hidden Steve. Her heart had ached for him, but she had not stirred. But now, with the prospect of allowing him to be boiled alive before her, she acted.

It is generally only on the stage that a little child comes to the rescue of adults at critical moments; but William Bannister was accorded the opportunity of doing so off it. It happened that at the moment of Mrs. Porter's entry Mamie had been standing near his cot, and she had not moved since. The consequence was that she was within easy reach of him; and, despair giving her what in the circumstances amounted to a flash of inspiration, she leaned quickly forward, even as Mrs. Porter's finger touched the knob, and gave the round head on the pillow a rapid push.

William Bannister sat up with a grunt, rubbed his eyes, and, seeing strangers, began to cry.

It was so obvious to Mrs. Porter and her companion, both from the evidence of their guilty consciences and the look of respectful reproach on Mamie's face, that the sound of their voices had disturbed the child, that they were routed from the start.

"Oh, dear me! He is awake," said the lady doctor.

"I am afraid we did not lower our voices," added Mrs. Porter. "And yet William is usually such a sound sleeper. Perhaps we had better—"

"Just so," said the doctor.

"—go downstairs while the nurse gets him off to sleep again."

"Quite."

The door closed behind them.

❦

"Oh, Steve!" said Mamie.

The White Hope had gone to sleep again with the amazing speed of childhood, and Mamie was looking pityingly at the bedraggled object which had emerged cautiously from behind the waterproof.

"I got mine," muttered Steve ruefully. "You ain't got a towel anywhere, have you, Mame?"

Mamie produced a towel and watched him apologetically as he attempted to dry himself.

"I'm so sorry, Steve."

"Cut it out. It was my fault. I oughtn't to have been there. Say, it was a bit of luck the kid waking just then."

"Yes," said Mamie.

Observe the tricks that conscience plays us. If Mamie had told Steve what had caused William to wake he would certainly have been so charmed by her presence of mind, exerted on his behalf to save him from the warm fate which Mrs. Porter's unconscious hand had been about to bring down upon him, that he would have forgotten his diffidence then and there and, as the poet has it, have eased his bosom of much perilous stuff.

But conscience would not allow Mamie to reveal the secret. Already she was suffering the pangs of remorse for having, in however good a cause, broken her idol's rest with a push that might have given the poor lamb a headache. She could not confess the crime even to Steve.

And if Steve had had the pluck to tell Mamie that he loved her, as he stood before her dripping with the water which he had suffered in silence rather than betray her, she would have fallen into his arms. For Steve at that moment had all the glamour for her of the self-sacrificing hero of a moving-picture film. He had not actually risked death for her, perhaps, but he had taken a sudden cold shower-bath without a murmur – all for her.

Mamie was thrilled. She looked at him with the gleaming eyes of devotion.

But Steve, just because he knew that he was wet and fancied that he must look ridiculous, held his peace.

And presently, his secret still locked in his bosom, and his collar sticking limply to his neck, he crept downstairs, avoiding the society of his fellow man, and slunk out into the night where, if there was no Mamie, there were, at any rate, dry clothes.

CHAPTER 4
THE WIDENING GAP

THE new life hit Kirk as a wave hits a bather; and, like a wave, swept him off his feet, choked him, and generally filled him with a feeling of discomfort.

He should have been prepared for it, but he was not. He should have divined from the first that the money was bound to produce changes other than a mere shifting of headquarters from Sixty-First Street to Fifth Avenue. But he had deluded himself at first with the idea that Ruth was different from other women, that she was superior to the artificial pleasures of the Society which is distinguished by the big S.

In a moment of weakness, induced by hair-ruffling, he had given in on the point of the hygienic upbringing of William Bannister; but there, he had imagined, his troubles were to cease. He had supposed that he was about to resume the old hermit's-cell life of the studio and live in a world which contained only Ruth, Bill, and himself.

He was quickly undeceived. Within two days he was made aware of the fact that Ruth was in the very centre of the social whirlpool and that she took it for granted that he would join her there. There was nothing of the hermit about Ruth now. She was amazingly undomestic.

Her old distaste for the fashionable life of New York seemed to have vanished absolutely. As far as Kirk could see, she was always entertaining or being entertained. He was pitched head-long into a world where people talked incessantly of things which bored him and did things which seemed to him simply mad. And Ruth, whom he had thought he understood, revelled in it all.

At first he tried to get at her point of view, to discover what she found to enjoy in this lunatic existence of aimlessness and futility. One night, as they were driving home from a dinner which had bored him unspeakably, he asked the question point-blank. It seemed to him incredible that she could take pleasure in an entertainment which had filled him with such depression.

"Ruth," he said impulsively, as the car moved off, "what do you see in this sort of thing? How can you stand these people? What have you in common with them?"

"Poor old Kirk. I know you hated it to-night. But we shan't be dining with the Baileys every night."

Bailey Bannister had been their host on that occasion, and the dinner had been elaborate and gorgeous. Mrs. Bailey was now one of the leaders of the younger set. Bailey, looking much more than a year older than when Kirk had seen him last, had presided at the head of the table with great dignity, and the meeting with him had not contributed to the pleasure of Kirk's evening.

"Were you awfully bored? You seemed to be getting along quite well with Sybil."

"I like her. She's good fun."

"She's certainly having good fun. I'd give anything to know what Bailey really thinks of it. She is the most shockingly extravagant little creature in New York. You know the Wilburs were quite poor, and poor Sybil was kept very short. I think that marrying Bailey and having all this money to play with has turned her head."

It struck Kirk that the criticism applied equally well to the critic.

"She does the most absurd things. She gave a freak dinner when you were away that cost I don't know how much. She is always doing something. Well, I suppose Bailey knows what he is about; but at her present pace she must be keeping him busy making money to pay for all her fads. You ought to paint a picture of Bailey, Kirk, as the typical patient American husband. You couldn't get a better model."

"Suggest it to him, and let me hide somewhere where I can hear what he says. Bailey has his own opinion of my pictures."

Ruth laughed a little nervously. She had always wondered exactly what had taken place that day in the studio, and the subject was one which she was shy of exhuming. She turned the conversation.

"What did you ask me just now? Something about—"

"I asked you what you had in common with these people."

Ruth reflected.

"Oh, well, it's rather difficult to say if you put it like that. They're just people, you know. They are amusing sometimes. I used to know most of them. I suppose that is the chief thing which brings us together. They happen to be there, and if you're travelling on a road you naturally talk to your fellow travellers. But why? Don't you like them? Which of them didn't you like?"

It was Kirk's turn to reflect.

"Well, that's hard to answer, too. I don't think I actively liked or disliked any of them. They seemed to me just not worth while. My point is, rather, why are we wasting a perfectly good evening mixing with them? What's the use? That's my case in a nut-shell."

"If you put it like that, what's the use of anything? One must do something. We can't be hermits."

A curious feeling of being infinitely far from Ruth came over Kirk. She dismissed his dream as a whimsical impossibility not worthy of serious consideration. Why could they not be hermits? They had been hermits before, and it had been the happiest period of both their lives. Why, just because an old man had died and left them money, must they rule out the best thing in life as impossible and plunge into a nightmare which was not life at all?

He had tried to deceive himself, but he could do so no longer. Ruth had changed. The curse with which his sensitive imagination had invested John Bannister's legacy was, after all no imaginary curse. Like a golden wedge, it had forced Ruth and himself apart.

Everything had changed. He was no longer the centre of Ruth's life. He was just an encumbrance, a nuisance who could not be got rid of and must remain a permanent handicap, always in the way.

So thought Kirk morbidly as the automobile passed through the silent streets. It must be remembered that he had been extremely bored for a solid three hours, and was predisposed, consequently, to gloomy thoughts.

Whatever his faults, Kirk rarely whined. He had never felt so miserable in his life, but he tried to infuse a tone of lightness into the conversation. After all, if Ruth's intuition fell short of enabling her to understand his feelings, nothing was to be gained by parading them.

"I guess it's my fault," he said, "that I haven't got abreast of the society game as yet. You had better give me a few pointers. My trouble is that, being new to them, I can't tell whether these people are types or exceptions. Take Clarence Grayling, for instance. Are there any more at home like Clarence?"

"My dear child, *all* Bailey's special friends are like Clarence, exactly like. I remember telling him so once."

"Who was the specimen with the little black moustache who thought America crude and said that the only place to live in was southern Italy? Is he an isolated case or an epidemic?"

"He is scarcer than Clarence, but he's quite a well-marked type. He is the millionaire's son who has done Europe and doesn't mean you to forget it."

"There was a chesty person with a wave of hair coming down over his forehead. A sickeningly handsome fellow who looked like a poet. I think they called him Basil. Does he run around in flocks, or is he unique?"

Ruth did not reply for a moment. Basil Milbank was a part of the past which, in the year during which Kirk had been away, had come rather startlingly to life.

There had been a time when Basil had been very near and important to her. Indeed, but for the intervention of Mrs. Porter, described in an earlier passage, she would certainly have married Basil. Then Kirk had crossed her path and had monopolized her. During the studio period the recollection of Basil had grown faint. After that, just at the moment when Kirk was not there to lend her strength, he had come back into her life. For nearly a year she had seen him daily; and gradually – at first almost with fear – she had realized that the old fascination was by no means such a thing of the past as she had supposed.

She had hoped for Kirk's return as a general, sorely pressed, hopes for reinforcements. With Kirk at her side she felt Basil would slip back into his proper place in the scheme of things. And, behold! Kirk had returned and still the tension remained unrelaxed.

For Kirk had changed. After the first day she could not conceal it from herself. That it was she who had changed did not present itself to her as a possible explanation of the fact that she now felt out of touch with her husband. All she knew was that they had been linked together by bonds of sympathy, and were so no longer.

She found Kirk dull. She hated to admit it, but the truth forced itself upon her. He had begun to bore her.

She collected her thoughts and answered his question.

"Basil Milbank? Oh, I should call him unique."

She felt a wild impulse to warn him, to explain the real significance of this man whom he classed contemptuously with Clarence Grayling and that absurd little Dana Ferris as somebody of no account. She wanted to cry out to him that she was in danger and that only he could help her. But she could not speak, and Kirk went on in the same tone of half-tolerant contempt:

"Who is he?"

She controlled herself with an effort, and answered indifferently.

"Oh, Basil? Well, you might say he's everything. He plays polo, leads cotillions, yachts, shoots, plays the piano wonderfully – everything. People usually like him very much." She paused. "Women especially."

She had tried to put something into her tone which might serve to awaken him, something which might prepare the way for what she wanted to say – and what, if she did not say it now – when the mood was on her, she could never say. But Kirk was deaf.

"He looks that sort of man," he said.

And, as he said it, the accumulated boredom of the past three hours found vent in a vast yawn.

Ruth set her teeth. She felt as if she had received a blow.

When he spoke again it was on the subject of street-paving defects in New York City.

❦

It was true, as Ruth had said, that they did not dine with the Baileys every night, but that seemed to Kirk, as the days went on, the one and only bright spot in the new state of affairs. He could not bring himself to treat life with a philosophical resignation. His was not open revolt. He was outwardly docile, but inwardly he rebelled furiously.

Perhaps the unnaturally secluded life which he had led since his marriage had unfitted him for mixing in society even more than nature had done. He had grown out of the habit of mixing. Crowds irritated him. He hated doing the same thing at the same time as a hundred other people.

Like most Bohemians, he was at his best in a small circle. He liked his friends as single spies, not in battalions. He was a man who should have had a few intimates and no acquaintances; and his present life was bounded north, south, east, and west by acquaintances. Most of the men to whom he spoke he did not even know by name.

He would seek information from Ruth as they drove home.

"Who was the pop-eyed second-story man with the bald head and the convex waistcoat who glued himself to me to-night?"

"If you mean the fine old gentleman with the slightly prominent eyes and rather thin hair, that was Brock Mason, the vice-president of consolidated groceries. You mustn't even think disrespectfully of a man as rich as that."

"He isn't what you would call a sparkling talker."

"He doesn't have to be. His time is worth a hundred dollars a minute, or a second – I forget which."

"Put me down for a nickel's worth next time."

And then they began to laugh over Ruth's suggestion that they should save up and hire Mr. Mason for an afternoon and make him keep quiet all the time; for Ruth was generally ready to join him in ridiculing their new acquaintances. She had none of that reverence for the great and the near-great which, running to seed, becomes snobbery.

It was this trait in her which kept alive, long after it might have died, the hope that her present state of mind was only a phase, and that, when she had tired of the new game, she would become the old Ruth of the studio. But, when he was honest with himself, he was forced to admit that she showed no signs of ever tiring of it.

They had drifted apart. They were out of touch with each other. It was not an uncommon state of things in the circle in which Kirk now found himself. Indeed, it seemed to him that the semi-detached couple was the rule rather than the exception.

But there was small consolation in this reflection. He was not at all interested in the domestic troubles of the people he mixed with. His own hit him very hard.

Ruth had criticized little Mrs. Bailey, but there was no doubt that she herself had had her head turned quite as completely by the new life.

The first time that Kirk realized this was when he came upon an article in a Sunday paper, printed around a blurred caricature which professed to be a photograph of Mrs. Kirk Winfield, in which she was alluded to with reverence and gusto as one of society's leading hostesses. In the course of the article reference was made to no fewer than three freak dinners of varying ingenuity which she had provided for her delighted friends.

It was this that staggered Kirk. That Mrs. Bailey should indulge in this particular form of insanity was intelligible. But that Ruth should have descended to it was another thing altogether.

He did not refer to the article when he met Ruth, but he was more than ever conscious of the gap between them – the gap which was widening every day.

The experiences he had undergone during the year of his wandering had strengthened Kirk considerably, but nature is not easily expelled; and the constitutional weakness of character which had hampered him through life prevented him from making any open protests or appeal. Moreover, he could understand now her point of view, and that disarmed him.

He saw how this state of things had come about. In a sense, it was the natural state of things. Ruth had been brought up in certain surroundings. Her love for him, new and overwhelming, had enabled her to free herself temporarily from these surroundings and to become reconciled to a life for which, he told himself, she had never been intended. Fate had thrown her back into her natural sphere. And now she revelled in the old environment as an exile revels in the life of the homeland from which he has been so long absent.

That was the crux of the tragedy. Ruth was at home. He was not. Ruth was among her own people. He was a stranger among strangers, a prisoner in a land where men spoke with an alien tongue.

There was nothing to be done. The gods had played one of their practical jokes, and he must join in the laugh against himself and try to pretend that he was not hurt.

CHAPTER 5
THE REAL THING

KIRK sat in the nursery with his chin on his hands, staring gloomily at William Bannister. On the floor William Bannister played some game of his own invention with his box of bricks.

They were alone. It was the first time they had been alone together for two weeks. As a rule, when Kirk paid his daily visit, Lora Delane Porter was there, watchful and forbidding, prepared, on the slightest excuse, to fall upon him with rules and prohibitions. To-day she was out, and Kirk had the field to himself, for Mamie, whose duty it was to mount guard, and who had been threatened with many terrible things by Mrs. Porter if she did not stay on guard, had once more allowed her too sympathetic nature to get the better of her and had vanished.

Kirk was too dispirited to take advantage of his good fortune. He had a sense of being there on parole, of being on his honour not to touch. So he sat in his chair, and looked at Bill; while Bill, crooning to himself, played decorously with bricks.

The truth had been a long time in coming home to Kirk, but it had reached him at last. Ever since his return he had clung to the belief that it was a genuine conviction of its merits that had led Ruth to support her aunt's scheme for Bill's welfare. He himself had always looked on the exaggerated precautions for the maintenance of the latter's health as ridiculous and unnecessary; but he had acquiesced in them because he thought that Ruth sincerely believed them indispensable.

After all, he had not been there when Bill so nearly died, and he could understand that the shock of that episode might have distorted the judgment even of a woman so well balanced as Ruth. He was quite ready to be loyal to her in the matter, however distasteful it might be to him.

But now he saw the truth. A succession of tiny incidents had brought light to him. Ruth might or might not be to some extent genuine in her belief in the new system, but her chief motive for giving it her support was something quite different. He had tried not to admit to himself, but he could do so no longer. Ruth allowed Mrs. Porter to have her way because it suited her to do so; because, with Mrs. Porter on the premises, she had more leisure in which to amuse herself; because, to put it in a word, the child had begun to bore her.

Everything pointed to that. In the old days it had been her chief pleasure to be with the boy. Their walks in the park had been a daily ceremony with which nothing had been allowed to interfere. But now she always had some excuse for keeping away from him.

Her visits to the nursery, when she did go there, were brief and perfunctory. And the mischief of it was that she always presented such admirable reasons for abstaining from Bill's society, when it was suggested to her that she should go to him, that it was impossible to bring her out into the open and settle the matter once and for all.

Patience was one of the virtues which set off the defects in Kirk's character; but he did not feel very patient now as he sat and watched Bill playing on the floor.

"Well, Bill, old man, what do you make of it all?" he said at last.

The child looked up and fixed him with unwinking eyes. Kirk winced. They were so exactly Ruth's eyes. That wide-open expression when somebody, speaking suddenly to her, interrupted a train of thought, was one of her hundred minor charms.

Bill had reproduced it to the life. He stared for a moment; then, as if there had been some telepathy between them, said: "I want mummy."

Kirk laughed bitterly.

"You aren't the only one. I want mummy, too."

"Where is mummy?"

"I couldn't tell you exactly. At a luncheon-party somewhere."

"What's luncheon-party?"

"A sort of entertainment where everybody eats too much and talks all the time without ever saying a thing that's worth hearing."

Bill considered this gravely.

"Why?"

"Because they like it, I suppose."

"Why do they like it?"

"Goodness knows."

"Does mummy like it?"

"I suppose so."

"Does mummy eat too much?"

"She doesn't. The others do."

"Why?"

William Bannister's thirst for knowledge was at this time perhaps his most marked characteristic. No encyclopaedia could have coped with it. Kirk was accustomed to do his best, cheerfully yielding up what little information on general subjects he happened to possess, but he was like Mrs. Partington sweeping back the Atlantic Ocean with her broom.

"Because they've been raised that way," he replied to the last question. "Bill, old man, when you grow up, don't you ever become one of these fellows who can't walk two blocks without stopping three times to catch up with their breath. If you get like that mutt Dana Ferris you'll break my heart. And you're heading that way, poor kid."

"What's Ferris?"

"He's a man I met at dinner the other night. When he was your age he was the richest child in America, and everybody fussed over him till he grew up into a wretched little creature with a black moustache and two chins. You ought to see him. He would make you laugh; and you don't get much to laugh at nowadays. I guess it isn't hygienic for a kid to laugh. Bill, honestly – what *do* you think of things? Don't you ever want to hurl one of those sterilized bricks of yours at a certain lady? Or has she taken all the heart out of you by this time?"

This was beyond Bill, as Kirk's monologues frequently were. He changed the subject.

"I wish I had a cat," he said, by way of starting a new topic.

"Well, why haven't you a cat? Why haven't you a dozen cats if you want them?"

"I asked Aunty Lora could I have a cat, and she said: 'Certainly not, cats are – cats are—'"

"Unhygienic?"

"What's that?"

"It's what your Aunt Lora might think a cat was. Or did she say pestilential?"

"I don't amember."

"But she wouldn't let you have one?"

"Mamie said a cat might scratch me."

"Well, you wouldn't mind that?" said Kirk anxiously.

He had come to be almost morbidly on the look-out for evidence which might go to prove that this cotton-wool existence was stealing from the child the birthright of courage which was his from both his parents. Much often depends on little things, and, if Bill had replied in the affirmative to the question, it would probably have had the result of sending Kirk there and then raging through the house conducting a sort of War of Independence.

The only thing that had kept him from doing so before was the reflection that Mrs. Porter's system could not be definitely taxed with any harmful results. But his mind was never easy. Every day found him still nervously on the alert for symptoms.

Bill soothed him now by answering "No" in a very decided voice. All well so far, but it had been an anxious moment.

It seemed incredible to Kirk that the life he was leading should not in time turn the child into a whimpering bundle of nerves. His conversations with Bill were, as a result, a sort of spiritual parallel to the daily taking of his temperature with the thermometer. Sooner or later he always led the talk round to some point where Bill must make a definite pronouncement which would show whether or not the insidious decay had begun to set in.

So far all appeared to be well. In earlier conversations Bill, subtly questioned, had stoutly maintained that he was not afraid of Indians, dogs, pirates, mice, cows, June-bugs, or noises in the dark. He had even gone so far as to state that if an Indian chief found his way into the nursery he, Bill, would chop his head off. The most exacting father could not have asked more. And yet Kirk was not satisfied: he remained uneasy.

It so happened that this afternoon Bill, who had had hitherto to maintain his reputation for intrepidity entirely by verbal statements, was afforded an opportunity of providing a practical demonstration that his heart was in the right place. The game he was playing with the bricks was one that involved a certain amount of running about with a puffing accompaniment of a vaguely equine nature. And while performing this part of the programme he chanced to trip. He hesitated for a moment, as if uncertain whether to fall or remain standing; then did the former with a most emphatic bump.

He scrambled up, stood looking at Kirk with a twitching lip, then gave a great gulp, and resumed his trotting. The whole exhibition of indomitable heroism was over in half a minute, and he did not even bother to wait for applause.

The effect of the incident on Kirk was magical. He was in the position of an earnest worshipper who, tortured with doubts, has prayed for a sign. This was a revelation. A million anti-Indian statements, however resolute, were nothing to this.

This was the real thing. Before his eyes this super-child of his had fallen in a manner which might quite reasonably have led to tears; which would, Kirk felt sure, have produced bellows of anguish from every other child in America. And what had happened? Not a moan. No, sir, not one solitary cry. Just a gulp which you had to strain your ears to hear, and which, at that, might have been a mere taking-in of breath such as every athlete must do, and all was over.

This child of his was the real thing. It had been proved beyond possibility of criticism.

There are moments when a man on parole forgets his promise. All thought of rules and prohibitions went from Kirk. He rose from his seat, grabbed his son with both hands, and hugged him. We cannot even begin to estimate the number of bacilli which must have rushed, whooping with joy, on to the unfortunate child. Under a microscope it would probably have looked like an Old Home Week. And Kirk did not care. He simply kept on hugging. That was the sort of man he was – thoroughly heartless.

"Bill, you're great!" he cried.

Bill had been an amazed party to the incident. Nothing of this kind had happened to him for so long that he had forgotten there were children to whom this sort of thing did happen. Then he recollected a similar encounter with a bearded man down in the hall when he came in one morning from his ride in the automobile. A moment later he had connected his facts.

This man who had no beard was the same man as the man who had a beard, and this behaviour was a personal eccentricity of his. The thought crossed his mind that Aunty Lora would not approve of this.

And then, surprisingly, there came the thought that he did not care whether Aunty Lora approved or not. *He* liked it, and that was enough for him.

The seeds of revolt had been sown in the bosom of William Bannister.

It happened that Ruth, returning from her luncheon-party, looked in at the nursery on her way upstairs. She was confronted with the spectacle of Bill seated on Kirk's lap, his face against Kirk's shoulder. Kirk, though he had stopped speaking as the door opened, appeared to be in the middle of a story, for Bill, after a brief glance at the newcomer, asked: "What happened then?"

"Kirk, really!" said Ruth.

Kirk did not appear in the least ashamed of himself.

"Ruth, this kid is the most amazing kid. Do you know what happened just now? He was running along and he tripped and came down flat. And he didn't even think of crying. He just picked himself up, and—"

"That was very brave of you, Billy. But, seriously, Kirk, you shouldn't hug him like that. Think what Aunt Lora would say!"

"Aunt Lora be—Bother Aunt Lora!"

"Well, I won't give you away. If she heard, she would write a book about it. And she was just starting to come up when I was downstairs. We came in together. You had better fly while there's time."

It was sound advice, and Kirk took it.

It was not till some time later, going over the incident again in his mind, he realized how very lightly Ruth had treated what, if she really adhered to Mrs. Porter's views on hygiene, should have been to her a dreadful discovery. The reflection was pleasant to him for a moment; it seemed to draw Ruth and himself closer together; then he saw the reverse side of it.

If Ruth did not really believe in this absurd hygienic nonsense, why had she permitted it to be practised upon the boy? There was only one answer, and it was the one which Kirk had already guessed at. She did it because it gave her more freedom, because it bored her to look after the child herself, because she was not the same Ruth he had left at the studio when he started with Hank Jardine for Colombia.

CHAPTER 6
THE OUTCASTS

THREE months of his new life had gone by before Kirk awoke from the stupor which had gripped him as the result of the general upheaval of his world. Ever since his return from Colombia he had honestly been intending to resume his painting, and, attacking it this time in a business-like way, to try to mould himself into the semblance of an efficient artist.

His mind had been full of fine resolutions. He would engage a good teacher, some competent artist whom fortune had not treated well and who would be glad of the job – Washington Square and its neighbourhood were full of them – and settle down grimly, working regular hours, to recover lost ground.

But the rush of life, as lived on the upper avenue, had swept him away. He had been carried along on the rapids of dinners, parties, dances, theatres, luncheons, and the rest, and his great resolve had gone bobbing away from him on the current.

He had recovered it now and climbed painfully ashore, feeling bruised and exhausted, but determined.

Among the motley crowd which had made the studio a home in the days of Kirk's bachelorhood had been an artist – one might almost say an ex-artist – named Robert Dwight Penway. An overfondness for rye whisky at the Brevoort cafe had handicapped Robert as an active force in the world of New York art. As a practical worker he was not greatly esteemed – least of all by the editors of magazines, who had paid advance cheques to him for work which, when delivered at all, was delivered too late for publication. These, once bitten, were now twice shy of Mr. Penway. They did not deny his great talents, which were, indeed, indisputable; but they were fixed in their determination not to make use of them.

Fate could have provided no more suitable ally for Kirk. It was universally admitted around Washington Square and – grudgingly

– down-town that in the matter of theory Mr. Penway excelled. He could teach to perfection what he was too erratic to practise.

Robert Dwight Penway, run to earth one sultry evening in the Brevoort, welcomed Kirk as a brother, as a rich brother. Even when his first impression, that he was to have the run of the house on Fifth Avenue and mix freely with touchable multi-millionaires, had been corrected, his altitude was still brotherly. He parted from Kirk with many solemn promises to present himself at the studio daily and teach him enough art to put him clear at the top of the profession. "Way above all these other dubs," asserted Mr. Penway.

Robert Dwight Penway's attitude toward his contemporaries in art bore a striking resemblance to Steve's estimate of his successors in the middle-weight department of the American prize-ring.

Surprisingly to those who knew him, Mr. Penway was as good as his word. Certainly Kirk's terms had been extremely generous; but he had thrown away many a contract of equal value in his palmy days. Possibly his activity was due to his liking for Kirk; or it may have been that the prospect of sitting by with a cigar while somebody else worked, with nothing to do all day except offer criticism, and advice, appealed to him.

At any rate, he appeared at the studio on the following afternoon, completely sober and excessively critical. He examined the canvases which Kirk had hauled from shelves and corners for his inspection. One after another he gazed upon them in an increasingly significant silence. When the last one was laid aside he delivered judgment.

"Golly!" he said.

Kirk flushed. It was not that he was not in complete agreement with the verdict. Looking at these paintings, some of which he had in the old days thought extremely good, he was forced to admit that "Golly" was the only possible criticism.

He had not seen them for a long time, and absence had enabled him to correct first impressions. Moreover, something had happened to him, causing him to detect flaws where he had seen only merits. Life had sharpened his powers of judgment. He was a grown man looking at the follies of his youth.

"Burn them!" said Mr. Penway, lighting a cigar with the air of one restoring his tissues after a strenuous ordeal. "Burn the lot. They're awful. Darned amateur nightmares. They offend the eye. Cast them into a burning fiery furnace."

Kirk nodded. The criticism was just. It erred, if at all, on the side of mildness. Certainly something had happened to him since he perpetrated those daubs. He had developed. He saw things with new eyes.

"I guess I had better start right in again at the beginning," he sad.

"Earlier than that," amended Mr. Penway.

So Kirk settled down to a routine of hard work; and, so doing, drove another blow at the wedge which was separating his life from Ruth's. There were days now when they did not meet at all, and others when they saw each other for a few short moments in which neither seemed to have much to say.

Ruth had made a perfunctory protest against the new departure.

"Really," she said, "it does seem absurd for you to spend all your time down at that old studio. It isn't as if you had to. But, of course, if you want to—"

And she had gone on to speak of other subjects. It was plain to Kirk that his absence scarcely affected her. She was still in the rapids, and every day carried her farther away from him.

It did not hurt him now. A sort of apathy seemed to have fallen on him. The old days became more and more remote. Sometimes he doubted whether anything remained of her former love for him, and sometimes he wondered if he still loved her. She was so different that it was almost as if she were a stranger. Once they had had everything in common. Now it seemed to him that they had nothing – not even Bill.

He did not brood upon it. He gave himself no time for that. He worked doggedly on under the blasphemous but efficient guidance of Mr. Penway. He was becoming a man with a fixed idea – the idea of making good.

He began to make headway. His beginnings were small, but practical. He no longer sat down when the spirit moved him to dash off vague masterpieces which might turn into something quite unexpected on the road to completion; he snatched at anything definite that presented itself.

Sometimes it was a couple of illustrations to a short story in one of the minor magazines, sometimes a picture to go with an eulogy of a patent medicine. Whatever it was, he seized upon it and put into it all the talent he possessed. And thanks to the indefatigable coaching of Robert Dwight Penway, a certain merit was beginning to creep into his work. His drawing was growing firmer. He no longer shirked difficulties.

Mr. Penway was good enough to approve of his progress. Being free from any morbid distaste for himself, he attributed that progress to its proper source. As he said once in a moment of expansive candour, he could, given a free hand and something to drink and smoke while doing it, make an artist out of two sticks and a lump of coal.

"Why, I've made *you* turn out things that are like something on earth, my boy," he said proudly. "And that," he added, as he reached out for the bottle of Bourbon which Kirk had provided for him, "is going some."

Kirk was far too grateful to resent the slightly unflattering note a more spirited man might have detected in the remark.

❦

Only once during those days did Kirk allow himself to weaken and admit to himself how wretched he was. He was drawing a picture of Steve at the time, and Steve had the sympathy which encourages weakness in others.

It was a significant sign of his changed attitude towards his profession that he was not drawing Steve as a figure in an allegorical picture or as "Apollo" or "The Toiler," but simply as a well-developed young man who had had the good sense to support his nether garments with Middleton's Undeniable Suspenders. The picture, when completed, would show Steve smirking down at the region of his waist-line and announcing with pride and satisfaction: "They're Middleton's!" Kirk was putting all he knew into the work, and his face, as he drew, was dark and gloomy.

Steve noted this with concern. He had perceived for some time that Kirk had changed. He had lost all his old boyish enjoyment of their sparring-bouts, and he threw the medicine-ball with an absent gloom almost equal to Bailey's.

It had not occurred to Steve to question Kirk about this. If Kirk had anything on his mind which he wished to impart he would say it. Meanwhile, the friendly thing for him to do was to be quiet and pretend to notice nothing.

It seemed to Steve that nothing was going right these days. Here was he, chafing at his inability to open his heart to Mamie. Here was Kirk, obviously in trouble. And – a smaller thing, but of interest, as showing how universal the present depression was – there was Bailey Bannister, equally obviously much worried over something or other.

For Bailey had reinstated Steve in the place he had occupied before old John Bannister had dismissed him, and for some time past Steve had marked him down as a man with a secret trouble. He had never been of a riotously cheerful disposition, but it had been possible once to draw him into conversation at the close of the morning's exercises. Now he hardly spoke. And often, when Steve arrived in the morning, he was informed that Mr. Bannister had started for Wall Street early on important business.

These things troubled Steve. His simple soul abhorred a mystery.

But it was the case of Kirk that worried him most, for he half guessed that the latter's gloom had to do with Ruth; and he worshipped Ruth.

Kirk laid down his sketch and got up.

"I guess that'll do for the moment, Steve," he said.

Steve relaxed the attitude of proud satisfaction which he had assumed in order to do justice to the Undeniable Suspenders. He stretched himself and sat down.

"You certainly are working to beat the band just now, squire," he remarked.

"It's a pretty good thing, work, Steve," said Kirk. "If it does nothing else, it keeps you from thinking."

He knew it was feeble of him, but he was powerfully impelled to relieve himself by confiding his wretchedness to Steve. He need not say much, he told himself plausibly – only just enough to lighten the burden a little.

He would not be disloyal to Ruth – he had not sunk to that – but, after all Steve was Steve. It was not like blurting out his troubles to a stranger. It would harm nobody, and do him a great deal of good, if he talked to Steve.

He relit his pipe, which had gone out during a tense spell of work on the suspenders.

"Well, Steve," he said, "what do you think of life? How is this best of all possible worlds treating you?"

Steve deposed that life was pretty punk.

"You're a great describer, Steve. You've hit it first time. Punk is the word. It's funny, if you look at it properly. Take my own case. The superficial observer, who is apt to be a bonehead, would say that I ought to be singing psalms of joy. I am married to the woman I wanted to marry. I have a son who, not to be fulsome, is a perfectly good sort of son. I have no financial troubles. I eat well. I have ceased to tremble when I see a job of work. In fact, I have advanced in my art to such an extent that shrewd business men like Middleton put the pictorial side of their Undeniable Suspenders in my hands and go off to play golf with their minds easy, having perfect confidence in my skill and judgment. If I can't be merry and bright, who can? Do you find me merry and bright, Steve?"

"I've seen you in better shape," said Steve cautiously.

"I've felt in better shape."

Steve coughed. The conversation was about to become delicate.

"What's eating you, colonel?" he asked presently.

Kirk frowned in silence at the Undeniable for a few moments. Then the pent-up misery of months exploded in a cascade of words. He jumped up and began to walk restlessly about the studio.

"Damn it! Steve, I ought not to say a word, I know. It's weak and cowardly and bad taste and everything else you can think of to speak of it – even to you. One's supposed to stand this sort of roasting at the stake with a grin, as if one enjoyed it. But, after all, you *are* different. It's not as if it was any one. You *are* different, aren't you?"

"Sure."

"Well, you know what's wrong as well as I do."

"Surest thing you know. It's hit me, too."

"How's that?"

"Well, things ain't the same. That's about what it comes to."

Kirk stopped and looked at him. His expression was wistful. "I ought not to be talking about it."

"You go right ahead, squire," said Steve soothingly. "I know just how you feel, and I guess talking's not going to do any harm. Act as if I wasn't here. Look on it as a monologue. I don't amount to anything."

"When did you go to the house last, Steve?"

Steve reflected.

"About a couple of weeks ago, I reckon."

"See the kid?"

Steve shook his head.

"Seeing his nibs ain't my long suit these days. I may be wrong, but I got the idea there was a dead-line for me about three blocks away from the nursery. I asked Keggs was the coast clear, but he said the Porter dame was in the ring, so I kind of thought I'd better away. I don't seem to fit in with all them white tiles and thermometers."

"You used to see him every day when we were here. And you didn't seem to contaminate him, as far as any one could notice."

There was a silence.

"Do you see him often, colonel?"

Kirk laughed.

"Oh, yes. I'm favoured. I pay a state visit every day. Think of that! I sit in a chair at the other end of the room while Mrs. Porter stands between to see that I don't start anything. Bill plays with his sterilized bricks. Occasionally he and I exchange a few civil words. It's as jolly and sociable as you could want. We have great times."

"Say, on the level, I wonder you stand for it."

"I've got to stand for it."

"He's your kid."

"Not exclusively. I have a partner, Steve."

Steve snorted dolefully.

"Ain't it hell the way things break loose in this world!" he sighed. "Who'd have thought two years ago—"

"Do you make it only two? I should have put it at about two thousand."

"Honest, squire, if any one had told me then that Miss Ruth had it in her to take up with all these fool stunts—"

"Well, I can't say I was prepared for it."

Steve coughed again. Kirk was in an expansive mood this afternoon, and the occasion was ideal for the putting forward of certain views which he had long wished to impart. But, on the other hand, the subject was a peculiarly delicate one. It has been well said that it is better for a third party to quarrel with a buzz-saw than to interfere between husband and wife; and Steve was constitutionally averse to anything that savoured of butting in.

Still, Kirk had turned the talk into this channel. He decided to risk it.

"If I were you," he said, "I'd get busy and start something."

"Such as what?"

Steve decided to abandon caution and speak his mind. Him, almost as much as Kirk, the existing state of things had driven to desperation. Though in a sense he was only a spectator, the fact that the altered conditions of Kirk's life involved his almost complete separation from Mamie gave him what might be called a stake in the affair. The brief and rare glimpses which he got of her nowadays made it absolutely impossible for him to conduct his wooing on a business-like basis. A diffident man cannot possibly achieve any success in odd moments. Constant propinquity is his only hope.

That fact alone, he considered, almost gave him the right to interfere. And, apart from that, his affection for Kirk and Ruth gave him a claim. Finally, he held what was practically an official position in the family councils on the strength of being William Bannister Winfield's godfather.

He loved William Bannister as a son, and it had been one of his favourite day dreams to conjure up a vision of the time when he should be permitted to undertake the child's physical training. He had toyed lovingly with the idea of imparting to this promising pupil all that he knew of the greatest game on earth. He had watched him in the old days staggering about the studio, and had pictured him grown to his full strength, his muscles trained, his brain full of the wisdom of one who, if his mother had not kicked, would have been middle-weight champion of America.

He had resigned himself to the fact that the infant's social status made it impossible that he should be the real White Hope whom he had once pictured beating all comers in the roped ring; but, after all, there was a certain mild fame to be acquired even by an amateur. And now that dream was over – unless Kirk could be goaded into strong action in time.

"Why don't you sneak the kid away somewhere?" he suggested. "Why don't you go right in at them and say: 'It's my kid, and I'm going to take him away into the country out of all this white-tile stuff and let him roll in the mud same as he used to.' Why, say, there's that shack of yours in Connecticut, just made for it. That kid would have the time of his life there."

"You think that's the solution, do you, Steve?"

"I'm dead sure it is." Steve's voice became more and more enthusiastic as the idea unfolded itself. "Why, it ain't only the kid I'm thinking of. There's Miss Ruth. Say, you don't mind me pulling this line of talk?"

"Go ahead. I began it. What about Miss Ruth?"

"Well, you know just what's the matter with her. She's let this society game run away with her. I guess she started it because she felt lonesome when you were away; and now it's got her and she can't drop it. All she wants is a jolt. It would slow her up and show her just where she was. She's asking for it. One good, snappy jolt would put the whole thing right. And this thing of jerking the kid away to Connecticut would be the right dope, believe *me*."

Kirk shook his head.

"It wouldn't do, Steve. It isn't that I don't want to do it; but one must play to the rules. I can't explain what I mean. I can only say it's impossible. Let's think of a parallel case. When you were in the ring, there must have been times when you had a chance of hitting your man low. Why didn't you do it? It would have jolted him, all right."

"Why, I'd have lost on a foul."

"Well, so should I lose on a foul if I started the sort of roughhouse you suggest."

"I don't get you."

"Well, if you want it in plain English, Ruth would never forgive me. Is that clear enough?"

"You're dead wrong, boss," said Steve excitedly. "I know her."

"I thought I did. Well, anyway, Steve, thanks for the suggestion; but, believe me, nothing doing. And now, if you feel like it, I wish you would resume your celebrated imitation of a man exulting over the fact that he is wearing Middleton's Undeniable. There isn't much more to do, and I should like to get through with it to-day, if possible. There, hold that pose. It's exactly right. The honest man gloating over his suspenders. You ought to go on the stage, Steve."

Chapter 7
Cutting the Tangled Knot

There are some men whose mission in life it appears to be to go about the world creating crises in the lives of other people. When there is thunder in the air they precipitate the thunderbolt.

Bailey Bannister was one of these. He meant extraordinarily well, but he was a dangerous man for that very reason, and in a properly constituted world would have been segregated or kept under supervision. He would not leave the tangled lives of those around him to adjust themselves. He blundered in and tried to help. He nearly always produced a definite result, but seldom the one at which he aimed.

That he should have interfered in the affairs of Ruth and Kirk at this time was, it must be admitted, unselfish of him, for just now he was having troubles of his own on a somewhat extensive scale. His wife's extravagance was putting a strain on his finances, and he was faced with the choice of checking her or increasing his income. Being very much in love, he shrank from the former task and adopted the other way out of the difficulty.

It was this that had led to the change in his manner noticed by Steve. In order to make more money he had had to take risks, and only recently had he begun to perceive how extremely risky these risks were. For the first time in its history the firm of Bannister was making first-hand acquaintance with frenzied finance.

It is, perhaps, a little unfair to lay the blame for this entirely at the door of Bailey's Sybil. Her extravagance was largely responsible; but Bailey's newly found freedom was also a factor in the developments of the firm's operations. If you keep a dog, a dog with a high sense of his abilities and importance, tied up and muzzled for a length of time and then abruptly set it free the chances are that it will celebrate its freedom. This had happened in the case of Bailey.

Just as her father's money had caused Ruth to plunge into a whirl of pleasures which she did not really enjoy, merely for the novelty of it, so the death of John Bannister and his own consequent accession to the throne had upset Bailey's balance and embarked him on an orgy of speculation quite foreign to his true nature. All their lives Ruth and Bailey had been repressed by their father, and his removal had unsteadied them.

Bailey, on whom the shadow of the dead man had pressed particularly severely, had been quite intoxicated by sudden freedom. He had been a cipher in the firm of Bannister & Son. In the firm of Bannister & Co. he was an untrammelled despot. He did that which was right in his own eyes, and there was no one to say him nay.

It was true that veteran members of the firm, looking in the glass, found white hairs where no white hairs had been and wrinkles on foreheads which, under the solid rule of old John Bannister, had been smooth; but it would have taken more than these straws to convince Bailey that the wind which was blowing was an ill-wind. He had developed in a day the sublime self-confidence of a young Napoleon. He was all dash and enterprise – the hurricane fighter of Wall Street.

With these private interests to occupy him, it is surprising that he should have found time to take the affairs of Ruth and Kirk in hand. But he did.

For some time he had watched the widening gulf between them with pained solicitude. He disliked Kirk personally; but that did not influence him. He conceived it to be his duty to suppress private prejudices. Duty seemed to call him to go to Kirk's aid and smooth out his domestic difficulties.

What urged him to this course more than anything else was Ruth's growing intimacy with Basil Milbank; for, in the period which had elapsed since the conversation recorded earlier in the story, when Kirk had first made the other's acquaintance, the gifted Basil had become a very important and menacing figure in Ruth's life.

To Ruth, as to most women, his gifts were his attraction. He danced well; he talked well; he did everything well. He appealed to a side of Ruth's nature which Kirk scarcely touched – a side which had only come into prominence in the last year.

His manner was admirable. He suggested sympathy without expressing it. He could convey to Ruth that he thought her a misunderstood and neglected wife while talking to her about the weather. He could make his own knight-errant attitude toward her perfectly plain without saying a word, merely by playing soft music to her on the piano; for he had the gift of saying more with his finger-tips than most men could have said in a long speech carefully rehearsed.

Kirk's inability to accompany Ruth into her present life had given Basil his chance. Into the gap which now lay between them he had slipped with a smooth neatness born of experience.

Bailey hated Basil. Men, as a rule, did, without knowing why. Basil's reputation was shady, without being actually bad. He was a suspect who had never been convicted. New York contained several husbands who eyed him askance, but could not verify their suspicions, and the apparent hopelessness of ever doing so made them look on Basil as a man who had carried smoothness into the realms of fine art. He was considered too gifted to be wholesome. The men of his set, being for the most part amiably stupid, resented his cleverness.

Bailey, just at present, was feeling strongly on the subject of Basil. He was at that stage of his married life when he would have preferred his Sybil to speak civilly to no other man than himself. And only yesterday Sybil had come to him to inform him with obvious delight that Basil Milbank had invited her to join his yacht party for a lengthy voyage.

This had stung Bailey. He was not included in the invitation. The whole affair struck him as sinister. It was true that Sybil had never shown any sign of being fascinated by Basil; but, he told himself, there was no knowing. He forbade Sybil to accept the invitation. To soothe her disappointment, he sent her off then and there to Tiffany's with a roving commission to get what she liked; for Bailey, the stern, strong man, the man who knew when to put his foot down, was no tyrant. But he would have been indignant at the suggestion that he had bribed Sybil to refuse Basil's invitation.

One of the arguments which Sybil had advanced in the brief discussion which had followed the putting down of Bailey's foot had been that Ruth had been invited and accepted, so why should not she? Bailey had not replied to this – it was at this point of the proceedings that the Tiffany motive had been introduced, but he had not forgotten it. He thought it over, and decided to call upon Ruth. He did so.

It was unfortunate that the nervous strain of being the Napoleon of Wall Street had had the effect of increasing to a marked extent the portentousness of Bailey's always portentous manner. Ruth rebelled against it. There was an insufferable suggestion of ripe old age and fatherliness in his attitude which she found irritating in the extreme. All her life she had chafed at authority, and now, when Bailey set himself up as one possessing it, she showed the worst side of herself to him.

He struck this unfortunate note from the very beginning.

"Ruth," he said, "I wish to speak seriously to you."

Ruth looked at him with hostile eyes, but did not speak. He did not know it, poor man, but he had selected an exceedingly bad moment for his lecture. It so happened that, only half an hour before, she and Kirk had come nearer to open warfare than they had ever come.

It had come about in this way. Kirk had slept badly the night before, and, as he lay awake in the small hours, his conscience had troubled him.

Had he done all that it was in him to do to bridge the gap between Ruth and himself? That was what his conscience had wanted to know. The answer was in the negative. On the following day, just before Bailey's call, he accordingly sought Ruth out, and – rather nervously, for Ruth made him feel nervous nowadays – suggested that he and she and William Bannister should take the air in each other's company and go and feed the squirrels in the park.

Ruth declined. It is possible that she declined somewhat curtly. The day was close and oppressive, and she had a headache and a general feeling of ill-will toward her species. Also, in her heart, she considered that the scheme proposed smacked too much of Sunday afternoon domesticity in Brooklyn. The idea of papa, mamma, and baby sporting together in a public park offended her sense of the social proprieties.

She did not reveal these thoughts to Kirk because she was more than a little ashamed of them. A year ago, she knew, she would not have objected to the idea. A year ago such an expedition would have been a daily occurrence with her. Now she felt if William Bannister wished to feed squirrels, Mamie was his proper companion.

She could not put all this baldly to Kirk, so she placed the burden of her refusal on the adequate shoulders of Lora Delane Porter. Aunt Lora, she said, would never hear of William Bannister wandering at large in such an unhygienic fashion. Upon which Kirk, whose patience was not so robust as it had been, and who, like Ruth, found the day oppressive and making for irritability, had cursed Aunt Lora heartily, given it as his opinion that between them she and Ruth were turning the child from a human being into a sort of spineless, effeminate exhibit in a museum, and had taken himself off to the studio muttering disjointed things.

Ruth was still quivering with the indignation of a woman who has been cheated of the last word when Bailey appeared and announced that he wished to speak seriously to her.

Bailey saw the hostility in her eyes and winced a little before it. He was not feeling altogether at his ease. He had had experience of Ruth in this mood, and she had taught him to respect it.

But he was not going to shirk his duty. He resumed:

"I am only speaking for your own good," he said. "I know that it is nothing but thoughtlessness on your part, but I am naturally anxious—"

"Bailey," interrupted Ruth, "get to the point."

Bailey drew a long breath.

"Well, then," he said, baulked of his preamble, and rushing on his fate, "I think you see too much of Basil Milbank."

Ruth raised her eyebrows.

"Oh?"

The mildness of her tone deceived Bailey.

"I do not like to speak of these things," he went on more happily; "but I feel that I must. It is my duty. Basil Milbank has not a good reputation. He is not the sort of man who – ah – who – in fact, he has not a good reputation."

"Oh?"

"I understand that he has invited you to form one of his yacht party."

"How did you know?"

"Sybil told me. He invited her. I refused to allow her to accept the invitation."

"And what did Sybil say?"

"She was naturally a little disappointed, of course, but she did as I requested."

"I wonder she didn't pack her things and go straight off."

"My dear Ruth!"

"That is what I should have done."

"You don't know what you are saying."

"Oh? Do you think I should let Kirk dictate to me like that?"

"He is certain to disapprove of your going when he hears of the invitation. What will you do?"

Ruth's eyes opened. For a moment she looked almost ugly.

"What shall I do? Why, go, of course."

She clenched her teeth. A woman's mind can work curiously, and she was associating Kirk with Bailey in what she considered an unwarrantable intrusion into her private affairs. It was as if Kirk, and not Bailey, were standing there, demanding that she should not associate with Basil Milbank.

"I shall make it my business," said Bailey, "to warn Kirk that this man is not a desirable companion for you."

The discussion of this miserable yacht affair had brought back to Bailey all the jealousy which he had felt when Sybil had first told him of it. All the vague stories he had ever heard about Basil were surging in his mind like waves of some corrosive acid. He had become a leading member of the extreme wing of the anti-Milbank party. He regarded Basil with the aversion which a dignified pigeon might feel for a circling hawk; and he was now looking on this yacht party as a deadly peril from which Ruth must be saved at any cost.

"I shall speak to him very strongly," he added.

Ruth's suppressed anger blazed up in the sudden way which before now had disconcerted her brother.

"Bailey, what do you mean by coming here and saying this sort of thing? You're becoming a perfect old woman. You spend your whole time prying into other people's affairs. I'm sorry for Sybil."

Bailey cast one reproachable look at her and left the room with pained dignity. Something seemed to tell him that no good could come to him from a prolongation of the interview. Ruth, in this mood, always had been too much for him, and always would be. Well, he had done his duty as far as he was concerned. It now remained to do the same by Kirk.

He hailed a taxi and drove to the studio.

Kirk was busy and not anxious for conversation, least of all with Bailey. He had not forgotten their last *tete-a-tete*.

Bailey, however, was regarding him with a feeling almost of friendliness. They were bound together by a common grievance against Basil Milbank.

"I came here, Winfield," he said, after a few moments of awkward conversation on neutral topics, "because I understand that this man Milbank has invited Ruth to join his yacht party."

"What yacht party?"

"This man Milbank is taking a party for a cruise shortly in his yacht."

"Who is Milbank?"

"Surely you have met him? Yes, he was at my house one night when you and Ruth dined there shortly after your return."

"I don't remember him. However, it doesn't matter. But why does the fact that he has asked Ruth on his yacht excite you? Are you nervous about the sea?"

"I dislike this man Milbank very much, Winfield. I think Ruth sees too much of him."

Kirk stiffened. His eyebrows rose the fraction of an inch.

"Oh?" he said.

It seemed to Bailey for an instant that he had been talking all his life to people who raised their eyebrows and said "Oh!" but he continued manfully.

"I do not think that Ruth should know him, Winfield."

"Wouldn't Ruth be rather a good judge of that?"

His tone nettled Bailey, but the man conscious of doing his duty acquires an artificial thickness of skin, and he controlled himself. But he had lost that feeling of friendliness, of sympathy with a brother in misfortune which he had brought in with him.

"I disagree with you entirely," he said.

"Another thing," went on Kirk. "If this man Milbank – I still can't place him – is such a thug, or whatever it is that he happens to be, how did he come to be at your house the night you say I met him?"

Bailey winced. He wished the world was not perpetually reminding him that Basil and Sybil were on speaking terms.

"Sybil invited him. I may say he has asked Sybil to make one of the yacht party. I absolutely forbade it."

"But, Heavens! What's wrong with the man?"

"He has a bad reputation."

"Has he, indeed!"

"And I wish my wife to associate with him as little as possible. And I should advise you to forbid Ruth to see more of him than she can help."

Kirk laughed. The idea struck him as comic.

"My good man, I don't forbid Ruth to do things."

Bailey, objecting to being called any one's good man, especially Kirk's, permitted his temper to get the better of him.

"Then you should," he snapped. "I have no wish to quarrel with you. I came in here in a friendly spirit to warn you; but I must say that for a man who married a girl, as you married Ruth, in direct opposition to the wishes of her family, you take a curious view of your obligations. Ruth has always been a headstrong, impulsive girl, and it is for you to see that she is protected from herself. If you are indifferent to her welfare, then all I can say is that you should not have married her. You appear to think otherwise. Good afternoon."

He stalked out of the studio, leaving Kirk uncomfortably conscious that he had had the worst of the argument. Bailey had been officious, no doubt, and his pompous mode of expression was not soothing, but there was no doubt that he had had right on his side.

Marrying Ruth did not involve obligations. He had never considered her in that light, but perhaps she was a girl who had to be protected from herself. She was certainly impulsive. Bailey had been right there, if nowhere else.

Who was this fellow Milbank who had sprung suddenly from nowhere into the position of a menace? What were Ruth's feelings toward him? Kirk threw his mind back to the dinner-party at Bailey's and tried to place him.

Was it the man – yes, he had it now. It was the man with the wave of hair over his forehead, the fellow who looked like a poet. Memory came to him with a rush. He recalled his instinctive dislike for the fellow.

So that was Milbank, was it? He got up and put away his brushes. There would be no more work for him that afternoon.

He walked slowly home. The heat of the day had grown steadily more oppressive. It was one of those airless, stifling afternoons which afflict New York in the summer. He remembered seeing something about a record in the evening paper which he had bought on his way to the studio, a whole column about heat and humidity. It certainly felt unusually warm even for New York.

It was one of those days when nerves are strained, when mole-hills become mountains, and mountains are all Everests. He had felt it when he talked with Ruth about Bill and the squirrels, and he felt it now. He was conscious of being extraordinarily irritated, not so much with any particular person as with the world in general. The very vagueness of Bailey's insinuations against Basil Milbank increased his resentment.

What a pompous ass Bailey was! What a fool he had been to give Bailey such a chance of snubbing him! What an extraordinarily futile and unpleasant world it was altogether!

He braced himself with an effort. It was this heat which was making him magnify trifles. Bailey was a fool. Probably there was nothing whatever wrong with this fellow Milbank. Probably he had some personal objection to the man, and that was all.

And yet the image of Basil which had come back to his mind was not reassuring. He had mistrusted him that night, and he mistrusted him now.

What should he do? Ruth was not Sybil. She was not the sort of woman a man could forbid to do things. It would require tact to induce her to refuse Basil's invitation.

As he reached the door an idea came to him, so simple that he wondered that it had not occurred to him before. It was, perhaps, an echo of his conversation with Steve.

He would get Ruth to come away with him to the shack in the Connecticut woods. As he dwelt on the idea the heat of the day seemed to become less oppressive and his heart leaped. How cool and pleasant it would be out there! They would take Bill with them and live the simple life again, in the country this time instead of in town. Perhaps out there, far away from the over-crowded city, he and Ruth would be able to come to an understanding and bridge over that ghastly gulf.

As for his work, he could do that as well in the woods as in New York. And, anyhow, he had earned a vacation. For days Mr. Penway had been hinting that the time had arrived for a folding of the hands.

Mr. Penway's views on New York and its record humidity were strong and crisply expressed. His idea, he told Kirk, was that some sport with a heart should loan him a couple of hundred bucks and let him beat it to the seashore before he melted.

169

In the drawing-room Ruth was playing the piano softly, as she had done so often at the studio. Kirk went to her and kissed her. A marked coolness in her reception of the kiss increased the feeling of nervousness which he had felt at the sight of her. It came back to him that they had parted that afternoon, for the first time, on definitely hostile terms.

He decided to ignore the fact. Something told him that Ruth had not forgotten, but it might be that cheerfulness now would blot out the resentment of past irritability.

But in his embarrassment he was more than cheerful. As Steve had been on the occasion of his visit to old John Bannister, he was breezy, breezy with an effort that was as painful to Ruth as it was to himself, breezy with a horrible musical comedy breeziness.

He could have adopted no more fatal tone with Ruth at that moment. All the afternoon she had been a complicated tangle of fretted nerves. Her quarrel with Kirk, Bailey's visit, a conscience that would not lie down and go to sleep at her orders, but insisted on running riot – all these things had unfitted her to bear up amiably under sudden, self-conscious breeziness.

And the heat of the day, charged now with the oppressiveness of long-overdue thunder, completed her mood. When Kirk came in and began to speak, the softest notes of the human voice would have jarred upon her. And Kirk, in his nervousness, was almost shouting.

His voice rang through the room, and Ruth winced away from it like a stricken thing. From out of the hell of nerves and heat and interfering brothers there materialized itself, as she sat there, a very vivid hatred of Kirk.

Kirk, meanwhile, uneasy, but a little guessing at the fury behind Ruth's calm face, was expounding his great scheme, his panacea for all the ills of domestic misunderstandings and parted lives.

"Ruth, old girl."

Ruth shuddered.

"Ruth, old girl, I've had a bully good idea. It's getting too warm for anything in New York. Did you ever feel anything like it is to-day? Why shouldn't you and I pop down to the shack and camp out there for a week or so? And we would take Bill with us. Just we three, with somebody to do the cooking. It would be great. What do you say?"

What Ruth said languidly was: "It's quite impossible."

It was damping; but Kirk felt that at all costs he must refuse to be damped. He clutched at his cheerfulness and held it.

"Nonsense," he retorted. "Why is it impossible? It's a great idea."

Ruth half hid a yawn. She knew she was behaving abominably, and she was glad of it.

"It's impossible as far as I'm concerned. I have a hundred things to do before I can leave New York."

"Well, I could do with a day or two to clear up a few bits of work I have on hand. Why couldn't we start this day week?"

"It is out of the question for me. About then I shall be on Mr. Milbank's yacht. He has invited me to join his party. The actual day is not settled, but it will be in about a week's time."

"Oh!" said Kirk.

Ruth said nothing.

"Have you accepted the invitation?"

"I have not actually answered his letter. I was just going to when you came in."

"But you mean to accept it?"

"Certainly. Several of my friends will be there. Sybil for one."

"Not Sybil."

"Oh, I know Bailey has made some ridiculous objection to her going, but I mean to persuade her."

Kirk did not answer. She looked at him steadily.

"So Bailey did call on you this afternoon? He told me he was going to, but I hoped he would think better of it. But apparently there are no limits to Bailey's stupidity."

"Yes, Bailey came to the studio. He seemed troubled about this yacht party."

"Did he advise you to forbid me to go?"

"Well, yes; he did."

"And now you have come to do it?"

"Not at all. I told Bailey that you were not the sort of woman one forbade to do things."

"I'm not."

There was a pause.

"All the same, I wish you wouldn't go."

Ruth did not answer.

"It would be very jolly out at the shack."

Ruth shuddered elaborately and gave a little laugh.

"Would it? It's rather a question of taste. Personally, I can't imagine anything more depressing and uncomfortable than being cooped up in a draughty frame house miles away from anywhere. There's no reason why you should not go, though, if you like that sort of thing. Of course, you must not take Bill."

"Why not?"

Kirk spoke calmly enough, but he was very near the breaking point. All his good resolutions had vanished under the acid of Ruth's manner.

"I couldn't let him rough it like that. Aunt Lora would have a fit."

Conditions being favourable, it only needs a spark to explode a powder magazine; and there are moments when a word can turn an outwardly calm and patient man into a raging maniac. This introduction of Mrs. Porter's name into the discussion at this particular point broke down the last remnants of Kirk's self-control.

For a few seconds his fury so mastered him that he could not speak. Then, suddenly, the storm passed and he found himself cool and venomous. He looked at Ruth curiously. It seemed incredible to him that he had ever loved her.

"We had better get this settled," he said in a hard, quiet voice.

Ruth started. She had never heard him speak like this before. She had not imagined him capable of speaking in that way. Even in the days when she had loved him most she had never looked up to him. She had considered his nature weak, and she had loved his weakness. Except in the case of her father, she had always dominated the persons with whom she mixed; and she had taken it for granted that her will was stronger than Kirk's. Something in his voice now told her that she had under-estimated him.

"Get what settled?" she asked, and was furious with herself because her voice shook.

"Is Mrs. Porter the mother of the child, or are you? What has Mrs. Porter to do with it? Why should I ask her permission? How does it happen to be any business of Mrs. Porter's at all?"

Ruth felt baffled. He was giving her no chance to take the offensive. There was nothing in his tone which she could openly resent. He was not shouting at her, he was speaking quietly. There was nothing for her to do but answer the question, and she knew that her answer would give him another point in the contest. Even as she spoke she knew that her words were ridiculous.

"Aunt Lora has been wonderful with him. No child could have been better looked after."

"I know she has used him as a vehicle for her particular form of insanity, but that's not the point. What I am asking is why she was introduced at all."

"I told you. When you were away, Bill nearly—"

"Died. I know. I'm not forgetting that. And naturally for a time you were frightened. It is just possible that for the moment you lost your head and honestly thought that Mrs. Porter's methods were the only chance for him. But that state of mind could not last all the time with you. You are not a crank like your aunt. You are a perfectly sensible, level-headed woman. And you must have seen the idiocy of it all long before I came back. Why did you let it go on?"

Ruth did not answer.

"I will tell you why. Because it saved you trouble. Because it gave you more leisure for the sort of futile waste of time which seems to be the only thing you care for nowadays. Don't trouble to deny it. Do you think I haven't seen in these last few months that Bill bores you to death? Oh, I know you always have some perfect excuse for keeping away from him. It's too much trouble for you to be a mother to him, so you hedge with your conscience by letting Mrs. Porter pamper him and sterilize his toys and all the rest of it, and try to make yourself think that you have done your duty to him. You know that, as far as everything goes that matters, any tenement child is better off than Bill."

"I—"

"You had better let me finish what I have got to say. I will be as brief as I can. That is my case as regards Bill. Now about myself. What do you think I am made of? I've stood it just as long as I could; you have tried me too hard. I'm through. Heaven knows why it should have come to this. It is not so very long ago that Bill was half the world to you and I was the other half. Now, apparently, there is not room in your world for either of us."

Ruth had risen. She was trembling.

"I think we had better end this."

He broke in on her words.

"End it? Yes, you're right. One way or the other. Either go back to the old life or start a new one. What we are living now is a horrible burlesque."

"What do you mean? How start a new life?"

"I mean exactly what I say. In the life you are living now I am an anachronism. I'm a survival. I'm out of date and in the way. You would be freer without me."

"That's absurd."

"Is the idea so novel? Is our marriage the only failure in New York?"

"Do you mean that we ought to separate?"

"Only a little more, a very little more, than we are separated now. Never see each other again instead of seeing each other for a few minutes every day. It's not a very big step to take."

Ruth sat down and rested her chin on her hand, staring at nothing. Kirk went to the window and looked out.

Over the park the sky was black. In the room behind him the light had faded till it seemed as if night were come. The air was heavy and stifling. A flicker of lightning came and went in the darkness over the trees.

He turned abruptly.

"It is the only reasonable thing to do. Our present mode of life is a farce. We are drifting farther apart every day. Perhaps I have changed. I know you have. We are two strangers chained together. We have made a muddle of it, and the best thing we can do is to admit it.

"I am no good to you. I have no part in your present life. You're the queen and I'm just the prince consort, the fellow who happens to be Mrs. Winfield's husband. It's not a pleasant part to have to play, and I have had enough of it. We had better separate before we hate each other. You have your amusements. I have my work. We can continue them apart. We shall both be better off."

He stopped. Ruth did not speak. She was still sitting in the same attitude. It was too dark to see her face. It formed a little splash of white in the dusk. She did not move.

Kirk went to the door.

"I'm going up to say good-bye to Bill. Have you anything to say against that? And I shall say good-bye to him in my own way."

She made no sign that she had heard him.

"Good-bye," he said again.

The door closed.

Up in the nursery Bill crooned to himself as he played on the floor. Mamie sat in a chair, sewing. The opening of the door caused them to look up simultaneously.

"Hello," said Bill.

His voice was cordial without being enthusiastic. He was glad to see Kirk, but tin soldiers were tin soldiers and demanded concentrated attention. When you are in the middle of intricate manoeuvres you cannot allow yourself to be more than momentarily distracted by anything.

"Mamie," said Kirk hoarsely, "go out for a minute, will you? I shan't be long."

Mamie obediently departed. Later, when Keggs was spreading the news of Kirk's departure in the servants' hall, she remembered that his manner had struck her as strange.

Kirk sat down in the chair she had left and looked at Bill. He felt choked. There was a mist before his eyes.

"Bill."

The child, absorbed in his game, did not look up.

"Bill, old man, come here a minute. I've something to say."

Bill looked up, nodded, moved a couple of soldiers, and got up. He came to Kirk's side. His chosen mode of progression at this time was a kind of lurch. He was accustomed to breathe heavily during the journey, and on arrival at the terminus usually shouted triumphantly.

Kirk put an arm round him. Bill stared gravely up into his face. There was a silence. From outside came a sudden rumbling crash. Bill jumped.

"Funder," he said in a voice that shook a little.

"Not afraid of thunder, are you?" said Kirk.

Bill shook his head stoutly.

"Bill."

"Yes, daddy?"

Kirk fought to keep his voice steady.

"Bill, old man, I'm afraid you won't see me again for some time. I'm going away."

"In a ship?"

"No, not in a ship."

"In a train?"

"Perhaps."

"Take me with you, daddy."

"I'm afraid I can't, Bill."

"Shan't I ever see you again?"

Kirk winced. How direct children are! What was it they called it in the papers? "The custody of the child." How little it said and how much it meant!

The sight of Bill's wide eyes and quivering mouth reminded him that he was not the only person involved in the tragedy of those five words. He pulled himself together. Bill was waiting anxiously for an answer to his question. There was no need to make Bill unhappy before his time.

"Of course you will," he said, trying to make his voice cheerful.

"Of course I will," echoed Bill dutifully.

Kirk could not trust himself to speak again. The old sensation of choking had come back to him. The room was a blur.

He caught Bill to him in a grip that made the child cry out, held him for a long minute, then put him gently down and made blindly for the door.

The storm had burst by the time Kirk found himself in the street. The thunder crashed and great spears of lightning flashed across the sky. A few heavy drops heralded the approach of the rain, and before he had reached the corner it was beating down in torrents.

He walked on, raising his face to the storm, finding in it a curious relief. A magical coolness had crept into the air, and with it a strange calm into his troubled mind. He looked back at the scene through which he had passed as at something infinitely remote. He could not realize distinctly what had happened. He was only aware that everything was over, that with a few words he had broken his life into small pieces. Too impatient to unravel the tangled knot, he had cut it, and nothing could mend it now.

"Why?"

The rain had ceased as suddenly as it had begun. The sun was struggling through a mass of thin cloud over the park. The world was full of the drip and rush of water. All that had made the day oppressive and strained nerves to breaking point had gone, leaving peace behind. Kirk felt like one waking from an evil dream.

"Why did it happen?" he asked himself. "What made me do it?"

A distant rumble of thunder answered the question.

CHAPTER 8
STEVE TO THE RESCUE

IT is an unfortunate fact that, when a powder-magazine explodes, the damage is not confined to the person who struck the match, but extends to the innocent bystanders. In the present case it was Steve Dingle who sustained the worst injuries.

Of the others who might have been affected, Mrs. Lora Delane Porter was bomb-proof. No explosion in her neighbourhood could shake her. She received the news of Kirk's outbreak with composure. Privately, in her eugenic heart, she considered his presence super-fluous now that William Bannister was safely launched upon his career.

In the drama of which she was the self-appointed stage-director, Kirk was a mere super supporting the infant star. Her great mind, occupied almost entirely by the past and the future, took little account of the present. So long as Kirk did not interfere with her management of Bill, he was at liberty, so far as she was concerned, to come or go as he pleased.

Steve could not imitate her admirable detachment. He was a poor philosopher, and all that his mind could grasp was that Kirk was in trouble and that Ruth had apparently gone mad.

The affair did not come to his ears immediately. He visited the studio at frequent intervals and found Kirk there, working hard and showing no signs of having passed through a crisis which had wrecked his life. He was quiet, it is true, but then he was apt to be quiet nowadays.

Probably, if it had not been for Keggs, he would have been kept in ignorance of what had happened for a time.

Walking one evening up Broadway, he met Keggs taking the air and observing the night-life of New York like himself.

Keggs greeted Steve with enthusiasm. He liked Steve, and it was just possible that Steve might not have heard about the great upheaval. He suggested a drink at a neighbouring saloon.

"We have not seen you at our house lately, Mr. Dingle," he re-marked, having pecked at his glass of beer like an old, wise bird.

He looked at Steve with a bright eye, somewhat puffy at the lids, but full of life.

"No," said Steve. "That's right. Guess I must have been busy."

Keggs uttered a senile chuckle and drank more beer.

"They're rum uns," he went on. "I've been in some queer places, but this beats 'em all."

"What do you mean?" inquired Steve, as a second chuckle escaped his companion.

"Why, it's come to an 'ead, things has, Mr. Dingle. That's what I mean. You won't have forgotten all about the pampering of that child what I told you of quite recent. Well, it's been and come to an 'ead."

"Yes? Continue, colonel. This listens good."

"You ain't 'eard?"

"Not a word."

Keggs smiled a happy smile and sipped his beer. It did the old man good, finding an entirely new audience like this.

"Why, Mr. Winfield 'as packed up and left."

Steve gasped.

"Left!" he cried. "Not *quit?* Not gone for good?"

"For his own good, I should say. Finds himself better off away from it all, if you ask me. But 'adn't you reelly heard, Mr. Dingle? God bless my soul! I thought it was public property by now, that little bit of noos. Why, Mr. Winfield 'asn't been living with us for the matter of a week or more."

"For the love of Mike!"

"I'm telling you the honest truth, Mr. Dingle. Two weeks ago come next Saturday Mr. Winfield meets me in the 'all looking wild and 'arassed – it was the same day there was that big thunder-storm – and he looks at me, glassy like, and says to me: 'Keggs, 'ave my bag packed and my boxes, too; I'm going away for a time. I'll send a messenger for 'em.' And out he goes into the rain, which begins to come down cats and dogs the moment he was in the street.

"I start to go out after him with his rain-coat, thinking he'd get wet before he could find a cab, they being so scarce in this city, not like London, where you simply 'ave to raise your 'and to 'ave a dozen flocking round you, but he don't stop; he just goes walking off through the rain and all, and I gets back into the house, not wishing to be wetted myself on account of my rheumatism, which is always troublesome in the damp weather. And I says to myself: "Ullo, 'ullo, 'ullo, what's all this?'

"See what I mean? I could tell as plain as if I'd been in the room with them that they had been having words. And since that day 'e ain't been near the 'ouse, and where he is now is more than I can tell you, Mr. Dingle."

"Why, he's at the studio."

"At the studio, is he? Well, I shouldn't wonder if he wasn't better off. 'E didn't strike me as a man what was used to the ways of society. He's happier where he is, I expect."

And, having summed matters up in this philosophical manner, Keggs drained his glass and cocked an expectant eye at Steve.

Steve obeyed the signal and ordered a further supply of the beer for which Mr. Keggs had a plebian and unbutlerlike fondness. His companion turned the conversation to the prospects of one of that group of inefficient middleweights whom Steve so heartily despised, between whom and another of the same degraded band a ten-round contest had been arranged and would shortly take place.

Ordinarily this would have been a subject on which Steve would have found plenty to say, but his mind was occupied with what he had just heard, and he sat silent while the silver-haired patron of sport opposite prattled on respecting current form.

Steve felt stunned. It was unthinkable that this thing had really occurred.

Mr. Keggs, sipping beer, discussed the coming fight. He weighed the alleged left hook of one principal against the much-advertised right swing of the other. He spoke with apprehension of a yellow streak which certain purists claimed to have discovered in the gladiator on whose chances he proposed to invest his cash.

Steve was not listening to him. A sudden thought had come to him, filling his mind to the exclusion of all else.

The recollection of his talk with Kirk at the studio had come back to him. He had advised Kirk, as a solution of his difficulties, to kidnap the child and take him to Connecticut. Well, Kirk was out of the running now, but he, Steve, was still in it.

He would do it himself.

The idea thrilled him. It was so in keeping with his theory of the virtue of the swift and immediate punch, administered with the minimum of preliminary sparring. There was a risk attached to the scheme which appealed to him. Above all, he honestly believed that it would achieve its object, the straightening out of the tangle which Ruth and Kirk had made of their lives.

When once an idea had entered Steve's head he was tenacious of it. He had come to the decision that Ruth needed what he called a jolt to bring her to herself, much as a sleep-walker is aroused by the touch of a hand, and he clung to it.

He interrupted Mr. Keggs in the middle of a speech touching on his man's alleged yellow streak.

"Will you be at home to-night, colonel?" he asked.

"I certainly will, Mr. Dingle."

"Mind if I look in?"

"I shall be delighted. I can offer you a cigar that I think you'll appreciate, and we can continue this little chat at our leisure. Mrs. Winfield's dining out, and that there Porter, thank Gawd, 'as gone to Boston."

CHAPTER 9
AT ONE IN THE MORNING

WILLIAM Bannister Winfield slept the peaceful sleep of childhood in his sterilized cot. The light gleamed faintly on the white tiles. It lit up the brass knobs on the walls, the spotless curtains, the large thermometer.

An intruder, interested in these things, would have seen by a glance at this last that the temperature of the room was exactly that recommended by doctors as the correct temperature for the nursery of a sleeping child; no higher, no lower. The transom over the door was closed, but the window was open at the top to precisely the extent advocated by the authorities, due consideration having been taken for the time of year and the condition of the outer atmosphere.

The hour was one in the morning.

Childhood is a readily adaptable time of life, and William Bannister, after a few days of blank astonishment, varied by open mutiny, had accepted the change in his surroundings and daily existence with admirable philosophy. His memory was not far-reaching, and, as time went on and he began to accommodate himself to the new situation, he had gradually forgotten the days at the studio, as, it is to be supposed, he had forgotten the clouds of glory which he had trailed on his entry into this world. If memories of past bear-hunts among the canvases on the dusty floor ever came to him now, he never mentioned it.

A child can weave romance into any condition of life in which fate places him; and William Bannister had managed to interest himself in his present existence with a considerable gusto. Scraps of conversation between Mrs. Porter and Mamie, overheard and digested, had given him a good working knowledge of the system of hygiene of which he was the centre. He was vague as to details, but not vaguer than most people.

He knew that something called "sterilizing" was the beginning and end of life, and that things known as germs were the Great Peril. He had expended much thought on the subject of germs. Mamie, questioned, could give him no more definite information than that they were "things which got at you and hurt you," and his awe of Mrs. Porter had kept him from going to the fountainhead of knowledge for further data.

Building on the information to hand, he had formed in his mind an odd kind of anthropomorphic image of the germ. He pictured it as a squat, thick-set man of repellent aspect and stealthy movements, who sneaked up on you when you were not looking and did unpleasant things to you, selecting as the time for his attacks those nights when you had allowed your attention to wander while saying your prayers.

On such occasions it was Bill's practice to fool him by repeating his prayers to himself in bed after the official ceremony. Some times, to make certain, he would do this so often that he fell asleep in mid-prayer.

He was always glad of the night-light. A germ hates light, preferring to do his scoundrelly work when it is so black that you can't see your hand in front of your face and the darkness presses down on you like a blanket. Occasionally a fear would cross his mind that the night-light might go out; but it never did, being one of Mr. Edison's best electric efforts neatly draped with black veiling.

Apart from this he had few worries, certainly none serious enough to keep him awake.

He was sleeping now, his head on his right arm, a sterilized Teddy-bear clutched firmly in his other hand, with the concentration of one engaged upon a feat at which he is an expert.

The door opened slowly. A head insinuated itself into the room, furtively, as if uncertain of its welcome. The door continued to open and Steve slipped in.

He closed the door as gently as he had opened it, and stood there glancing about him. A slow grin appeared upon his face, to be succeeded by an expression of serious resolve. For Steve was anxious.

It was still Steve's intention to remove, steal, purloin, and kidnap William Bannister that night, but now that the moment had come for doing it he was nervous.

He was not used to this sort of thing. He was an honest ex-middleweight, not a burglar; and just now he felt particularly burglarious. The stillness of the house oppressed him. He had not relished the long wait between the moment of his apparent departure and that of his entry into the nursery.

He had acted with simple cunning. He had remained talking pugilism with Keggs in the pantry till a prodigious yawn from his host had told him that the time was come for the breaking up of the party. Then, begging Keggs not to move, as he could find his way out, he had hurried to the back door, opened and shut it, and darted into hiding. Presently Keggs, yawning loudly, had toddled along the passage, bolted the door, and made his way upstairs to bed, leaving Steve to his vigil.

Steve's reflections during this period had not been of the pleasantest. Exactly what his explanation was to be, if by any mischance he should make a noise and be detected, he had been unable to decide. Finally he had dismissed the problem as insoluble, and had concentrated his mind on taking precautions to omit any such noise.

So far he had succeeded. He had found his way to the nursery easily enough, having marked the location earnestly on his previous visits. During the whole of his conversation with Keggs in the pantry he had been repeating to himself the magic formula which began: "First staircase to the left – turn to the right—" and here he was now at his goal and ready to begin.

But it was just this question of beginning which exercised him so grievously. How was he to begin? Should he go straight to the cot and wake the kid? Suppose the kid was scared and let out a howl?

A warm, prickly sensation about the forehead was Steve's silent comment on this reflection. He took a step forward and stopped again. He was conscious of tremors about the region of the spine.

The thought crossed his mind at that moment that burglars earned their money.

As he stood, hesitating, his problem was solved for him. There came a heavy sigh from the direction of the cot which made him start as if a pistol had exploded in his ear; and then he was aware of two large eyes staring at him.

There was a tense pause. A drop of perspiration rolled down his cheek-bone and anchored itself stickily on the angle of his jaw. It tickled abominably, but he did not dare to move for fear of unleashing the scream which brooded over the situation like a cloud.

At any moment now a howl of terror might rip the silence and bring the household on the run. And then – the explanations! A second drop of perspiration started out in the wake of the first.

The large eyes continued to inspect him. They were clouded with sleep. Suddenly a frightened look came into them, and, as he saw it, Steve braced his muscles for the shock.

"Here it comes!" he said miserably to himself. "Oh, Lord! We're off!"

He searched in his brain for speech, desperately, as the best man at a wedding searches for that ring while the universe stands still, waiting expectantly.

He found no speech.

The child's mouth opened. Steve eyed him, fascinated. No bird, encountering a snake, was ever so incapable of movement as he.

"Are you a germ?" inquired William Bannister.

Steve tottered to the cot and sat down on it. The relief was too much for him.

"Gee, kid!" he said, "you had my goat then. I've got to hand it to you."

His sudden approach had confirmed William Bannister's worst suspicions. This was precisely how he had expected the germ to behave. He shrank back on the pillow, gulping.

"Why, for the love of Mike," said Steve, "don't you know me, kid? I'm not a porch-climber. Don't you remember Steve who used to raise Hades with you at the studio? Darn it, I'm your godfather! I'm Steve!"

William Bannister sat up, partially reassured.

"What's Steve?" he inquired.

"I'm Steve."

"Why?"

"How do you mean – why?"

The large eyes inspected him gravely.

"I remember," he said finally.

"Well, don't go forgetting, kid. I couldn't stand a second session like that. I got a weak heart."

"You're Steve."

"That's right. Stick to that and we'll get along fine."

"I thought you were a germ."

"A what?"

"They get at you and hurt you."

"Who said so?"

"Mamie."

"Are you scared of germs?"

The White Hope nodded gravely.

"I have to be sterilized because of them. Are you sterilized?"

"Nobody ever told me so. But, say, kid, you don't want to be frightened of germs or microbes or bacilli or any of the rest of the circus. You don't want to be frightened of nothing. You're the White Hope, the bear-cat that ain't scared of anything on earth. What's this germ thing like, anyway?"

"It's a—I've never seen one, but Mamie says they get at you and hurt you. I think it's a kind of big sort of ugly man that creeps in when you're asleep."

"So that's why you thought I was one?"

The White Hope nodded.

"Forget it!" said Steve. "Mamie is a queen, all right, believe me, but she's got the wrong dope on this microbe proposition. You don't need to be scared of them any more. Why, some of me best pals are germs."

"What's pals?"

"Why, friends. You and me are pals. Me and your pop are pals."

"Where's pop?"

"He's gone away."

"I remember."

"He thought he needed a change of air. Don't you ever need a change of air?"

"I don't know."

"Well, you do. Take it from me. This is about the punkest joint I ever was in. You don't want to stay in a dairy-kitchen like this."

"What's dairy-kitchen?"

"This is. All these white tiles and fixings. It makes me feel like a pint of milk to look at 'em."

"It's because of the germs."

"Ain't I telling you the germs don't want to hurt you?"

"Aunt Lora told Mamie they do."

"Say, cull, you tell your Aunt Lora to make a noise like an ice-cream in the sun and melt away. She's a prune, and what she says don't go. Do you want to know what a germ or a microbe – it's the same thing – really is? It's a fellow that has the best time you can think of. They've been fooling you, kid. They saw you were easy, so they handed it to you on a plate. I'm the guy that can put you wise about microbes."

"Tell me."

"Sure. Well, a microbe is a kid that just runs wild out in the country. He don't have to hang around in a white-tiled nursery and eat sterilized junk and go to bed when they tell him to. He has a swell time out in the woods, fishing and playing around in the dirt and going after birds' eggs and picking berries, and – oh, shucks, anything else you can think of. Wouldn't you like to do that?"

William Bannister nodded.

"Well, say, as it happens, there's a fine chance for you to be a germ right away. I know a little place down in the Connecticut woods which would just hit you right. You could put on overalls—"

"What's overalls?"

"Sort of clothes. Not like the fussed-up scenery you have to wear now, but the real sort of clothes which you can muss up and nobody cares a darn. You can put 'em on and go out and tear up Jack like a regular kid all you want. Say, don't you remember the fool stunts you and me used to pull off in the studio?"

"What studio?"

"Gee! you're a bit shy on your English, ain't you? It makes it sort of hard for a guy to keep up what you might call a flow of talk. Still, you should worry. Why, don't you remember where you used to live before you came to this joint? Big, dusty sort of place, where you and me used to play around on the floor?"

The White Hope nodded.

"Well, wouldn't you like to do that again?"

"Yes."

"And be a regular microbe?"

"Yes."

Steve looked at his watch.

"Well, that's lucky," he said. "It happens to be exactly the right time for starting out to be one. That's curious, ain't it?"

"Yes."

"I've got a pal – friend, you know—"

"Is he a germ?"

"Sure. He's waiting for me now in an automobile in the park—"

"Why?"

"Because I asked him to. He owns a garage. Place where automobiles live, you know. I asked him to bring out a car and wait around near by, because I might be taking a pal of mine – that's you – for a ride into the country to-night. Of course, you don't have to come if you don't want to. Only it's mighty nice out there. You can spend all to-morrow rolling about in the grass and listening to the birds. I shouldn't wonder if we couldn't borrow a farmer's kid for you to play with. There's lots of them around. He should show you the best time you've had in months."

William Bannister's eyes gleamed. The finer points of the scheme were beginning to stand out before him with a growing clarity.

"Would I have to take my bib?" he asked excitedly.

Steve uttered a scornful laugh.

"No, *sir!* We don't wear bibs out there."

As far as William Bannister was concerned, this appeared to settle it. Of all the trials of his young life he hated most his bib.

"Let's go!"

Steve breathed a sigh of relief.

"Right, squire; we will," he said. "But I guess we had best leave a letter for Mamie, so's she won't be wondering where you've got to."

"Will Mamie be cross?"

"Not on your life. She'll be tickled to death."

He scribbled a few lines on a piece of paper and left them on the cot, from which William Bannister had now scrambled.

"Can you dress yourself?" asked Steve.

"Oh, yes." It was an accomplishment of which the White Hope was extremely proud.

"Well, go to it, then."

"Steve."

"Hello?"

"Won't it be a surprise for Mamie?"

"You bet it will. And she won't be the only one, at that."

"Will mother be surprised?"

"She sure will."

"And pop?"

"You bet!"

William Bannister chuckled delightedly.

"Ready?" said Steve.

"Yes."

"Now listen. We've got to get out of this joint as quiet as mice. It would spoil the surprise if they was to hear us and come out and ask what we were doing. Get that?"

"Yes."

"Well, see how quiet you can make it. You don't want even to breathe more than you can help."

They left the room and crept down the dark stairs. In the hall Steve lit a match and switched on the electric light. He unbolted the door and peered out into the avenue. Close by, under the trees, stood an automobile, its headlights staring into the night.

"Quick!" cried Steve.

He picked up the White Hope, closed the door, and ran.

CHAPTER 10
ACCEPTING THE GIFTS OF THE GODS

IT was fortunate, considering the magnitude of the shock which she was to receive, that circumstances had given Steve's Mamie unusual powers of resistance in the matter of shocks. For years before her introduction into the home of the Winfield family her life had been one long series of crises. She had never known what the morrow might bring forth, though experience had convinced her that it was pretty certain to bring forth something agitating which would call for all her well-known ability to handle disaster.

The sole care of three small brothers and a weak-minded father gives a girl exceptional opportunities of cultivating poise under difficult conditions. It had become second nature with Mamie to keep her head though the heavens fell.

Consequently, when she entered the nursery next morning and found it empty, she did not go into hysterics. She did not even scream. She read Steve's note twice very carefully, then sat down to think what was her best plan of action.

Her ingrained habit of looking on the bright side of things, the result of a life which, had pessimism been allowed to rule it, might have ended prematurely with what the papers are fond of calling a "rash act," led her to consider first those points in the situation which she labelled in her meditations as "bits of luck."

It was a bit of luck that Mrs. Porter happened to be away for the moment. It gave her time for reflection. It was another bit of luck that, as she had learned from Keggs, whom she met on the stairs on her way to the nursery, a mysterious telephone-call had caused Ruth to rise from her bed some three hours before her usual time and depart hurriedly in a cab. This also helped.

Keggs had no information to give as to Ruth's destination or the probable hour of her return. She had vanished without a word, except a request to Keggs to tell the driver of her taxi to go to the Thirty-Third Street subway.

"Must 'a' 'ad bad noos," Keggs thought, "because she were look'n' white as a sheet."

Mamie was sorry that Ruth had had bad news, but her departure certainly helped to relieve the pressure of an appalling situation.

With the absence of Ruth and Mrs. Porter the bits of luck came to an end. Try as she would, Mamie could discover no other silver linings in the cloud-bank. And even these ameliorations of the disaster were only temporary.

Ruth would return. Worse, Mrs. Porter would return. Like two Mother Hubbards, they would go to the cupboard, and the cupboard would be bare. And to her, Mamie, would fall the task of explanation.

The only explanation that occurred to her was that Steve had gone suddenly mad. He had given no hint of his altruistic motives in the hurried scrawl which she had found on the empty cot. He had merely said that he had taken away William Bannister, but that "it was all right."

Why Steve should imagine that it was all right baffled Mamie. Anything less all right she had never come across in a lifetime of disconcerting experiences.

She was aware that things were not as they should be between Ruth and Kirk, and the spectacle of the broken home had troubled her gentle heart; but she failed to establish a connection between Kirk's departure and Steve's midnight raid.

After devoting some ten minutes to steady brainwork she permitted herself the indulgence of a few tears. She did not often behave in this shockingly weak way, her role in life hitherto having been that of the one calm person in a disrupted world. When her father had lost his job, and the rent was due, and Brother Jim had fallen in the mud to the detriment of his only suit of clothes, and Brothers Terence and Mike had developed respectively a sore throat and a funny feeling in the chest, she had remained dry-eyed and capable. Her father had cried, her brother Jim had cried, her brother Terence had cried, and her brother Mike had cried in a manner that made the weeping of the rest of the family seem like the uncanny stillness of a summer night; but she had not shed a tear.

Now, however, she gave way. She buried her little face on the pillow which so brief a while before had been pressed by the round head of William Bannister and mourned like a modern Niobe.

At the end of two minutes she rose, sniffing but courageous, herself again. In her misery an idea had come to her. It was quite a simple and obvious idea, but till now it had eluded her.

She would go round to the studio and see Kirk. After all, it was his affair as much as anybody else's, and she had a feeling that it would be easier to break the news to him than to Ruth and Mrs. Porter.

She washed her eyes, put on her hat, and set out.

Luck, however, was not running her way that morning. Arriving at the studio, she rang the bell, and rang and rang again without result except a marked increase in her already substantial depression. When it became plain to her that the studio was empty she desisted.

It is an illustration of her remarkable force of character that at this point, refusing to be crushed by the bludgeoning of fate, she walked to Broadway and went into a moving-picture palace. There was nothing to be effected by staying in the house and worrying, so she resolutely declined to worry.

From this point onward her day divided itself into a series of three movements repeated at regular intervals. From the moving pictures she went to the house on Fifth Avenue. Finding that neither Ruth nor Mrs. Porter had returned, she went to the studio. Ringing the bell there and getting no answer, she took in the movies once more.

Mamie was a philosopher.

The atmosphere of the great house was still untroubled on her second visit. The care of the White Hope had always been left exclusively in the hands of the women, and the rest of the household had not yet detected his absence. It was not their business to watch his comings in and his goings out. Besides, they had other things to occupy them.

The unique occasion of the double absence of Ruth and Mrs. Porter was being celebrated by a sort of Saturnalia or slaves' holiday. It was true that either or both might return at any moment, but there was a disposition on the part of the domestic staff to take a chance on it.

Keggs, that sinful butler, had strolled round to an apparently untenanted house on Forty-First Street, where those who knew their New York could, by giving the signal, obtain admittance and the privilege of losing their money at the pleasing game of roulette with a double zero.

George, the footman, in company with Henriette, the lady's-maid, and Rollins, the chauffeur, who had butted in absolutely uninvited to George's acute disgust, were taking the air in the park. The rest of the staff, with the exception of a house-maid, who had been bribed, with two dollars and an old dress which had once been Ruth's and was now the property of Henriette, to stand by the ship, were somewhere on the island, amusing themselves in the way that seemed best to them. For all practical purposes, it was a safe and sane Fourth provided out of a blue sky by the god of chance.

It was about five o'clock when Mamie, having, at a modest estimate, seen five hundred persecuted heroes, a thousand ill-used heroines, several regiments of cowboys, and perhaps two thousand comic men pursued by angry mobs, returned from her usual visit to the studio.

This time there were signs of hope in the shape of a large automobile opposite the door. She rang the bell, and there came from within the welcome sound of footsteps. An elderly man of a somewhat dissipated countenance opened the door.

"I want to see Mr. Winfield," said Mamie.

Mr. Penway, for it was he, gave her the approving glance which your man of taste and discrimination does not fail to bestow upon youth and beauty and bawled over his shoulder –

"Kirk!"

Kirk came down the passage. He was looking brown and healthy. He was in his shirt-sleeves.

"Oh, Mr. Winfield. I'm in such trouble."

"Why, Mamie! What's the matter? Come in."

Mamie followed him into the studio, eluding Mr. Penway, whose arm was hovering in the neighbourhood of her waist.

"Sit down," said Kirk. "What's the trouble? Have you been trying to get at me before? We've been down to Long Beach."

"A delightful spot," observed Mr. Penway, who had followed. "Sandy, but replete with squabs. Why didn't you come earlier? We could have taken you."

"May I talk privately with you, Mr. Winfield?"

"Sure."

Kirk looked at Mr. Penway, who nodded agreeably.

"Outside for Robert?" he inquired amiably. "Very well. There is no Buttinsky blood in the Penway family. Let me just fix myself a high-ball and borrow one of your cigars and I'll go and sit in the car and commune with nature. Take your time."

"Just a moment, Mamie," said Kirk, when he had gone. He picked up a telegram which lay on the table. "I'll read this and see if it's important, and then we'll get right down to business. We only got back a moment before you arrived, so I'm a bit behind with my correspondence."

As he read the telegram a look of astonishment came into his face. He sat down and read the message a second time. Mamie waited patiently.

"Good Lord!" he muttered.

A sudden thought struck Mamie.

"Mr. Winfield, is it from Steve?" she said.

Kirk started, and looked at her incredulously.

"How on earth did you know? Good Heavens! Are you in this, Mamie, too?"

Mamie handed him her note. He read it without a word. When he had finished he sat back in his chair, thinking.

"I thought Steve might have telegraphed to you," said Mamie.

Kirk roused himself from his thoughts.

"Was this what you came to see me about?"

"Yes."

"What does Ruth – what do they think of it – up there?"

"They don't know anything about it. Mrs. Winfield went away early this morning. Mr. Keggs said she had had a telephone call, Mrs. Porter is in Boston. She will be back to-day some time. What are we to do?"

"Do!" Kirk jumped up and began to pace the floor. "I'll tell you what I'm going to do. Steve has taken the boy up to my shack in Connecticut. I'm going there as fast as the auto can take me."

"Steve's mad!"

"Is he? Steve's the best pal I've got. For two years I've been aching to get at this boy, and Steve has had the sense to show me the way."

He went on as if talking to himself.

"Steve's a man. I'm just a fool who hangs round without the nerve to act. If I had had the pluck of a rabbit I'd have done this myself six months ago. But I've hung round doing nothing while that damned Porter woman played the fool with the boy. I'll be lucky now if he remembers who I am."

He turned abruptly to Mamie.

"Mamie, you can tell them whatever you please when you get home. They can't blame you. It's not your fault. Tell them that Steve was acting for me with my complete approval. Tell them that the kid's going to be brought up right from now on. I've got him, and I'm going to keep him."

Mamie had risen and was facing him, a very determined midget, pink and resolute.

"I'm not going home, Mr. Winfield."

"What?"

"If you are going to Bill, I am coming with you."

"Nonsense."

"That's my place – with him."

"But you can't. It's impossible."

"Not more impossible than what has happened already."

"I won't take you."

"Then I'll go by train. I know where your house is. Steve told me."

"It's out of the question."

Mamie's Irish temper got the better of her professional desire to maintain the discreetly respectful attitude of employee toward employer.

"Is it then? We'll see. Do you think I'm going to leave you and Steve to look after my Bill? What do men know about taking care of children? You would choke the poor mite or let him kill himself a hundred ways."

She glared at him defiantly. He glared back at her. Then his sense of humour came to his rescue. She looked so absurdly small standing there with her chin up and her fists clenched. He laughed delightedly. He went up to her and placed a hand on each of her shoulders, looking down at her. He felt that he loved her for her championship of Bill.

"You're a brick, Mamie. Of course you shall come. We'll call at the house and you can pack your grip. But, by George, if you put that infernal thermometer in I'll run the automobile up against a telegraph-pole, and then Bill will lose us both."

"Finished?" said a voice. "Oh, I beg your pardon. Sorry."

Mr. Penway was gazing at them with affectionate interest from the doorway. Kirk released Mamie and stepped back.

"I only looked in," explained Mr. Penway. "Didn't mean to intrude. Thought you might have finished your chat, and it was a trifle lonely communing with nature."

"Bob," said Kirk, "you'll have to get on without me for a day or two. Make yourself at home. You know where everything is."

"I can satisfy my simple needs. Thinking of going away?"

"I've got to go up to Connecticut. I don't know how long I shall be away."

"Take your time," said Mr. Penway affably. "Going in the auto?"

"Yes."

"The weather is very pleasant for automobiling just now," remarked Mr. Penway.

❧

Ten minutes later, having thrown a few things together into a bag, Kirk took his place at the wheel. Mamie sat beside him. The bag had the rear seat to itself.

"There seems to be plenty of room still," said Mr. Penway. "I have half a mind to come with you."

He looked at Mamie.

"But on reflection I fancy you can get along without me."

He stood at the door, gazing after the motor as it moved down the street. When it had turned the corner he went back into the studio and mixed himself a high-ball.

"Kirk does manage to find them," he said enviously.

CHAPTER 11
MR. PENWAY ON THE GRILL

FATE moves in a mysterious way. Luck comes hand in hand with misfortune. What we lose on the swings we make up on the roundabouts. If Keggs had not seen twenty-five of his hard-earned dollars pass at one swoop into the clutches of the *croupier* at the apparently untenanted house on Forty-First Street, and become disgusted with the pleasing game of roulette, he might have delayed his return to the house on Fifth Avenue till a later hour; in which case he would have missed the remarkable and stimulating spectacle of Kirk driving to the door in an automobile with Mamie at his side; of Mamie, jumping out and entering the house; of Mamie leaving the house with a suit-case; of Kirk helping her into the automobile, and of the automobile disappearing with its interesting occupants up the avenue at a high rate of speed.

Having lost his money, as stated, and having returned home, he was enabled to be a witness, the only witness, of these notable events, and his breast was filled with a calm joy in consequence. This was something special. This was exclusive, a scoop. He looked forward to the return of Mrs. Porter with an eagerness which, earlier in the day, he would have considered impossible. Somehow Ruth did not figure in his picture of the delivery of the sensational news that Mr.

194

Winfield had eloped with the young person engaged to look after her son. Mrs. Porter's was one of those characters which monopolize any stage on which they appear. Besides, Keggs disliked Mrs. Porter, and the pleasure of the prospect of giving her a shock left no room for other thoughts.

It was nearly seven o'clock when Mrs. Porter reached the house. She was a little tired from the journey, but in high good humour. She had had a thoroughly satisfactory interview with her publishers – satisfactory, that is to say, to herself; the publishers had other views.

"Is Mrs. Winfield in?" she asked Keggs as he admitted her.

Ruth was always sympathetic about her guerrilla warfare with the publishers. She looked forward to a cosy chat, in the course of which she would trace, step by step, the progress of the late campaign which had begun overnight and had culminated that morning in a sort of Gettysburg, from which she had emerged with her arms full of captured flags and all the other trophies of conquest.

"No, madam," said Keggs. "Mrs. Winfield has not yet returned."

Keggs was an artist in tragic narration. He did not give away his climax; he led up to it by degrees as slow as his audience would permit.

"Returned? I did not know she intended to go away. Her yacht party is next week, I understand."

"Yes, madam."

"Where has she gone?"

"To Tuxedo, madam."

"Tuxedo?"

"Mrs. Winfield has just rung us up from there upon the telephone to request that necessaries for an indefinite stay be despatched to her. She is visiting Mrs. Bailey Bannister."

If Mrs. Porter had been Steve, she would probably have said "For the love of Mike!" at this point. Being herself, she merely repeated the butler's last words.

"If I may be allowed to say so, madam, I think that there must have been trouble at Mrs. Bannister's. A telephone-call came from her very early this morning for Mrs. Winfield which caused Mrs. Winfield to rise and leave in a taximeter-cab in an extreme hurry. If I might be allowed to suggest it, it is probably a case of serious illness. Mrs. Winfield was looking very disturbed."

"H'm!" said Mrs. Porter. The exclamation was one of disappointment rather than of apprehension. Sudden illnesses at the Bailey
home did not stir her, but she was annoyed that her recital of the
squelching of the publishers would have to wait.

She went upstairs. Her intention was to look in at the nursery
and satisfy herself that all was well with William Bannister. She had
given Mamie specific instructions as to his care on her departure;
but you never knew. Perhaps her keen eye might be able to detect
some deviation from the rules she had laid down.

It detected one at once. The nursery was empty. According to
schedule, the child should have been taking his bath.

She went downstairs again. Keggs was waiting in the hall. He
had foreseen this return. He had allowed her to go upstairs with his
story but half heard because that appealed to his artistic sense. This
story, to his mind, was too good to be bolted at a sitting; it was the
ideal serial.

"Keggs."

"Madam?"

"Where is Master William?"

"I fear I do not know, madam."

"When did he go out? It is seven o'clock; he should have been in
an hour ago."

"I have been making inquiries, madam, and I regret to inform
you that nobody appears to have seen Master William all day."

"What?"

"It not being my place to follow his movements, I was unaware
of this until quite recently, but from conversation with the other
domestics, I find that he seems to have disappeared!"

"Disappeared?"

A glow of enjoyment such as he had sometimes experienced
when the ticker at the Cadillac Hotel informed him that the man he
had backed in some San Francisco fight had upset his opponent for
the count began to permeate Keggs.

"Disappeared, madam," he repeated.

"Perhaps Mrs. Winfield took him with her to Tuxedo."

"No, madam. Mrs. Winfield was alone. I was present when she
drove away."

"Send Mamie to me at once," said Mrs. Porter.

Keggs could have whooped with delight had not such an action seemed to him likely to prejudice his chances of retaining a good situation. He contented himself with wriggling ecstatically. "The young person is not in the house, madam."

"Not in the house? What business has she to be out? Where is she?"

"I could not tell you, madam." Keggs paused, reluctant to deal the final blow, as a child lingers lovingly over the last lick of ice-cream in a cone. "I last saw her at about five o'clock, driving off with Mr. Winfield in an automobile."

"What!"

Keggs was content. His climax had not missed fire. Its staggering effect was plain on the face of his hearer. For once Mrs. Porter's poise had deserted her. Her one word had been a scream.

"She did not tell me her destination, madam," went on Keggs, making all that could be made of what was left of the situation after its artistic finish. "She came in and packed a suit-case and went out again and joined Mr. Winfield in the automobile, and they drove off together."

Mrs. Porter recovered herself. This was a matter which called for silent meditation, not for chit-chat with a garrulous butler.

"That will do, Keggs."

"Very good, madam."

Keggs withdrew to his pantry, well pleased. He considered that he had done himself justice as a raconteur. He had not spoiled a good story in the telling.

Mrs. Porter went to her room and sat down to think. She was a woman of action, and she soon reached a decision.

The errant pair must be followed, and at once. Her great mind, playing over the situation like a searchlight, detected a connection between this elopement and the disappearance of William Bannister. She had long since marked Kirk down as a malcontent, and she now labelled the absent Mamie as a snake in the grass who had feigned submission to her rule, while meditating all the time the theft of the child and the elopement with Kirk. She had placed the same construction on Mamie's departure with Kirk as had Mr. Penway, showing that it is not only great minds that think alike.

A latent conviction as to the immorality of all artists, which had been one of the maxims of her late mother, sprang into life. She blamed herself for having allowed a nurse of such undeniable physical attractions to become a member of the household. Mamie's very quietness and apparent absence of bad qualities became additional evidence against her now, Mrs. Porter arguing that these things indicated deep deceitfulness. She told herself, what was not the case, that she had never trusted that girl.

But Lora Delane Porter was not a woman to waste time in retrospection. She had not been in her room five minutes before her mind was made up. It was improbable that Kirk and his guilty accomplice had sought so near and obvious a haven as the studio, but it was undoubtedly there that pursuit must begin. She knew nothing of his way of living at that retreat, but she imagined that he must have appointed some successor to George Pennicut as general factotum, and it might be that this person would have information to impart.

The task of inducing him to impart it did not daunt Mrs. Porter. She had a just confidence in her powers of cross-examination.

She went to the telephone and called up the garage where Ruth's automobiles were housed. Her plan of action was now complete. If no information were forthcoming at the studio, she would endeavour to find out where Kirk had hired the car in which he had taken Mamie away. He would probably have secured it from some garage near by. But this detective work would be a last resource. Like a good general, she did not admit of the possibility of failing in her first attack.

And, luck being with her, it happened that at the moment when she set out, Mr. Penway, feeling pretty comfortable where he was, abandoned his idea of going out for a stroll along Broadway and settled himself to pass the next few hours in Kirk's armchair.

Mr. Penway's first feeling when the bell rang, rousing him from his peaceful musings, was one of mild vexation. A few minutes later, when Mrs. Porter had really got to work upon him, he would not have recognized that tepid emotion as vexation at all.

Mrs. Porter wasted no time. She perforated Mr. Penway's spine with her eyes, reduced it to the consistency of summer squash, and drove him before her into the studio, where she took a seat and motioned him to do the same. For a moment she sat looking at him, by way of completing the work of subjection, while Mr. Penway writhed uneasily on his chair and thought of past sins.

"My name is Mrs. Porter," she began abruptly.

"Mine's Penway," said the miserable being before her. It struck him as the only thing to say.

"I have come to inquire about Mr. Winfield."

As she paused Mr. Penway felt it incumbent upon him to speak again.

"Dear old Kirk," he mumbled.

"Nothing of the kind," said Mrs. Porter sharply. "Mr. Winfield is a scoundrel of the worst type, and if you are as intimate a friend of his as your words imply, it does not argue well for your respectability."

Mr. Penway opened his mouth feebly and closed it again. Having closed it, he reopened it and allowed it to remain ajar, as it were. It was his idea of being conciliatory.

"Tell me." Mr. Penway started violently. "Tell me, when did you last see Mr. Winfield?"

"We went to Long Beach together this afternoon."

"In an automobile?"

"Yes."

"Ah! Were you here when Mr. Winfield left again?"

For the life of him Mr. Penway had not the courage to say no. There was something about this woman's stare which acted hypnotically upon his mind, never at its best as early in the evening.

He nodded.

"There was a young woman with him?" pursued Mrs. Porter.

At this moment Mr. Penway's eyes, roving desperately about the room, fell upon the bottle of Bourbon which Kirk's kindly hospitality had provided. His emotions at the sight of it were those of the shipwrecked mariner who see a sail. He sprang at it and poured himself out a stiff dose. Before Mrs. Porter's disgusted gaze he drained the glass and then turned to her, a new man.

The noble spirit restored his own. For the first time since the interview had begun he felt capable of sustaining his end of the conversation with ease and dignity.

"How's that?" he said.

"There was a young woman with him?" repeated Mrs. Porter.

Mr. Penway imagined that he had placed her by this time. Here, he told himself in his own crude language, was the squab's mother camping on Kirk's trail with an axe. Mr. Penway's moral code was of the easiest description. His sympathies were entirely with Kirk.

Fortified by the Bourbon, he set himself resolutely to the task of lying whole-heartedly on behalf of his absent friend.

"No," he said firmly.

"No!" exclaimed Mrs. Porter.

"No," repeated Mr. Penway with iron resolution. "No young woman. No young woman whatsoever. I noticed it particularly, because I thought it strange, don't you know – what I mean is, don't you know, strange there shouldn't be!"

How tragic is a man's fruitless fight on behalf of a friend! For one short instant Mrs. Porter allowed Mr. Penway to imagine that the victory was his, then she administered the *coup-de-grace*.

"Don't lie, you worthless creature," she said. "They stopped at my house on their way while the girl packed a suitcase."

Mr. Penway threw up his brief. There are moments when the stoutest- hearted, even under the influence of old Bourbon, realize that to fight on is merely to fight in vain.

He condensed his emotions into four words.

"Of all the chumps!" he remarked, and, pouring himself out a further instalment of the raw spirit, he sat down, a beaten man.

Mrs. Porter continued to harry him.

"Exactly," she said. "So you see that there is no need for any more subterfuge and concealment. I do not intend to leave this room until you have told me all you have to tell, so you had better be quick about it. Kindly tell me the truth in as few words as possible – if you know what is meant by telling the truth."

A belated tenderness for his dignity came to Mr. Penway.

"You are insulting," he remarked. "You are – you are – most insulting."

"I meant to be," said Mrs. Porter crisply. "Now. Tell me. Where has Mr. Winfield gone?"

Mr. Penway preserved an offended silence. Mrs. Porter struck the table a blow with a book which caused him to leap in his seat.

"Where has Mr. Winfield gone?"

"How should I know?"

"How should you know? Because he told you, I should imagine. Where – has – Mr. – Winfield – gone?"

"C'nnecticut," said Mr. Penway, finally capitulating.

"What part of Connecticut?"

"I don't know."

"What part of Connecticut?"

"I tell you I don't know. He said: 'I'm off to Connecticut,' and left." It suddenly struck Mr. Penway that his defeat was not so overwhelming as he had imagined. "So you haven't got much out of me, you see, after all," he added.

Mrs. Porter rose.

"On the contrary," she said; "I have got out of you precisely the information which I required, and in considerably less time than I had supposed likely. If it interests you, I may tell you that Mr. Winfield has gone to a small house which he owns in the Connecticut woods."

"Then what," demanded Mr. Penway indignantly, "did you mean by keeping on saying 'What part of C'nnecticut? What part of C'nnecticut? What part—'"

"Because Mr. Winfield's destination has only just occurred to me." She looked at him closely. "You are a curious and not uninteresting object, Mr. Penway."

Mr. Penway started. "Eh?"

"Object lesson, I should have said. I should like to exhibit you as a warning to the youth of this country."

"What!"

"From the look of your frame I should imagine that you were once a man of some physique. Your shoulders are good. Even now a rigorous course of physical training might save you. I have known more helpless cases saved by firm treatment. You have allowed yourself to deteriorate much as did a man named Pennicut who used to be employed here by Mr. Winfield. I saved him. I dare say I could make something of you. I can see at a glance that you eat, drink, and smoke too much. You could not hold out your hand now, at this minute, without it trembling."

"I could," said Mr. Penway indignantly.

He held it out, and it quivered like a tuning-fork.

"There!" said Mrs. Porter calmly. "What do you expect? You know your own business best, I suppose, but I should like to tell you that if you do not become a teetotaller instantly, and begin taking exercise, you will probably die suddenly within a very few years. Personally I shall bear the calamity with fortitude. Good evening, Mr. Penway."

For some moments after she had gone Mr. Penway sat staring before him. His eyes wore a glassy look. His mouth was still ajar.

"Damn woman!" he said at length.

He turned to his meditations.

"Damn impertinent woman!"

Another interval for reflection, and he spoke again.

"Damn impertinent, interfering woman that!"

He reached out for the bottle of Bourbon and filled his glass. He put it to his lips, then slowly withdrew it.

"Damn impertinent, inter – I wonder!"

There was a small mirror on the opposite wall. He walked unsteadily toward it and put out his tongue. He continued in this attitude for a time, then, with increased dejection, turned away.

He placed a hand over his heart. This seemed to depress him still further. Finally he went to the table, took up the glass, poured its contents carefully back into the bottle, which he corked and replaced on the shelf.

On the floor against the wall was a pair of Indian clubs. He picked these up and examined them owlishly. He gave them little tentative jerks. Finally, with the air of a man carrying out a great resolution, he began to swing them. He swung them in slow, irregular sweeps, his eyes the while, still glassy, staring fixedly at the ceiling.

CHAPTER 12
DOLLS WITH SOULS

RUTH had not seen Bailey since the afternoon when he had called to warn her against Basil Milbank. Whether it was offended dignity that kept him away, or merely pressure of business, she did not know.

That pressure of business existed, she was aware. The papers were full, and had been full for several days, of wars and rumours of wars down in Wall Street; and, though she understood nothing of finance, she knew that Bailey was in the forefront of the battle. Her knowledge was based partly on occasional references in the papers to the firm of Bannister & Co. and partly on what she heard in society.

She did not hear all that was said in society about Bailey's financial operations – which, as Bailey had the control of her money, was unfortunate for her. The manipulation of money bored her, and she had left the investing of her legacy entirely to Bailey. Her father, she knew, had always had a high opinion of Bailey's business instincts, and that was good enough for her.

She could not know how completely revolutionized the latter's mind had become since the old man's death, and how freedom had turned him from a steady young man of business to a frenzied financier.

It was common report now that Bailey was taking big chances. Some went so far as to say that he was "asking for it," "it" in his case being presumably the Nemesis which waits on those who take big chances in an uncertain market. It was in the air that he was "going up against" the Pinkey-Dowd group and the Norman-Graham combination, and everybody knew that the cemeteries of Wall Street were full of the unhonoured graves of others who in years past had attempted to do the same.

Pinkey, that sinister buccaneer, could have eaten a dozen Baileys. Devouring aspiring young men of the Bailey type was Norman's chief diversion.

Ruth knew nothing of these things. She told herself that it was her abruptness that had driven Bailey away.

Weariness and depression had settled on Ruth since that afternoon of the storm. It was as if the storm had wrought an awakening in her. It had marked a definite point of change in her outlook. She felt as if she had been roused from a trance by a sharp blow.

If Steve had but known, she had had the "jolt" by which he set such store. She knew now that she had thrown away the substance for the shadow.

Kirk's anger, so unlike him, so foreign to the weak, easy-going person she had always thought him, had brought her to herself. But it was too late. There could be no going back and picking up the threads. She had lost him, and must bear the consequences.

The withdrawal of Bailey was a small thing by comparison, a submotive in the greater tragedy. But she had always been fond of Bailey, and it hurt her to think that she should have driven him out of her life.

It seemed to her that she was very much alone now. She was marooned on a desert island of froth and laughter. Everything that mattered she had lost.

Even Bill had gone from her. The bitter justice of Kirk's words came home to her now in her time of clear thinking. It was all true. In the first excitement of the new life he had bored her. She had looked upon Mrs. Porter as a saviour who brought her freedom together with an easy conscience. It had been so simple to deceive herself, to cheat herself into the comfortable belief that all that could be done for him was being done, when, as concerned the essential thing, as Kirk had said, there was no child of the streets who was not better off.

She tramped her round of social duties mechanically. Everything bored her now. The joy of life had gone out of her. She ate the bread of sorrow in captivity.

And then, this morning, had come a voice from the world she had lost – little Mrs. Bailey's voice, small and tearful.

Could she possibly come out by the next train? Bailey was very ill. Bailey was dying. Bailey had come home last night looking ghastly. He had not slept. In the early morning he had begun to babble – Mrs. Bailey's voice had risen and broken on the word, and Ruth at the other end of the wire had heard her frightened sobs. The doctor had come. The doctor had looked awfully grave. The doctor had telephoned to New York for another doctor. They were both upstairs now. It was awful, and Ruth must come at once.

This was the bad news which had brought about the pallor which had impressed Mr. Keggs as he helped Ruth into her cab.

Little Mrs. Bailey was waiting for her on the platform when she got out of the train. Her face was drawn and miserable. She looked like a beaten kitten. She hugged Ruth hysterically.

"Oh, my dear, I'm so glad you've come. He's better, but it has been awful. The doctors have had to *fight* him to keep him in bed. He was crazy to get to town. He kept saying over and over again that he must be at the office. They gave him something, and he was asleep when I left the house."

She began to cry helplessly. The fates had not bestowed upon Sybil Bannister the same care in the matter of education for times of crisis which they had accorded to Steve's Mamie. Her life till now had been sheltered and unruffled, and disaster, swooping upon her, had found her an easy victim.

She was trying to be brave, but her powers of resistance were small like her body. She clung to Ruth as a child clings to its mother. Ruth, as she tried to comfort her, felt curiously old. It occurred to her with a suggestion almost of grotesqueness that she and Sybil had been debutantes in the same season.

They walked up to the house. The summer cottage which Bailey had taken was not far from the station. On the way, in the intervals of her sobs, Sybil told Ruth the disjointed story of what had happened.

Bailey had not been looking well for some days. She had thought it must be the heat or business worries or something. He had not eaten very much, and he had seemed too tired to talk when he got home each evening. She had begged him to take a few days' rest. That had been the only occasion in the whole of the last week when she had heard him laugh; and it had been such a horrid, ugly sort of laugh that she wished she hadn't.

He had said that if he stayed away from the office for some time to come it would mean love in a cottage for them for the rest of their lives – and not a summer cottage at Tuxedo at that. "'My dear child,'" he had gone on, "and you know when Bailey calls me that," said Sybil, "it means that there is something the matter; for, as a rule, he never calls me anything but my name, or baby, or something like that."

Which gave Ruth a little shock of surprise. Somehow the idea of the dignified Bailey addressing his wife as baby startled her. She was certainly learning these days that she did not know people as completely as she had supposed. There seemed to be endless sides to people's characters which had never come under her notice. A sudden memory of Kirk on that fateful afternoon came to her and made her wince.

Mrs. Bailey continued: "'My dear child,' he went on, 'this week is about the most important week you and I are ever likely to live through. It's the show-down. We either come out on top or we blow up. It's one thing or the other. And if I take a few days' holiday just now you had better start looking about for the best place to sell your jewellery.'

"Those were his very words," she said tearfully. "I remember them all. It was so unlike his usual way of talking."

Ruth acknowledged that it was. More than ever she felt that she did not know the complete Bailey.

"He was probably exaggerating," she said for the sake of saying something.

Sybil was silent for a moment.

"It isn't that that's worrying me," she went on then. "Somehow I don't seem to care at all whether we come out right or not, so long as he gets well. Last night, when I thought he was going to die, I made up my mind that I couldn't go on living without him. I wouldn't have, either."

This time the shock of surprise which came to Ruth was greater by a hundred-fold than the first had been. She gave a quick glance at Sybil. Her small face was hard, and the little white teeth gleamed between her drawn lips. It was the face, for one brief instant, of a fanatic. The sight of it affected Ruth extraordinarily. It was as if she had seen a naked soul where she had never imagined a soul to be.

She had weighed Sybil in the same calm, complacent almost patronizing fashion in which she had weighed Bailey, Kirk, everybody. She had set her down as a delightful child, an undeveloped, feather-brained little thing, pleasant to spend an afternoon with, but not to be taken seriously by any one as magnificent and superior as Ruth Winfield. And what manner of a man must Bailey be, Bailey whom she had always looked on as a dear, but as quite a joke, something to be chaffed and made to look foolish, if he was capable of inspiring love like this?

A wave of humility swept over her. The pygmies of her world were springing up as giants, dwarfing her. The pinnacle of superiority on which she had stood so long was crumbling into dust.

She was finding herself. She winced again as the thought stabbed her that she was finding herself too late.

They reached the house in silence, each occupied with her own thoughts. The defiant look had died out of Sybil's face and she was once more a child, crying because unknown forces had hurt it. But Ruth was not looking at her now.

She was too busy examining this new world into which she had been abruptly cast, this world where dolls had souls and jokes lost their point.

At the cottage good news awaited them. The crisis was past. Bailey was definitely out of danger. He was still asleep, and sleeping easily. It had just been an ordinary breakdown, due to worrying and overwork, said the doctor, the bigger of the doctors, the one who had been summoned from New York.

"All your husband needs now, Mrs. Bannister, is rest. See that he is kept quiet. That's all there is to it."

As if by way of a commentary on his words, a small boy on a bicycle rode up with a telegram.

Sybil opened it. She read it, and looked at Ruth with large eyes.

"From the office," she said, handing it to her.

Ruth read it. It was a C. D. Q., an S.O.S. from the front; an appeal for help from the forefront of the battle. She did not understand the details of it, but the purport was clear. The battle had begun, and Bailey was needed. But Bailey lay sleeping in his tent.

She handed it back in silence. There was nothing to be done.

The second telegram arrived half an hour after the first. It differed from the first only in its greater emphasis. Panic seemed to be growing in the army of the lost leader.

The ringing of the telephone began almost simultaneously with the arrival of the second telegram. Ruth went to the receiver. A frantic voice was inquiring for Mr. Bannister even as she put it to her ear.

"This is Mrs. Winfield speaking," she said steadily, "Mr. Bannister's sister. Mr. Bannister is very ill and cannot possibly attend to any business."

There was a silence at the other end of the wire. Then a voice, with the calm of desperation, said: "Thank you." There was a pause. "Thank you," said the voice again in a crushed sort of way, and the receiver was hung up. Ruth went back to Sybil.

The hours passed. How she got through them Ruth hardly knew. Time seemed to have stopped. For the most part they sat in silence. In the afternoon Sybil was allowed to see Bailey for a few minutes. She returned thoughtful. She kissed Ruth before she sat down, and once or twice after that Ruth, looking up, found her eyes fixed upon her. It seemed to Ruth that there was something which she was trying to say, but she asked no questions.

After dinner they sat out on the porch. It was a perfect night. The cool dusk was soothing.

Ruth broke a long silence.

"Sybil!"

"Yes, dear?"

"May I tell you something?"

"Well?"

"I'm afraid it's bad news."

Sybil turned quickly.

"You called up the office while I was with Bailey?"

Ruth started.

"How did you know?"

"I guessed. I have been trying to do it all day, but I hadn't the pluck. Well?"

"I'm afraid things are about as bad as they can be. A Mr. Meadows spoke to me. He was very gloomy. He told me a lot of things which I couldn't follow, details of what had happened, but I understood all that was necessary, I'm afraid—"

"Bailey's ruined?" said Sybil quietly.

"Mr. Meadows seemed to think so. He may have exaggerated."

Sybil shook her head.

"No. Bailey was talking to me upstairs. I expected it."

There was a long silence.

"Ruth."

"Yes?"

"I'm afraid – "

Sybil stopped.

"Yes?"

A sudden light of understanding came to Ruth. She knew what it was that Sybil was trying to say, had been trying to say ever since she spoke with Bailey.

"My money has gone, too? Is that it?"

Sybil did not answer. Ruth went quickly to her and took her in her arms.

"You poor baby," she cried. "Was that what was on your mind, wondering how you should tell me? I knew there was something troubling you."

Sybil began to sob.

"I didn't know how to tell you," she whispered.

Ruth laughed excitedly. She felt as if a great weight had been lifted from her shoulders – a weight which had been crushing the life out of her. In the last few days the scales had fallen from her eyes and she had seen clearly.

She realized now what Kirk had realized from the first, that what had forced his life apart from hers had been the golden wedge of her father's money. It was the burden of wealth that had weighed her down without her knowing it. She felt as if she had been suddenly set free.

"I'm dreadfully sorry," said Sybil feebly.

Ruth laughed again.

"I'm not," she said. "If you knew how glad I was you would be congratulating me instead of looking as if you thought I was going to bite you."

"Glad!"

"Of course I'm glad. Everything's going to be all right again now. Sybil dear, Kirk and I had the most awful quarrel the other day. We – we actually decided it would be better for us to separate. It was all my fault. I had neglected Kirk, and I had neglected Bill, and Kirk couldn't stand it any longer. But now that this has happened, don't you see that it will be all right again? You can't stand on your dignity when you're up against real trouble. If this had not happened, neither of us would have had the pluck to make the first move; but now, you see, we shall just naturally fall into each other's arms and be happy again, he and I and Bill, just as we were before."

"It must be lovely for you having Bill," said little Mrs. Bailey wistfully. "I wish – "

She stopped. There was a corner of her mind into which she could not admit any one, even Ruth.

"Having him ought to have been enough for any woman." Ruth's voice was serious. "It was enough for me in the old days when we were at the studio. What fools women are sometimes! I suppose I lost my head, coming suddenly into all that money – I don't know why; for it was not as if I had not had plenty of time, when father was alive, to get used to the idea of being rich. I think it must have been the unexpectedness of it. I certainly did behave as if I had gone mad. Goodness! I'm glad it's over and that we can make a fresh start."

"What is it like being poor, Ruth? Of course, we were never very well off at home, but we weren't really poor."

"It's heaven if you're with the right man."

Mrs. Bailey sighed.

"Bailey's the right man, as far as I'm concerned. But I'm wondering how he will bear it, poor dear."

Ruth was feeling too happy herself to allow any one else to be unhappy if she could help it.

"Why, of course he will be splendid about it," she said. "You're letting your imagination run away with you. You have got the idea of Bailey and yourself as two broken creatures begging in the streets. I don't know how badly Bailey will be off after this smash, but I do know that he will have all his brains and his energy left."

Ruth was conscious of a momentary feeling of surprise that she should be eulogizing Bailey in this fashion, and – stranger still – that she should be really sincere in what she said. But to-day seemed to have changed everything, and she was regarding her brother with a new-born respect. She could still see Sybil's face as it had appeared in that memorable moment of self-revelation. It had made a deep impression upon her.

"A man like Bailey is worth a large salary to any one, even if he may not be able to start out for himself again immediately. I'm not worrying about you and Bailey. You will have forgotten all about this crash this time next year." Sybil brightened up. She was by nature easily moved, and Ruth's words had stimulated her imagination.

"He *is* awfully clever," she said, her eyes shining.

"Why, this sort of thing happens every six months to anybody who has anything to do with Wall Street," proceeded Ruth, fired by her own optimism. "You read about it in the papers every day. Nobody thinks anything of it."

Sybil, though anxious to look on the bright side, could not quite rise to these heights of scorn for the earthquake which had shaken her world.

"I hope not. It would be awful to go through a time like this again."

Ruth reassured her, though it entailed a certain inconsistency on her part. She had a true woman's contempt for consistency.

"Of course you won't have to go through it again. Bailey will be careful in future not to – not to do whatever it is that he has done."

She felt that the end of her inspiring speech was a little weak, but she did not see how she could mend it. Her talk with Mr. Meadows on the telephone had left her as vague as before as to the actual details of what had been happening that day in Wall Street. She remembered stray remarks of his about bulls, and she had gathered that something had happened to something which Mr. Meadows called G.R.D.'s, which had evidently been at the root of the trouble; but there her grasp of high finance ended.

Sybil, however, was not exigent. She brightened at Ruth's words as if they had been an authoritative pronouncement from an expert.

"Bailey is sure to do right," she said. "I think I'll creep in and see if he's still asleep."

Ruth, left alone on the porch, fell into a pleasant train of thought. There was something in her mental attitude which amused her. She wondered if anybody had ever received the announcement of financial ruin in quite the same way before. Yet to her this attitude seemed the only one possible.

How simple everything was now! She could go to Kirk and, as she had said to Sybil, start again. The golden barrier between them had vanished. One day had wiped out all the wretchedness of the last year. They were back where they had started, with all the accumulated experience of those twelve months to help them steer their little ship clear of the rocks on its new voyage.

❧

She was roused from her dream by the sound of an automobile drawing up at the door. A voice that she recognised called her name. She went quickly down the steps.

"Is that you, Aunt Lora?"

Mrs. Porter, masterly woman, never wasted time in useless chatter.

"Jump in, my dear," she said crisply. "Your husband has stolen William and eloped with that girl Mamie (whom I never trusted) to Connecticut."

Chapter 13
Pastures New

Steve had arrived at the Connecticut shack in the early dawn of the day which had been so eventful to most of his friends and acquaintances. William Bannister's interest in the drive, at first acute, had ceased after the first five miles, and he had passed the remainder of the journey in a sound sleep from which the stopping of the car did not awaken him.

Steve jumped down and stretched himself. There was a wonderful freshness in the air which made him forget for a moment his desire for repose. He looked about him, breathing deep draughts of its coolness. The robins which, though not so well advertised, rise just as punctually as the lark, were beginning to sing as they made their simple toilets before setting out to attend to the early worm. The sky to the east was a delicate blend of pinks and greens and yellows, with a hint of blue behind the grey which was still the prevailing note.

A vaguely sentimental mood came upon Steve. In his heart he knew perfectly well that he could never be happy for any length of time out of sight and hearing of Broadway cars; but at that moment, such was the magic of the dawn, he felt a longing to settle down in the country and pass the rest of his days a simple farmer with beard unchecked by razor. He saw himself feeding the chickens and addressing the pigs by their pet names, while Mamie, in a cotton frock, called cheerfully to him to come in because breakfast was ready and getting cold.

Mamie! Ah!

His sigh turned into a yawn. He realized with the abruptness which comes to a man who stands alone with nature in the small hours that he was very sleepy. The excitement which had sustained him till now had begun to ebb. The free life of the bearded farmer seemed suddenly less attractive. Bed was what he wanted now, not nature.

He opened the door of the car and lifted William Bannister out, swathed in rugs. The White Hope gurgled drowsily, but did not wake. Steve carried him on to the porch and laid him down. Then he turned his attention to the problem of effecting an entry.

Once an honest man has taken to amateur burgling he soon picks up the tricks of it. To open his knife and shoot back the catch of the nearest window was with Steve the work, if not of a moment, of a very few minutes. He climbed in and unlocked the front door. Then he carried his young charge into the sitting-room and laid him down on a chair, a step nearer his ultimate destination – bed.

Steve's faculties were rapidly becoming numb with approaching sleep, but he roused himself to face certain details of the country life which till now had escaped him. His earnest concentration on the main plank of his platform, the spiriting away of William Bannister, had caused him to overlook the fact that no preparations had been made to welcome him on his arrival at his destination. He had treated the shack as if it had been a summer hotel, where he could walk in and engage a room. It now struck him that there was much to be attended to before he could, as he put it to himself, hit the hay. There was the White Hope's bed to be made, and, by the way of a preliminary to that, sheets must be found and blankets, not to mention pillows.

Yawning wearily he set out on his search.

He found sheets, but mistrusted them. They might or might not be perfectly dry. He did not care to risk his godson's valuable health in the experiment. A hazy notion that blankets were always safe restored his spirits, and he became cheerful on reflecting that a child with William Bannister's gift for sleep would not be likely to notice the absence of linen in his bed.

The couch which he finally passed adequate would have caused Lora Delane Porter's hair to stand erect, but it satisfied Steve. He went downstairs, and, returning with William Bannister, placed him carefully on it and tucked him in. The White Hope slept on.

Having assured himself that all was well, Steve made up a similar nest for himself, and, removing his coat and shoes, crawled under the blankets. Five minutes later rhythmical snores proclaimed the fact that nature had triumphed over all the discomforts of one of the worst-made beds in Connecticut.

The sun was high when Steve woke. He rose stiffly and went into the other room. William Bannister still slept.

Steve regarded him admiringly.

"For the dormouse act," he mused, "that kid certainly stands alone. You got to hand it to him."

An aching void within him called his mind to the question of breakfast. It began to come home to him that he had not planned out this expedition with that thoroughness which marks the great general.

"I guess I'll have to get out to the nearest village in the bubble," he said. "And while I'm there maybe I'd better send Kirk a wire.

And I reckon I'll have to take the kid. If he wakes up and finds me gone he'll throw fits. Up you get, squire."

He kneaded the recumbent form of his godson with a large hand until he had massaged out of him the last remains of his great sleep. It took some time, but it was effective. The White Hope sat up, full of life and energy. He inspected Steve gravely for a moment, endeavouring to place him.

"Hello, Steve," he said at length.

"Hello, kid."

"Where am I?"

"In the country. In Connecticut."

"What's 'Necticut?"

"This is. Where we are."

"Where are we?"

"Here. In Connecticut."

"Why?"

Steve raised a protesting hand.

"Not so early in the day, kid; not before breakfast," he pleaded. "Honest, I'm not strong enough. It ain't as if we was a vaudeville team that had got to rehearse."

"What's rehearse?"

Steve changed the subject.

"Say, kid, ain't you feeling like you could bite into something? I got an emptiness inside me as big as all outdoors. How about a mouthful of cereal and a shirred egg? Now, for the love of Mike," he went on quickly, as his godson opened his mouth to speak, "don't say 'What's shirred?' It's something you do to eggs. It's one way of fixing 'em."

"What's fixing?" inquired William Bannister brightly.

Steve sighed. When he spoke he was calm, but determined.

"That'll be all the dialogue for the present," he said. "We'll play the rest of our act in dumb show. Get a move on you, and I'll take you out in the bubble – the automobile, the car, the chug-chug wagon, the thing we came here in, if you want to know what bubble is – and we'll scare up some breakfast."

Steve's ignorance of the locality in which he found himself was complete; but he had a general impression that farmers as a class were people who delighted in providing breakfasts for the needy, if the needy possessed the necessary price. Acting on this assumption, he postponed his trip to the nearest town and drove slowly along the roads with his eyes open for signs of life.

He found a suitable farm and, applying the brakes, gathered up William Bannister and knocked at the door.

His surmise as to the hospitality of farmers proved correct, and presently they were sitting down to a breakfast which it did his famished soul good to contemplate.

William Bannister seemed less enthusiastic. Steve, having disposed of two eggs in quick succession, turned to see how his young charge was progressing with his repast, and found him eyeing a bowl of bread-and-milk in a sort of frozen horror.

"What's the matter, kid?" he asked. "Get busy."

"No paper," said William Bannister.

"For the love of Pete! Do you expect your morning paper out in the woods?"

"No paper," repeated the White Hope firmly.

Steve regarded him thoughtfully.

"I didn't have this trip planned out right," he said regretfully. "I ought to have got Mamie to come along. I bet a hundred dollars she would have got next to your meanings in a second. I pass. What's your kick, anyway? What's all this about paper?"

"Aunty Lora says not to eat bread that doesn't come wrapped up in paper," said the White Hope, becoming surprisingly lucid. "Mamie undoes it out of crinkly paper."

"I get you. They feed you rolls at home wrapped up in tissue-paper, is that it?"

"What's tissue?"

"Same as crinkly. Well, see here. You remember what we was talking about last night about germs?"

"Yes."

"Well, that's one thing germs never do, eat bread out of crinkly paper. You want to forget all the dope they shot into you back in New York and start fresh. You do what I tell you and you can't go wrong. If you're going to be a regular germ, what you've got to do is to wrap yourself round that bread-and-milk the quickest you can. Get me? Till you do that we can't begin to start out to have a good time."

William Bannister made no more objections. He attacked his meal with an easy conscience, and about a quarter of an hour later leaned back with a deep sigh of repletion.

Steve, meanwhile had entered into conversation with the lady of the house.

"Say, I guess you ain't got a kid of your own anywheres, have you?"

"Sure I have," said the hostess proudly. "He's out in the field with his pop this minute. His name's Jim."

"Fine. I want to get hold of a kid to play with this kid here. Jim sounds pretty good to me. About the same age as this one?"

"For the Lord's sake! Jim's eighteen and weighs two hundred pounds."

"Cut out Jim. I thought from the way you spoke he was a regular kid. Know any one in these parts who's got something about the same weight as this one?"

The farmer's wife reflected.

"Kids is pretty scarce round here," she said. "I reckon you won't get one that I knows of. There's that Tom Whiting, but he's a bad boy. He ain't been raised right."

"What's the matter with him?"

"I don't want to speak harm of no one, but his father used to be a low prize-fighter, and you know what they are."

Steve nodded sympathetically.

"Regular plug-uglies," he said. "A friend of mine used to have to mix with them quite a lot, poor fellah! He used to say they was none of them truly refined. And this kid takes after his pop, eh? Kind of scrappy kid, is that it?"

"He's a bad boy."

"Well, maybe I'd better look him over, just in case. Where's he to be found?"

"They live in the cottage by the big house you can see through them trees. His pop looks after Mr. Wilson's prize dawgs. That's his job."

"What's Wilson?" asked the White Hope, coming out of his stupor.

"You beat me to it by a second, kid. I was just going to ask it myself."

"He's one of them rich New Yawkers. He has his summer place here, and this Whiting looks after his prize dawgs."

"Well, I guess I'll give him a call. It's going to be lonesome for my kid if he ain't got some one to show him how to hit it up. He's not used to country life. Come along. We'll get into the bubble and go and send your pop a telegram."

"What's telegram?" asked William Bannister.

"I got you placed now," said Steve, regarding him with interest. "You're not going to turn into an ambassador or an artist or any of them things. You're going to be the greatest district attorney that ever came down the pike."

CHAPTER 14
THE SIXTY-FIRST STREET CYCLONE

IT was past seven o'clock when Kirk, bending over the wheel, with Mamie at his side came in sight of the shack. The journey had been checked just outside the city by a blow-out in one of the back tyres. Kirk had spent the time, while the shirt-sleeved rescuer from the garage toiled over the injured wheel, walking up and down with a cigar. Neither he nor Mamie had shown much tendency towards conversation. Mamie was habitually of a silent disposition, and Kirk's mind was too full of his thoughts to admit of speech.

Ever since he had read Steve's telegram he had been in the grip of a wild exhilaration. He had not stopped to ask himself what this mad freak of Steve's could possibly lead to in the end – he was satisfied to feel that its immediate result would be that for a brief while, at any rate, he would have his son to himself, away from all the chilling surroundings which had curbed him and frozen his natural feelings in the past.

He tried to keep his mind from dwelling upon Ruth. He had thought too much of her of late for his comfort. Since they had parted that day of the thunder-storm the thought that he had lost her had stabbed him incessantly. He had tried to tell himself that it was the best thing they could do, to separate, since it was so plain that their love had died; but he could not cheat himself into believing it.

It might be true in her case – it must be, or why had she let him go that afternoon? – but, for himself, the separation had taught him that he loved her as much as ever, more than ever. Absence had purified him of that dull anger which had been his so short a while before. He looked back and marvelled that he could ever have imagined for a moment that he had ceased to love her.

Now, as he drove along the empty country roads, he forced his mind to dwell, as far as he could, only upon his son. There was a mist before his eyes as he thought of him. What a bully lad he had been! What fun they had had in the old days! But that brought his mind back to Ruth, and he turned his mind resolutely to the future again.

He chuckled silently as he thought of Steve. Of all the mad things to do! What had made him think of it? How had such a wild scheme ever entered his head? This, he supposed, was what Steve called punching instead of sparring. But he had never given him credit for the imagination that could conceive a punch of this magnitude.

And how had he carried it out? He could hardly have broken into the house. Yet that seemed the only way in which it could have been done.

From Steve his thoughts returned to William Bannister. He smiled again. What a time they would have – while it lasted! The worst of it was, it could not last long. To-morrow, he supposed, he would have to take the child back to his home. He could not be a party to this kidnapping raid for any length of time. This must be looked on as a brief holiday, not as a permanent relief.

That was the only flaw in his happiness as he stopped the car at the door of the shack, for by now he had succeeded at last in thrusting the image of Ruth from his mind.

There was a light in the ground-floor window. He raised his head and shouted:

"Steve!"

The door opened.

"Hello, Kirk. That you? Come along in. You're just in time for the main performance."

He caught sight of Mamie standing beside Kirk.

"Who's that?" he cried. For a moment he thought it was Ruth, and his honest heart leaped at the thought that his scheme had worked already and brought Kirk and her together again.

"It's me, Steve," said Mamie in her small voice. And Steve, as he heard it, was seized with the first real qualm he had had since he had embarked upon his great adventure.

As Kirk had endeavoured temporarily to forget Ruth, so had he tried not to think of Mamie. It was the only thing he was ashamed of in the whole affair, the shock he must have given her.

"Hello, Mamie," he said sheepishly, and paused. Words did not come readily to him.

Mamie entered the house without speaking. It seemed to Steve that invective would have been better than this ominous silence. He looked ruefully at her retreating back and turned to greet Kirk.

"You're mighty late," he said.

"I only got your telegram toward the end of the afternoon. I had been away all day. I came here as fast as I could hit it up directly I read it. We had a blow-out, and that delayed us."

Steve ventured a question.

"Say, Kirk, why 'us,' while we're talking of it? How does Mamie come to be here?"

"She insisted on coming. It seems that everybody in the house was away to-day, so she tells me, so she came round to me with your note."

"I guess this has put me in pretty bad with Mamie," observed Steve regretfully. "Has she been knocking me on the trip?"

"Not a word."

Steve brightened, but became subdued again next moment.

"I guess she's just saving it," he said resignedly.

"Steve, what made you do it?"

"Oh, I reckoned you could do with having the kid to yourself for a spell," said Steve awkwardly.

"You're all right, Steve. But how did you manage it? I shouldn't have thought it possible."

"Oh, it wasn't so hard, that part. I just hid in the house, and – but say, let's forget it; it makes me feel kind of mean, somehow. It seems to me I may have lost Mamie her job. It's mighty hard to do the right thing by every one in this world, ain't it? Come along in and see the kid. He's great. Are you feeling ready for supper? Him and me was just going to start."

It occurred to Kirk for the first time that he was hungry.

"Have you got anything to eat, Steve?"

Steve brightened again.

"Have we?" he said. "We've got everything there is in Connecticut! Why, say, we're celebrating. This is our big day. Know what's happened? Why – "

He stopped short, as if somebody had choked him. They had gone into the sitting-room while he was speaking. The table was laid for supper. A chafing-dish stood at one end, and the remainder of the available space was filled with a collection of foods, from cold chicken to candy, which did credit to Steve's imagination.

But it was not the sight of these that checked his flow of speech. It was the look on Mamie's face as he caught sight of it in the lamplight. The White Hope was sitting at the table in the attitude of one who has heard the gong and is anxious to begin; while Mamie, bending over him, raised her head as the two men entered and fixed Steve with a baleful stare.

"What have you been doing to the poor mite?" she demanded fiercely, "to get his face scratched this way?"

There was no doubt about the scratch. It was a long, angry red line running from temple to chin. The White Hope, becoming conscious of the fact that the attention of the public was upon him, and diagnosing the cause, volunteered an explanation.

"Bad boy," he said, and looked meaningly again at the candy.

"What does he mean by 'bad boy'?"

"Just what he says, Mamie, honest. Gee! you don't think *I* done it, do you?"

"Have you been letting the precious lamb *fight?*" cried Mamie, her eyes two circles of blue indignation.

Steve's enthusiasm overcame his sense of guilt. He uttered a whoop.

"*Letting* him! Gee! Listen to her! Why, say, that kid don't have to be let! He's a scrapper from Swatville-on-the-Bingle. Honest! That's what all this food is about. We're celebrating. This is a little supper given in his honour by a few of his admirers and backers, meaning me. Why, say, Kirk, that kid of yours is just the greatest thing that ever happened. Get that chafing-dish going and I'll tell you all about it."

"How did he come by that scratch?" said Mamie, coldly sticking to her point.

"I'll tell you quick enough. But let's start in on the eats first. You wouldn't keep a coming champ waiting for his grub, would you? Look how he's lamping that candy."

"Were you going to let the poor mite stuff himself with candy, Steve Dingle?"

"Sure. Whatever he says goes. He owns the joint after this afternoon."

Mamie swiftly removed the unwholesome delicacy.

"The idea!"

Kirk was busying himself with the chafing-dish.

"What have you got in here, Steve?"

"Lobster, colonel. I had to do thirty miles to get it, too."

Mamie looked at him fixedly.

"Were you going to feed lobster to this child?" she asked with ominous calm. "Were you intending to put him to bed full of broiled lobster and marshmallows?"

"Nix on the rough stuff, Mamie," pleaded the embarrassed pugilist. "How was I to know what kids feed on? And maybe he would have passed up the lobster at that and stuck to the sardines."

"Sardines!"

"Ain't kids allowed sardines?" said Steve anxiously. "The guy at the store told me they were wholesome and nourishing. It looked to me as if that ought to hit young Fitzsimmons about right. What's the matter with them?"

"A little bread-and-milk is all that he ever has before he goes to bed."

Steve detected a flaw in this and hastened to make his point.

"Sure," he said, "but he don't win the bantam-weight champeenship of Connecticut every night."

"Is that what he's done to-day, Steve?" asked Kirk.

"It certainly is. Ain't I telling you?"

"That's the trouble. You're not. You and Mamie seem to be having a discussion about the nourishing properties of sardines and lobster. What has been happening this afternoon?"

"Bad boy," remarked William Bannister with his mouth full.

"That's right," said Steve. "That's it in a nutshell. Say, it was this way. It seemed to me that, having no kid of his own age to play around with, his nibs was apt to get lonesome, so I asked about and found that there was a guy of the name of Whiting living near here who had a kid of the same age or thereabouts. Maybe you remember him? He used to fight at the feather-weight limit some time back. Called himself Young O'Brien. He was a pretty good scrapper in his time, and now he's up here looking after some gent's prize dogs.

"Well, I goes to him and borrows his kid. He's a scrappy sort of kid at that and weighs ten pounds more than his nibs; but I reckoned he'd have to do, and I thought I could stay around and part 'em if they got to mixing it."

Mamie uttered an indignant exclamation, but Kirk's eyes were gleaming proudly.

"Well?" he said.

Steve swallowed lobster and resumed.

"Well, you know how it is. You meet a guy who's been in the same line of business as yourself and you find you've got a heap to talk about. I'd never happened across the gink Whiting, but I knew of him, and, of course, he'd heard of me, and we got to discussing things. I seen him lose on a foul to Tommy King in the eighteenth round out in Los Angeles, and that kept us busy talking, him having it that he hadn't gone within a mile of fouling Tommy and me saying I'd been in a ring-seat and had the goods on him same as if I'd taken a snap-shot. Well, we was both getting pretty hot under the collar about it when suddenly there's the blazes of a noise behind us, and there's the two kids scrapping all over the lot. The Whiting kid had started it, mind you, and him ten pounds heavier than Bill, and tough, too."

The White Hope confirmed this.

"Bad boy," he remarked, and with a deep breath resumed excavating work on a grapefruit.

"Well, I was just making a jump to separate them when this Whiting gook says, 'Betcha a dollar my kid wins!' and before I knew what I was doing I'd taken him. It wasn't that that stopped me, though. It was his saying that his kid took after his dad and could eat up anything of his own age in America. Well, darn it, could I take that from a slob of a mixed-ale scrapper when it was handed out at the finest kid that ever came from New York?"

"Of course not," said Kirk indignantly, and even Mamie forbore to criticize. She bent over the White Hope and gave his grapefruit-stained cheek a kiss.

"Well, I *should* say not!" cried Steve. "I just hollered to his nibs, 'Soak it to him, kid! for the honour of No. 99'; and, believe me, the young bear-cat sort of gathered himself together, winked at me, and began to hammer the stuffing out of the scrappy kid. Say, there wasn't no sterilized stuff about his work. You were a regular germ, all right, weren't you squire?"

"Germ," agreed the White Hope. He spoke drowsily.

"Gee!" Steve resumed his saga in a whirl of enthusiasm. "Gee! if they're right to start with, if they're born right, if they've got the grit in them, you can't sterilize it out of 'em if you use up half the germ-killer in the country. From the way that kid acted you'd have thought he'd been spending the last year in a training-camp. The other kid rolled him over, but he come up again as if that was just the sort of stuff he liked, and pretty soon I see that he's uncovered a yellow streak in the Whiting kid as big as a barn door. You were on it, weren't you, colonel?"

But the White Hope had no remarks to offer this time. His head had fallen forward and was resting peacefully in his grapefruit.

"He's asleep," said Mamie.

She picked him up gently and carried him out.

"He's a champeen at that too," said Steve. "I had to pull him out of the hay this morning. Well, I guess he's earned it. He's had a busy day."

"What happened then, Steve?"

"Why, after that there wasn't a thing to it. Whiting, poor simp, couldn't see it. 'Betcha ten dollars my kid wins,' he hollers. 'He's got him going.' 'Take you,' I shouts; and at that moment the scrappy kid sees it's all over, so he does the old business of fouling, same as his pop done when he fought Tommy King. It's in the blood, I guess. He takes and scratches poor Bill on the cheek."

"That was enough for me. I jumps in. 'All over,' I says. 'My kid wins on a foul.' 'Foul nothing,' says Whiting. 'It was an accident, and you lose because you jumped into the fight, same as Connie McVey did when Corbett fought Sharkey. Think you can get away with it, pulling that old-time stuff?' I didn't trouble to argue with him. 'Oh,' I says, 'is that it? Say, just take a slant at your man. If you don't stop him quick he'll be in Texas.'

"For the scrappy kid was beating it while the going was good and was half a mile away, running hard. Well, that was enough even for the Whiting guy. 'I guess we'll call it a draw,' he says, 'and all bets off.' I just looks at him and says, quite civil and polite: 'You darned half-baked slob of a rough-house scrapper,' I says, 'it ain't a draw or anything like it. My kid wins, and I'll trouble you now to proceed to cash in with the dough, or else I'm liable to start something.' So he paid up, and I took the White Hope indoors and give him a wash and brush-up, and we cranks up the bubble and hikes off to the town and spends the money on getting food for the celebration supper. And what's over I slips into the kid's pocket and says: 'That's your first winner's end, kid, and you've earned it.'"

Steve paused and filled his glass.

"I'm on the waggon as a general thing nowadays," he said; "but I reckon this an occasion. Right here is where we drink his health."

And, overcome by his emotion, he burst into discordant song.

"Fo-or he's a jolly good fellow," bellowed Steve. "For he's a jolly good fellow. For he's – "

There was a sound of quick footsteps outside, and Mamie entered the room like a small whirlwind.

"Be quiet!" she cried. "Do you want to wake him?"

"Wake him?" said Steve. "You can't wake that kid with dynamite."

He raised his glass.

"Ladeez'n gentlemen, the boy wonder! Here's to him! The bantam-weight champeen of Connecticut. The Sixty-First Street Cyclone! The kid they couldn't sterilize! The White Hope!"

"The White Hope!" echoed Kirk.

"Fo-or he's a jolly good fellow – " sang Steve.

"Be quiet!" said Mrs. Porter from the doorway, and Steve, wheeling round, caught her eye and collapsed like a pricked balloon.

CHAPTER 15
MRS. PORTER'S WATERLOO

OF the little band of revellers it would be hard to say which was the most taken aback at this invasion. The excitement of the moment had kept them from hearing the sound of the automobile which Mrs. Porter, mistrusting the rough road that led to the shack, had stopped some distance away.

Perhaps, on the whole, Kirk was more surprised than either of his companions. Their guilty consciences had never been quite free from the idea of the possibility of pursuit; but Kirk, having gathered from Mamie that neither Ruth nor her aunt was aware of what had happened, had counted upon remaining undisturbed till the time for return came on the morrow.

He stood staring at Ruth, who had followed Mrs. Porter into the room.

Mrs. Porter took charge of the situation. She was in her element. She stood with one hand resting on the table as if she were about to make an after-dinner speech – as indeed she was.

Lora Delane Porter was not dissatisfied with the turn events had taken. On the whole, perhaps, it might be said that she was pleased. She intended, when she began to speak, to pulverize Kirk and the abandoned young woman whom he had selected as his partner in his shameful escapade, but in this she was swayed almost entirely by a regard for abstract morality.

As concerned Ruth, she felt that the situation was, on the whole, the best thing that could have happened. To her Napoleonic mind, which took little account of the softer emotions, concerning itself entirely with the future of the race, Kirk had played his part and was now lagging superfluous on the stage. His tendency, she felt, was to retard rather than to assist William Bannister's development. His influence, such as it was, clashed with hers. She did not forget that there had been a time when Ruth, having practically to choose between them, had chosen to go Kirk's way and had abandoned herself to a life which could only be considered unhygienic and retrograde. Her defeat in the matter of Whiskers, the microbe-harbouring dog from Ireland, still rankled.

It was true that in what might be called the return match she had utterly routed Kirk; but until this moment she had always been aware of him as an opponent who might have to be reckoned with. She was quite convinced that it would be in the best interests of everybody, especially of William Bannister, if he could be eliminated. There were signs of human weakness in Ruth which sometimes made her uneasy. Ruth, she told herself, might "bear the torch," but when it came to "not faltering" she was less certain of her.

Ruth, it was true, had behaved admirably in the matter of the upbringing of William from the moment of her conversion till now, but might she not at any moment become a backslider and fill the white-tiled nursery with abominable long-haired dogs? Most certainly she might. In a woman who had once been a long-haired dogist there are always possibilities of a relapse into long-haired dogism, just as in a converted cannibal there are always possibilities of a return to the gods of wood and stone and the disposition to look on his fellow-man purely in the light of breakfast-food.

For these reasons Mrs. Porter was determined to push home her present advantage, to wipe Kirk off the map as an influence in Ruth's life. It was her intention, having recovered William Bannister and bathed him from head to foot in a weak solution of boric acid, to stand over Ruth while she obtained a divorce. That done, she would be in a position to defy Kirk and all his antagonistic views on the subject of the hygienic upbringing of children.

She rapped the table and prepared to speak.

Even a Napoleon, however, may err from lack of sufficient information; and there was a flaw in her position of which she was unaware. From the beginning of the drive to the end of it Ruth had hardly spoken a word, and Mrs. Porter, in consequence, was still in ignorance of what had been happening that day in Wall Street and the effect of these happenings on her niece's outlook on life. Could she have known it, the silent girl beside her had already suffered the relapse which she had feared as a remote possibility.

Ruth's mind during that drive had been in a confusion of regrets and doubts and hopes. There were times when she refused absolutely to believe the story of Kirk's baseness which her aunt poured into her ear during the first miles of the journey. It was absurd and incredible. Yet, as they raced along the dark roads, doubt came to her and would not be driven out.

A single unfortunate phrase of Kirk's, spoken in haste, but remembered at leisure, formed the basis of this uncertainty. That afternoon when he had left her he had said that Mamie was the real mother of the child. Could it be that Mamie's undeviating devotion to the boy had won the love which she had lost? It was possible. Considered in the light of what Mrs. Porter had told her, it seemed, in her blackest moments, certain.

She knew how wrapped up in the boy Kirk had been. Was it not a logical outcome of his estrangement from herself that he should have turned for consolation to the one person in sympathy with him in his great love for his child?

She tried to read his face as he stood looking at her now, but she could find no hope in it. The eyes that met hers were cold and expressionless.

Mrs. Porter rapped the table a second time.

"Mr. Winfield," she said in the metallic voice with which she was wont to cow publishers insufficiently equipped with dash and enterprise in the matter of advertising treatises on the future of the race, "I have no doubt you are surprised to see us. You appear to be looking your wife in the face. It speaks well for your courage but badly for your sense of shame. If you had the remnants of decent feeling in you, you would be physically incapable of the feat. If you would care to know how your conduct strikes an unprejudiced spectator, I may tell you that I consider you a scoundrel of the worst type and unfit to associate with any but the low company in which I find you."

Steve, who had been listening with interest, and indeed, a certain relish while Kirk was, as he put it to himself, "getting his" in this spirited fashion, started at the concluding words of the address, which, in his opinion, seemed slightly personal. He had long ago made up his mind that Lora Delane Porter, though an entertaining woman and, on the whole, more worth while than a moving-picture show, was quite mad; but, he felt, even lunatics ought to realize that there is a limit to what they may say.

He moaned protestingly, and rashly, for he drew the speaker's attention upon himself.

"This person," went on Mrs. Porter, indicating Steve with a wave of her hand which caused him to sidestep swiftly and throw up an arm, as had been his habit in the ring when Battling Dick or Fighting Jack endeavoured to blot him out with a right swing, "who, I observe, retains the tattered relics of a conscience, seeing that he winces, you employed to do the only dangerous part of your dirty work. I hope he will see that he gets his money. In his place I should be feeling uneasy."

"Ma'am!" protested Steve.

Mrs. Porter silenced him with a gesture.

"Be quiet!" she said.

Steve was quiet.

Mrs. Porter returned to Kirk.

227

Of all her burning words, Kirk had not heard one. His eyes had never left Ruth's. Like her, he was trying to read a message from a face that seemed only cold. In this crisis of their two lives he had no thought for anybody but her. He had a sense of great issues, of being on the verge of the tremendous; but his brain felt numbed and heavy. He could not think. He could see nothing except her eyes.

His inattention seemed to communicate itself to Mrs. Porter. She rapped imperatively upon the table for the third time. The report galvanized Steve, as, earlier in the day, a similar report had galvanized Mr. Penway; but Kirk did not move.

"Mr. Winfield!"

Still Kirk made no sign that he had heard her. It was discouraging, but Lora Delane Porter was not made of the stuff that yields readily to discouragement. She resumed:

"As for this wretched girl" – she indicated the silent Mamie with a wave of her hand – "this abandoned creature whom you have led astray, this shameless partner of your—"

"Say!"

The exclamation came from Steve, and it stopped Mrs. Porter like a bullet. To her this interruption from one whom she had fallen upon and wiped out resembled a voice from the tomb. She was not accustomed to having her victims rise up and cut sharply, even peremptorily, into the flow of her speech. Macbeth, confronted by the ghost of Banquo, may have been a little more taken aback, but not much.

She endeavoured to quell Steve with a glance, but it was instantly apparent that he was immune for the time being to quelling glances. His brown eyes were fixed upon her in a cold stare which she found arresting and charged with menace. His chin protruded and his upper lip was entirely concealed behind its fellow in a most uncomfortable manner.

She had never had the privilege of seeing Steve in the active exercise of his late profession, or she would have recognized the look. It was the one which proclaims the state of mind commonly known as "being fighting mad," and in other days had usually heralded a knock-out for some too persistent opponent.

"Say, ma'am, you want to cut that out. That line of talk don't go."

Great is the magic of love that can restore a man in an instant of time from being an obsequious wreck to a thing of fire and resolution. A moment before Steve's only immediate object in life had been to stay quiet and keep out of the way as much as possible. He had never been a man of ready speech in the presence of an angry woman; words intimidated him as blows never did, especially the whirl of words which were at Lora Delane Porter's command in moments of emotion.

But this sudden onslaught upon Mamie, innocent Mamie who had done nothing to anybody, scattered his embarrassment and filled him with much the same spirit which sent bantam-weight knights up against heavy-weight dragons in the Middle Ages. He felt inspired.

"Nix on the 'abandoned creature,'" he said with dignity. "You're on the wrong wire! This here lady is my affianced wife!"

He went to Mamie and, putting his arm round her waist, pressed her to him. He was conscious, as he did so, of a sensation of wonderment at himself. This was the attitude he had dreamed of a thousand times and had been afraid to assume. For the last three years he had been picturing himself in precisely this position, and daily had cursed the lack of nerve which had held him back. Yet here he was, and it had all happened in a moment. A funny thing, life.

"What!" exclaimed Mrs. Porter.

"Sure thing," said Steve. His coolness, the ease with which he found words astonished him as much as his rapidity of action.

"I stole the kid," he said, "and it was my idea at that. Kirk didn't know anything about it. I wired to him to-day what I had done and that he was to come right along. And," added Steve in a burst of inspiration, "I said bring along Mamie, too, as the kid's used to her and there ought to be a woman around. And she could be here, all right, and no harm, she being my affianced wife." He liked that phrase. He had read it in a book somewhere, and it was the goods.

He eyed Mrs. Porter jauntily. Mrs. Porter's gaze wavered. She was not feeling comfortable. Hers was a nature that did not lend itself easily to apologies, yet apologies were obviously what the situation demanded. The thought of all the eloquence which she had expended to no end added to her discomfort. For the first time she was pleased that Kirk had so manifestly not been listening to a word of it.

"Oh!" she said.

She paused.

"That puts a different complexion on this affair."

"Betcha life!"

She paused once more. It was some moments before she could bring herself to speak. She managed it at last.

"I beg your pardon," she said.

"Mine, ma'am?" said Steve grandly. Five minutes before, the idea that he could ever speak grandly to Lora Delane Porter would have seemed ridiculous to him; but he was surprised at nothing now.

"And the young wom— And the future Mrs. Dingle's," said Mrs. Porter with an effort.

"Thank you, ma'am," said Steve, and released Mamie, who forthwith bolted from the room like a scared rabbit.

Steve had started to follow her when Mrs. Porter, magnificent woman, snatching what was left from defeat, stopped him.

"Wait!" she said. "What you have said alters the matter in one respect; but there is another point. On your own confession you have been guilty of the extremely serious offence, the penal offence of kidnapping a child who – "

"Drop me a line about it, ma'am," said Steve. "Me time's rather full just now."

He disappeared into the outer darkness after Mamie.

⚇

In the room they had left, Kirk and Ruth faced each other in silence. Lora Delane Porter eyed them grimly. It was the hour of her defeat, and she knew it. Forces too strong for her were at work. Her grand attack, the bringing of these two together that Ruth might confront Kirk in his guilt, had recoiled upon her. The Old Guard had made their charge up the hill, and it had failed. Victory had become a rout. With one speech Steve had destroyed her whole plan of campaign.

She knew it was all over, that in another moment if she remained, she would be compelled to witness the humiliating spectacle of Ruth in Kirk's arms, stammering the words which intuition told her were even now trembling on her lips. She knew Ruth. She could read her like a primer. And her knowledge told her that she was about to capitulate, that all her pride and resentment had been swept away, that she had gone over to the enemy.

Elemental passions were warring against Lora Delane Porter, and she bowed before them.

"Mr. Winfield," she said sharply, her voice cutting the silence like a knife, "I beg your pardon. I seem to have made a mistake. Good night."

Kirk did not answer.

"Good night, Ruth."

Ruth made no sign that she had heard.

Mrs. Porter, grand in defeat, moved slowly to the door.

But even in the greatest women there is that germ of feminine curiosity which cannot be wholly eliminated, that little grain of dust that asserts itself and clogs the machinery. It had been Mrs. Porter's intention to leave the room without a glance, her back defiantly toward the foe. But, as she reached the door, there came from behind her a sound of movement, a stifled cry, a little sound whose meaning she knew too well.

She hesitated. She stood still, fighting herself. But the grain of dust had done its work. For an instant she ceased to be a smoothly working machine and became a woman subject to the dictates of impulse.

She turned.

Intuition had not deceived her. Ruth had gone over to the enemy. She was in Kirk's arms, holding him to her, her face hidden against his shoulder, for all the world as if Lora Delane Porter, her guiding force, had ceased to exist.

Mrs. Porter closed the door and walked stiffly through the scented night to where the headlights of her automobile cleft the darkness. Birds, asleep in the trees, fluttered uneasily at the sudden throbbing of the engine.

CHAPTER 16
THE WHITE-HOPE LINK

THE White Hope slept. The noise of the departing car, which had roused the birds, had made no impression on him. As Steve had said, dynamite could not do it. He slumbered on, calmly detached, unaware of the remarkable changes which, in the past twenty-four hours, had taken place in his life. An epoch had ended and a new one begun, but he knew it not.

And probably, if Kirk and Ruth, who were standing at his bedside, watching him, had roused him and informed him of these facts, he would have displayed little excitement. He had the philosophical temperament. He took things as they came. Great natural phenomena, like Lora Delane Porter, he accepted as part of life. When they were in his life, he endured them stoically. When they went out of it, he got on without them. Marcus Aurelius would have liked William Bannister Winfield. They belonged to the same school of thought.

The years have a tendency to destroy this placidity towards life and to develop in man a sense of gratitude to fate for its occasional kindnesses; and Kirk, having been in the world longer than William Bannister, did not take the gifts of the gods so much for granted. He was profoundly grateful for what had happened. That Lora Delane Porter should have retired from active interference with his concerns was much; but that he should have had the incredible good fortune to be freed from the burden of John Bannister's money was more.

If ever money was the root of all evil, this had been. It had come into his life like a poisonous blight, withering and destroying wherever it touched. It had changed Ruth; it had changed William Bannister; it had changed himself; it was as if the spirit of the old man had lived on, hating him and working him mischief. He always had superstitious fear of it; and events had proved him right.

And now the cloud had rolled away. A few crowded hours of Bailey's dashing imbecility had removed the curse forever.

He was alone with Ruth and his son in a world that contained only them, just as in the old days of their happiness. There was something symbolic, something suggestive of the beginning of a new order of things, in their isolation at this very moment. Steve had gone. Only he and Ruth and the child were left.

The child – the White Hope – he was the real hero of the story, the real principal of the drama of their three lives. He was the link that bound them together, the force that worked for coherence and against chaos. He stood between them, his hands in theirs; and while he did so there could be no parting of the ways. His grip was light, but as strong as steel. Time would bring troubles, moods, misunderstandings, for they were both human; but, while that grip held, there could be no gulf dividing Ruth and himself, as it had divided them in the past.

He faced the future calmly, with open eyes. It would be rough going at first, very rough going. It meant hard work, incessant work. No more vague masterpieces which might or might not turn into "Carmen" or "The Spanish Maiden." No more delightful idle days to be loafed through in the studio or the shops. No more dreams, seen hazily through the smoke of a cigar, as he lay on the couch and stared at the ceiling, of what he would do to-morrow. To-morrow must look after itself. His business was with the present and the work of the present.

He braced himself to the fight, confident of his power to win. He had found himself.

Bill stirred in his sleep and muttered. Ruth bent over him and kissed the honourable scratch on his cheek.

"Poor little chap! You'll wake up and find that you aren't a millionaire baby after all! I wonder if you'll mind. Kirk, do *you* mind?"

"Mind!"

"I don't," said Ruth. "I think it will be rather fun being poor again."

"Who's poor?" said Kirk stoutly. "I'm not. I've got you and I've got Bill. Do you remember – ages ago – what that Vince girl, the model, you know, said that her friend had called me? A plute. That's me. I'm the richest man in the world."

THE END

www.ArcWodehouse.com